I0547488

Bridle Path
Press

Also by Melissa Westemeier

Whipped, Not Beaten
Kicks Like a Girl

Across the River

a novel

Melissa Westemeier

Across the River is a work of fiction. Names, characters, places, and incidents are the products of the author's imagination or are used fictitiously. Any resemblance to actual events, locales, or persons, living or dead, is entirely coincidental.

Copyright © 2016 by Melissa Westemeier

All rights reserved.

No part of this book may be reproduced or transmitted in any manner whatsoever without permission from the publisher except in the case of brief quotations for purpose of critical articles or reviews.

For information or permission contact:

Bridle Path Press, LLC
8419 Stevenson Road
Baltimore, MD 21208

www.bridlepathpress.com

Direct orders to the above address.

Printed in the United States of America.
First Edition.
ISBN: 978-0-9908287-4-7

Library of Congress Control Number: 2016935371

Book Design by Elizabeth Ryan Cole
Cover Design by Mitch Miskoviak

Bridle Path
Press

With gratitude to all the storytellers who sat around the Bridge Bar in Fremont, Wisconsin. I tried to protect the innocent—and the guilty—in this fictional version of events.

Across the River

ONE

Early March

Home. MONA BUTTERFIELD FELT contentment settle inside her chest like a deep sigh as she drove past the familiar billboard on Rural Route 20. The billboard depicted a giant wide-mouthed bass, its body arched in a shower of splashing water, a cartoon-ish fisherman triumphantly reeling it in. Beneath the picture large red letters announced *Welcome to Bassville—The White Bass Capital of the Western Hemisphere.* Two miles east of the sign, minding the sneaky decrease in speed limit designed to trap out-of-town visitors, Mona reached the stop sign before the two-lane bridge connecting both sides of town and glimpsed the Wissipaw River. The pocked gray surface of the frozen water stretched between the banks and around the bends where Mona knew ice shanties still stood in shaded spots. Their owners played the odds every year, leaving them near open water that grew wider with each passing hour of springtime thaw.

Ever since the new state highway routed traffic two miles east,

Bassville didn't get much traffic. Now the town appeared abruptly if you took a wrong turn on a back road, interrupting the curving of rural road between trees and fields. Whenever Mona returned home, this time from a trip to Northport to renew her driver's license at the DMV and snag a winter jacket on clearance at Kmart, she felt a sudden sense of relief, as though the act of leaving had somehow disrupted her equilibrium. Arriving home felt like stepping out of a roller coaster car and back on to the safety of solid ground. It didn't help that she'd gotten lost *again* in Northport. Constant development redefined the landmarks and borders as Northport sprawled across former meadows, forests and cornfields. New construction out by the mall had caused a traffic detour, and she'd wound up five miles out of her way at a truck stop asking for directions. Here in Bassville she could depend on finding each street and building exactly the way she'd left it.

Halfway across the bridge Mona checked the little blue cottage for signs of life, and seeing none—and no black pick-up truck parked nearby—she sped up and continued driving towards her parents' farm, singing along with Sheena Easton's voice playing on the car radio. "My baby takes the morning train, he works from nine to five and then . . . "

Bassville straddled the river. The town hall, cheese factory, two taverns, a marina and several houses lined the east side. The west side boasted most of the houses, grocery store, gas stations, eight taverns, two bait shops and random stores lining Main Street, and the school. Crooked sidewalks and gutters edged the two main streets, Main and Fulton, punctuated by five streetlights and two stop signs. Main Street had never been paved and every spring it thawed into a long stretch of mud. Drivers were often stranded after a heavy rain, tires sunk in wet and greasy slicks. Locals drove with one set of tires on the sidewalks when it rained or thawed, a practice Joe the Cop,

Bassville's only full-time officer, ignored.

Within a month the tiny river town would become crowded with fishermen parking their boat trailers wherever they could find space and trawling the river first for walleye and then white bass. Locals tolerated the annual flux since seasonal tourism provided their bread and butter for a few months while leaving everyone behind to enjoy the peace and quiet for the rest of the year. Without fishermen driving hundreds of miles to spend their money on beer, bait and beds, Bassville's economy would limp along at poverty level. The current balance in Mona Butterfield's checkbook indicated that it was time to welcome the fishermen with open arms.

Mona turned into the gravel driveway leading to the farm and blinked at the sight of Sean's car parked beside the windbreak of pine trees. She yanked open her car door and ran up the steps leading to her parents' back door two at a time.

Slamming the kitchen door shut with her shoulder she cried, "Sean! What are you doing here?" She ran to him, pressing her cheek against his chest and wrapping her arms around his lanky frame. Three years and thirteen inches separated the siblings and she beamed up at his scruffy face. The happy surprise of her younger brother's visit from college was the first bright spot since Christmas.

"Spring break. No money for an ocean view in Panama City, so I scraped together enough cash for gas to take me to the sweet shores of the Wissipaw River." Sean grinned down at her and slid back onto the counter by the sink. His long legs nearly reached the floor and his size fourteen sneakers tapped against the cupboard doors.

"How's school going? Hi, Mom." Mona kissed her mother's cheek before pulling out a chair at the kitchen table.

"It's nice to have you both home for a change," June Butterfield said and grabbed a red-checked potholder, pulled a pan of brownies out of the oven, and set them on the stovetop to cool. She wiped her

3

hands across her blue jeans, then poured out three cups of coffee into a series of mismatched mugs and sat down across from her daughter.

"It's great. I've been up to my eyeballs applying for grants for our department chair—" Sean began in a rush.

"Why are you doing that?" June interrupted. "Sean, you're almost done. You graduate in June." Her voice was sharp as the crease between her eyebrows.

Sean shrugged and started to crack his knuckles, a habit he'd picked up to loosen his hands before playing his trumpet. "Doesn't hurt to have experience, Mom." With the pretense of drinking his coffee, he fell silent.

"Have you been out to the barn yet?" Mona asked him and stirred two spoonfuls of sugar into her cup. He'd tell her everything when they were alone. He always did.

"No. Dad's out there I suppose." Sean hesitated before pushing himself off the countertop to land on the faded linoleum floor with a thud.

"And he'd love some help with the chores. Get out there and help him while I finish making dinner." June shooed them out the back door and closed it tight against the cold wind. She watched them cross the frozen turf, their bouncing gaits identical, before resuming her spot at the stove, her delicate features furrowed with concern.

Even with overhead lights swaying overhead, the barn was dim, and felt cozy with the humid air. The heavy wooden door groaned shut behind them and Mona and Sean waved to their father on the far end of the stalls. Their boots scuffed across the forage-strewn floor, mixing with the sound of cows stomping their feet and lowing.

"This is a nice surprise," Loyal called to them over the mechanical hum of the milking machine. "Does June know you're here?" He slapped the rear of the cow he'd just milked and crossed over to his children.

"We've already been in the house. She sent us out to help you," Sean said.

"I'm always glad to have extra hands on deck. I can't wait for you to be around when school lets out. I might even take a vacation after we get you settled back here." Loyal said and grinned. "Take your mother someplace tropical, maybe Florida."

"She'd love that," Mona said.

Sean shot a look at his sister and put his hands on his hips. "What do you need us to do?"

"I'm about done with milking. Why don't you two tackle the bedding." Loyal nodded and waved his gloved hand to indicate the hay bales lined up in the aisle between the stalls. "Have at her, you know what to do."

Sean nudged Mona with his elbow and pointed at a pitchfork leaning against the wall. "Pitch or muck?" he asked.

"You muck." Mona grabbed the pitchfork's wooden handle and began prying a bale of hay loose. "Hey, sweetie," she murmured to the Holstein in the nearest stall.

Sean began scraping the first stall with a shovel, shoving the waste towards the long aisle that stretched the length of the barn. "I hate this work."

"I don't know, it's not so bad," Mona said. "It beats sitting around at a desk all day. I think it feels good to get a little sweaty." She kicked at the edge of the bale to loosen the tightly packed straw. "Plus you get to go outside and even though milking's the same every day, the rest of your chores change with the seasons."

"I'm not doing it," Sean declared. "I'm going to get my graduate degree. I got accepted into the program at Ohio State."

Mona stopped and turned to stare at her brother. "Have you told Dad?" She glanced across the barn at their father who was bent over

5

the task of sterilizing the teats of another cow before attaching the cups to milk it. "He's counting on you coming back."

"That's why I'm here. To tell him in person." Sean clenched his jaw.

"He's going to be pissed."

"I have to do this. You have no idea. At college everything is so … ," he cast around for the right words. "New. Exciting. Every day I meet new people. Talk about new ideas. This town, it's full of the same old same old every single day. I need more than that. And I love the lab. I love working with smart people, solving problems. That makes me feel alive. This place?" Sean flung out his arms. "It makes me feel like I'm dying."

Mona studied her brother's frantic expression while poking the tines of the pitchfork into a seam in the concrete floor. Deep down she always knew he'd never come back to farming, but hearing him say it felt final. A calico barn cat rubbed its head against her rubber boot. "I get it," she said. "I don't completely understand it, but I get what you mean about wanting to feel a certain way."

"Thanks. I don't think anyone else here will." He banged the broad side of the shovel once before turning back to the next stall.

While she neatly laid fresh bedding for the Sissy, a gentle, black-faced Holstein that she'd bottle-fed as a calf, Mona wondered if she'd ever want to change her life as badly as Sean did. She didn't think so, she decided. She'd miss the familiar things too much. She glanced up at the rusted metal sign that read "Butterfield's Best" nailed to the wall above the barn door. Except for the milk pipeline, its long stainless steel pipes snaking from stall to stall, everything in the barn was probably the same as when their great-grandfather had built it. Sean's decision not to continue the family business would not go down well with their dad.

Forty-seven head of cattle, Mona and Sean returned from the barn.

They took turns washing up in the kitchen sink before joining their parents in the dining room. June had laid out her mother's china for the occasion of Sean's homecoming and steam rose from periwinkle-patterned serving bowls heaped with mashed potatoes, gravy, chicken and rolls. Loyal already sat at the head of the table, his greying head bowed patiently while he waited for his children to sit.

"Father, bless this food and our family. Thank you for your bounteous grace. In Your name, Amen." Loyal Butterfield opened his eyes and grabbed his fork. "Where's the meat? When do we eat?"

Agreeable laughter at Loyal's trademark ending to the suppertime prayer trickled around the table. Sean poured glasses of milk for everyone while Mona reached for a roll.

"You hear anything from Alaska, Mona?" Sean asked.

"No," Mona said and shrugged. The yeasty smell of warm bread filled her nostrils when she pried the crust apart.

"Sean," June warned.

"It's okay, Mom. People always ask." Mona turned to look her brother fully in the face. "Last I heard, T.C. was working on a fishing boat. We don't really keep in touch. Besides, I'd hate living in some mountain cabin all by myself while he fished all week long. I'm happier here."

"He likes it then?" Sean asked.

"Loves it, according to his dad." Mona opened a plastic carton of Butterfield's Best and dipped her knife into the pale yellow whipped butter. "We had a good run of it—three years is a long time—but he wasn't going to stay and I didn't want to leave and that's that." She still missed him sometimes, everyone did. Stocky, cocky, with a head of thick curly hair and a strong jaw, T.C. flooded a room with his charisma. Standing beside him was like Christmas morning, bright and breathless. For months after he'd left town the usual crowd seemed more sober without him. But he'd been gone for ten months now, and the stab of their break-up had dulled. It hurt to let him go, but it would have hurt more to follow him so far from home. At least that's what Mona told herself every night before falling asleep.

"You'll have a new boyfriend before the end of summer," Sean predicted.

Mona felt the flush rise up her neck to her cheeks and bent her head to let her hair swing forward and hide her face. She wished Jake Paulick were her new boyfriend, but no way would she tell anyone that, not even Sean.

"Did you tell Sean about Angie Trayson?" June asked her husband.

"I didn't." Loyal stabbed a few pieces of chicken off the serving platter before passing it over to Sean. "She's got some kind of cancer," Loyal said to his son.

"What do you mean? She's just a kid—like only ten or something."

"Eleven," June supplied.

"Geez." Sean shook his head. "What kind of cancer?"

"Leukemia," Mona told him around a mouthful of potatoes.

"She'd been feeling poorly all winter," June said. "Headaches, dizzy, tired and achy. They thought she had the flu. A couple weeks ago, Dottie brought her to the doctor and a week later she was down at Children's Hospital in Milwaukee for tests. They're treating her with chemotherapy right now. That radiation's awful stuff, almost worse than the cancer. She's lost ten pounds and has begun to lose her hair."

"Wow. Poor kid." Sean frowned. "Is she going to make it?"

"The doctors decided to try something called a bone marrow transplant. The radiation treatment hasn't worked. They say she's a good candidate because of her age, but now they're in limbo until they can find a match to donate to her. It's hard on everyone, as you can imagine. Dottie stays down at the hospital with her while she's getting treatment, so Scotty's had to help his dad out at their farm on top of his carpentry work at the hotel."

"Whoa—" Sean looked across at Loyal. "Do they have insurance for her—I mean, being farmers and all?"

"I don't know," Loyal said.

"Dottie told me the insurance covers most of it, but they won't cover transplants. So far the only help they take from anyone are casseroles from the church ladies." June pointed to the mashed potatoes. "Anyone want seconds?"

"No thanks," Loyal said. "It's a tough thing to watch a kid go through that."

After a moment of brooding silence, Mona changed the topic. "So, Sean," Mona said, "any chance you'll come back for fishing season?"

"Funny you should ask," Sean said and reached again for the platter of chicken. "I've got some big news." He cleared his throat while his parents and sister set down their forks and gave him their full attention. The grandfather clock in the hallway filled the silence with baritone chimes. "I've been accepted at Ohio State."

A long pause followed. Mona picked golden french-fried onions off of her beans and laid them along the edge of her plate. She knew what was coming and her heart pounded hard in her chest. The worst moments always unfolded in slow motion while the best raced by— as if God kept an omnipotent finger on some mystical remote control ordained to torment people.

Loyal drew his bushy eyebrows together with a confused scowl. "What do you mean? You're about to graduate." He leaned forward, carefully placed his forearms on the table and clasped his chapped hands.

"Yes, Dad. And I want to go on. I got into their graduate program. They're offering me a great package. I'll have to kick in for room and board, but the tuition is free. I'll assist three sections of freshman chemistry and get to contribute to some serious research." Sean's blue

9

eyes blazed while he anxiously glanced from his mother's face to his father's, willing them to be happy for him.

June dropped her hands and began folding her napkin one inch at a time across her lap. She watched her calloused fingers crease the linen fabric, reluctant to take sides in the battle brewing at her dining room table. The farm was their life, but her son's happiness—that was important, too. A hangnail caught in the weave of the napkin, the rasp of the jagged edge barely audible.

"But that's not our agreement," Loyal enunciated slowly. "We paid for four years. Then you said you'd come back to take over the farm."

"That's what *you* said, Dad. *I* said I wanted to go to college. I never said I wanted to farm."

"You never said that you didn't." Loyal clenched his jaw and the cords of his neck stood out above the collar of his flannel shirt. "Sean, you can't turn your back on this farm. On seventy years of Butterfield tradition."

"This wasn't an easy choice." Sean's voice rose and his cheeks flushed red. "But I don't want to spend the next forty years of my life tied to cow teats."

"Sean!" June's voice lashed out at him like a slap.

"Sorry." Sean exhaled. "I know it's hard for you to understand, but it's my life—my decision. Not yours."

"And what of this? What about this family? What happens here if you don't come back?" Loyal never shouted. But he also never fathomed his only son would refuse to take over their farm.

Sean stared at his plate. Heat from the untouched chicken breast had begun melting the edges of the mound of cherry Jell-O. Rivulets of red sweetness drained into the white lump of mashed potatoes. "I'm sorry."

"Bullshit. You're selfish."

"Loyal!" June gasped.

10

"I said I'm sorry." Sean stood. He walked around to his mother and bent down to kiss her cheek. June gazed straight ahead at her husband. "I didn't expect you to understand," Sean said bitterly. His footsteps echoed down the hall and the back door slammed before anyone at the table spoke.

"Now what?" Loyal asked his wife, hopelessness shading his voice.

Mona pushed back her chair with a reverberating scrape and followed Sean outside; the door banged shut behind her in a sudden gust of wind. She caught up to him at his car and grabbed the sleeve of his jacket. "You can't leave like this." How cruel to have slow motion and fast forward, but no rewind button to press.

"Mona," Sean grabbed her shoulders so tightly she flinched. "This town's a dead end. If you have any sense at all, you'll leave too. Go to college. You're smart enough. Hell, move to Northport and start at the tech. But get out while you still have the chance."

He leaned his forehead against hers, a gesture of affection they'd shared since he was a baby in his high chair and Mona would feed him Cheerios with grubby, pudgy fingers. Then he folded his tall body into his car. Mona watched him drive away and hugged her arms tight against the chill in the air, strands of her hair catching in her half-open mouth and wetly stinging her cheeks.

Mona returned to the house to hear the familiar clink and clatter of supper dishes being cleared.

"Where did we go wrong? My son. The son I raised to take over this farm." Loyal stood by the back door and stared at the black shadows of the barns, silo, clothesline poles and fence line. His broad back was rigid and June stepped behind him, reaching up to trace her fingertips across his shoulders.

"Maybe I could do it, Dad." The words came out suddenly, surprising them all. Mona hardly knew if she meant them or not.

Loyal turned to look at his daughter and his expression softened when he spoke. "You're sweet to want to keep the peace, Pumpkin." He shook his head. "Sean was supposed to be the farmer here."

"No," Mona protested, moving towards her father. "He doesn't want to—he hasn't for a long time." She paused, searching for the words to express the ideas now buzzing in her head. She didn't think she wanted to leave like Sean did. Maybe not having a better plan was a sign that she belonged where everyone thought *he* belonged. "I'm not going anywhere. I could learn how to do it."

Loyal reached over to brush a strand of hair off her face, careful not to touch the bangs she relentlessly teased and sprayed stiff each day. "You're a hard worker, but farming—it's a tough go of it anymore. That's why we sent Sean to school. Milk prices are down, interest rates are up, the cost of feed and insurance always rises—hell, farming is more business and math than milking these days. You never showed any interest in college and whoever takes over needs to understand more than how to operate a tractor and a milking machine. I know you're trying to be helpful, but this is between me and Sean."

June moved between them, pulling them both into a hug. "We'll let this rest until tomorrow. It'll all work out."

Mona leaned into her mother's soft embrace and wondered, *Will it?* She closed her eyes. *I never saw myself tied to the farm anyway.* She kissed them goodnight. "I'm going home. It's getting late."

Zipping her new winter jacket against the cold night wind, Mona started her car and turned towards the one-bedroom house she'd bought a month before T.C. left. Buying the old Zimmer cottage advanced the inevitable end of things, pressing her roots deeper while he'd cashed out his assets to head west. He took the proceeds from his boat and snowmobile to fund his escape while she picked up a second job cleaning summer cottages to scrape up a down payment to stay put.

It only took five minutes to drive from her parents' farm to her house in town, not enough time for her car's heater to kick in. She glanced across the river as she crossed the bridge and saw the lights were on in the little blue cottage. Jake Paulick was home now. Funny how he'd come back to town. She'd always pegged him as someone who'd go places. She let the thought of him carry her home where she draped her jacket over the back of a kitchen chair and walked towards the glowing fluorescent grow light hanging over the countertop. There, in empty Butterfield's Best containers, grew five rows of young plants. Mona gently ruffled the tips of their fuzzy leaves, inhaling the earthy aroma of potting soil and green—that peculiar green smell that only comes from tomato plants.

Bold black letters on popsicle sticks tagged their identities—"Mr. Stripy" and "Brandywine" tomatoes, "Delicata Squash," "Lemon Cucumber." Mona found the seeds in February after Grandma Butterfield died. They'd been in her dresser drawer, twenty-two envelopes labeled with her shaky, spidery handwriting. As a sort of tribute to her grandmother and the memory of the huge gardens she'd maintained around the farmhouse, Mona tried to germinate the seeds. Out of the hundreds of seeds Grandma had saved, these straggly green plants sprung hopeful towards the light. A new vision of her back yard had sprung into Mona's mind since this modest success—a garden. Not just any garden, but a garden full of old-fashioned plants that most people didn't grow any more. Eggplants and beets. Celeriac. Huge yellow-striped tomatoes. A garden like Grandma's.

"Too bad Dad's not a vegetable farmer or I'd step up in Sean's place," Mona murmured before switching off the grow light purchased last month at Fleet Farm. She watched the kitchen window rattle in the wind before turning towards her bedroom.

14

TWO

Barrel-sized chunks of ice sped down the river, spinning when they rammed into each other. The river gleamed black and dangerous where it rose up the banks, pouring over docks and smacking the pilings. It slopped onto lawns, raced across parking lots and flooded the boat landing. Beneath the murky current walleye searched for food along the river floor, snapping at minnows.

A tiny clapboard building with peeling white paint and drooping gutters stood beside the highway, about a hundred feet past the billboard. A neon sign flickered "Open" behind smeared windows, where the dried carcasses of a million mosquitoes and flies lay heaped between glass panes and torn screens. Inside the shop a portly, bearded man dipped minnows in a huge aluminum tank. He alternately swigged Mountain Dew out of a can and dragged on a cigarette with his free hand while listening to the stereo propped on the shelf behind the cash register.

Maw Cooper suffered through the steady trickle of walleye fishermen, preferring the chaotic rush of the amateurs looking to hook white bass. Those fishing walleye came in slowly throughout the day, politely requesting their choice of bait and paying cash. These men knew what they wanted, and they didn't want to stand around talking about it. No hassling with credit cards or novice questions for these expert fishermen, thank you very much. That would wait until May when the city slickers sped into town in their shiny SUVs, eager to "live off the land" for three or four days out of the year before returning to their high-speed, sterilized lives behind cubicle walls. Maw liked his cash register full as much as the next guy, so he helpfully sold the weekend fishermen more bait than they'd ever use in a three-day weekend, and outfitted them with new rods and reels to boot. Yes sir, he preferred business in May, when the hours flew past punctuated by the constant ring of his register drawer opening.

Adam Lewsciewski, who everybody called "The Pole" for short, Scotty Trayson and Jake Paulick banged through the door, startling Maw out of his white bass daydream. The Pole was a tall, broad-shouldered carpenter who wore a perpetual grin. Scotty and Jake were several years younger than their fishing companion, Scotty deceptively innocent-looking with his huge brown eyes and brown curly hair. Jake had the athletic physique, cleft chin and thick blonde hair commonly seen on male models in the J.C. Penney catalog. The men clumped across the scuffed wood floor in their work boots. Maw emerged from behind a tank of minnows, happy for the interruption because his morning had been lonely. Only two customers since four o'clock and now it was almost seven.

"Maw! Did we scare you?" Jake asked. He plucked a pack of Big Red off the display rack and dropped a dollar on the counter before tearing it open. "It's walleye season, this place should be hopping—where are all your customers?"

"Not buying bait today, that's for sure," Maw said.

Scotty opened the back cooler and grabbed a six-pack of beer and a Styrofoam container of wax worms from the same shelf. Maw stocked his store by convenience, without regard for sanitary regulations. The Pole pulled out his wallet and plucked a ten-dollar bill with his thumb and forefinger.

"Don't you guys work for a living?" Maw quipped while he counted out The Pole's change.

"Not on a day like today. We're taking the morning off to catch supper. Jake told me last night they're biting well over by the railroad bridge. Don't tell our boss we're playing hooky." The Pole winked at Maw. "She thinks we're getting lumber up in Northport."

Two things always pleased Maw: taking a day off to fish and watching others take a day off to fish, especially when it involved a good cover story. He gave The Pole his change and reached under the counter.

"Try these." His stubby hands held out two heavy crankbaits. "They're on me."

"Thanks. These are wobblers." Scotty jiggled the two minnow-shaped crankbaits in his palm and tugged his jeans up a notch. He wore a thermal undershirt beneath a plaid flannel button-down with the sleeves cut off—a style Maw referred to as "Northwoods Hillbilly." "We'll let you know how we do."

"How's Angie?" Maw asked him.

"Fighting. She's still down at Children's Hospital, but my folks hope to bring her home in a couple weeks. It depends on how she responds to the chemo treatments. So far so good though." Scotty adjusted his faded Milwaukee Brewers cap over his thick brown curls. "Thanks for asking about her. We'll see you later, Maw." He gave Maw a nod and followed his friends out the door.

"We'll call you if we find out they're biting anywhere else," Jake called before slamming the door of his pickup truck and pulling out.

Side one of AC/DC's *Highway to Hell* had played out and he hated side two, so Maw hit rewind on the tape deck. While he waited for his music Maw wiped his glasses clean with the edge of his T-shirt and straightened a display of cigarettes. The tape deck ground to a stop and Maw punched "play." Then he returned to the minnow tanks and leaned above the swirling water to check the water temperature once more before adjusting a valve. "That oughta do it," he announced to the empty store before returning to his stool behind the counter.

Looking through the bug-smeared window at the faint daylight spreading across the sky, Maw noticed two of the light bulbs on his sign outside needed replacing. "Best get after that," he muttered. "Don't want to be known as 'Ma's Bat and Tackle'."

He tore yesterday's page off his Word of the Day calendar and read the word for March 12th. "Jactation—noun—the act of bragging, a false boast or false statement that causes harm to another person. Relentless tossing or jerking of the body in severe illness." Maw loved long, obscure words that nobody else heard of. He thought it made him sound smart when he said things like "fistulous" and "polygenesis" in the middle of a conversation. Since 1978 he'd religiously studied the daily offering in the Word of the Day calendar. "Jactation." He considered it for a moment before trying it out. "I don't think it's jactation to say my minnows are the best in town."

He had just nudged through the door of the storage room at the back of his shop, carrying his can of Mountain Dew and cradling two light bulbs in his arm, when the phone's ring pierced the quiet gurgle of the minnow tanks and the serene hum of the coolers. Maw started and the bulbs slid out of his arm, their fragile glass shells shattering on the floor. "Shit!" Maw kicked at the glass shards with his scuffed sneakers, turned down the wail of "Girls Got Rhythm" and reached across the counter to grab the phone receiver.

"Maw here," he snapped and shrugged the phone cord off his shoulder.

18

"Good morning. Am I talking to Maw's Bait and Tackle?" asked a low voice smoother than aged whiskey.

"Yeah. I'm Maw."

"Well, hello, *Maw*. This is Dave LaMay calling from Chicago. What's the fishing report for the week up there in *Bassville*?"

"Well, hello, *Dave LaMay from Chicago*." Maw adopted the caller's condescending tone in his gravelly voice. "The fishing report for the week is fair to middlin' provided you know where to fish and what to use for bait."

The voice on the other line rumbled with laughter at this response and went on to explain that he, Dave LaMay from Chicago, was a disc jockey at a radio station downtown. Knowing a number of Chicago natives made their way north to fish each spring, he thought he'd incorporate a fishing report into his morning program. Maw's happened to be the number provided to him by a friendly operator.

Maw recognized an opportunity for free advertising as fast as a sturgeon could gulp down a frog, so he launched into his pitch without missing a beat.

"Dave LaMay from Chicago, you tell your listeners that the best fishing is done with a minnow for bait. A fierce minnow. A minnow that goes after the fish itself instead of waiting passively for the fish to come find it in the murky depths of the Wissipaw River. You tell your listeners that very minnow is bred and raised and sold exclusively at Maw's Bait and Tackle right here in Bassville."

"Is that a fact?"

"Yup. Just off the highway. You can see my sign. Actually it reads 'Ma's Bat and Tackle' just now. I was on my way to replace a couple of bulbs in the "W" when you called. Could change the name to 'Ma's Bat and Tackle' and skip changing light bulbs, but I'd end up with a different business entirely, don't you know. But tell your listeners it's *MAW'S BAIT AND TACKLE*! Maw spelled with a 'W'."

Dave LaMay agreed his listeners would indeed know where to go since this phone call was live, on the air, at this very moment.

Maw grinned, delighted to have commercial air time at no personal expense. "It's not jactation, Dave LaMay," he paused to let Chicago absorb his intelligence, "when I tell you that I sell the best minnows around. Tell you what, Dave, anyone comes into my shop mentioning your show, I'll give 'em a free dozen of my specialty minnows. "

"That's quite a deal, Maw."

"Listen, call back tomorrow and I'll give you another report. About twenty guys in suits just came through my front door talking about some radio guy named Dave LaMay and free minnows. I gotta go."

"Until tomorrow then, Maw."

Maw hung up the phone and raised his "Born to Fish" coffee mug high in the air. "To Maw Cooper! Salesman extraordinaire! Come on, May! Come on, you fabulously wealthy anglers of the south!" He choked down a swig of cold coffee because a toast didn't count unless you took a sip, and whispered, "Call again tomorrow. Please."

Meanwhile, in the seventeenth floor of an office building overlooking the heart of Chicago's Rush Street, Dave LaMay announced the next song and pushed aside the microphone. He tilted back his head and closed his eyes and laughed. "I was supposed to talk to some country bumpkin, Will," he told his manager after catching his breath.

"I'm telling you, I just took the first number the operator gave me."

"We gotta call this guy again tomorrow. What a character!" Dave LaMay slapped his knees and thumbed through a stack of CDs. "He's almost as funny as me!"

THREE

Mona gazed out the Pub's front window, bar rag and bottle of Windex forgotten as she imagined living in the little blue cottage across the river. She'd add window boxes filled with lemon-scented geraniums and switch out the dingy brown blinds to curtains. Maybe a masculine plaid to keep the flowers from making the place *too* girly. They could put a wrought iron table and chairs and eat supper on the porch when the weather was nice … A yelp outside broke her reverie and she tore her gaze from the windows overlooking the river to the windows facing Main Street. Her grandparents inched across the muddy street toward her. Grandma Nancy rocked back and forth in her wheelchair, her puffy white face creased with glee. "Oh shit!" she cheered when Grandpa Frank plunged her through another waterlogged pothole and shoved her chair up to the sidewalk.

He paused for breath at the bottom of the ramp into the Bassville Pub before leaning his weight behind her chair once more, pushing her up the wooden structure which had been specially built for her.

Mona met them at the door, holding it open as they squeaked past her over the tile floor.

"Good morning!" Mona yelled to greet them since Grandpa Frank was mostly deaf. "Cold enough for ya?" She kissed them each on the cheek.

Grandpa Frank stopped and considered Mona's inquiry. "It is cold out. It was colder yesterday. Do you have French toast today? We want to eat French toast."

"You bet we have French toast. Go back and she'll take care of you," Mona shouted, returning to her post behind the bar while Grandpa Frank steered Grandma Nancy back to their favorite table overlooking the river.

Arlyce Shanski left her coffee and newspaper in the kitchen to take their order; Mona could hear their voices clearly over the hum of the coolers and the radio. A moment later Arlyce joined her behind the bar to get their water and coffee.

"Nancy's sure yelling at Frank today," Arlyce said, her mouth drawn down from a combination of too many cigarettes and too many worries, giving her an expression most people read as disapproving. "Guess he didn't want to leave the house."

"Why not?" Mona asked, stepping aside to let Arlyce get at the ice bin.

"Too cold, he says. Too cold and too much work. Told her he'd just come and get food to bring home to her." A sensible plan in her view.

"Like Grandma'd stand for that!" Mona said.

"No shit!" Arlyce said, her voice a perfect raspy mimic of Nancy's. Arlyce exchanged a grin with Mona before heading back to flip the French toast on the grill.

Since her stroke seven years ago, Nancy Alderidge could not speak to be understood by anyone, except her husband. It was amazing how they could sit and talk for hours, when the only decipherable words from Nancy's end were "yeah," "naw," and "oh shit." Fortunately, those three phrases were pretty useful in most situations. Anyone listening closely to the pair swore she crooned like a bird and Frank knew exactly what each sound meant.

Before the stroke, Frank and Nancy owned the Riverside Bar for twenty-two years. At the end of the pool league season every year (a few weeks before the walleye run got started), the teams had a huge party. Nancy always arrived wearing full-length sequined dresses and fur stoles, dripping with rhinestone necklaces and bracelets—one year she even donned a tiara. Frank would trail behind looking like her chauffeur in his one good pair of dress slacks and a navy suit coat. The two made such a happy, unlikely couple—Nancy, gregarious and loud, Frank, mousy and quiet. After her stroke, Frank put a For Sale sign in the bar's front window and turned the key over to a realtor. They moved into a first floor apartment in the old bank building downtown, and he had cared for her every day since.

Their daily routine included a long breakfast at the Bassville Pub. Both bound by Nancy's wheelchair, June handled most of their errands and all of their driving. Frank and Nancy spent their afternoons parked outside the door of their apartment, waving at every car and person passing their corner before returning indoors promptly at six to watch *Wheel of Fortune* and eat microwaved popcorn.

Arlyce carried two orders of French toast and a plate of sausages out to the dining room. "Here you go," she announced grandly, flourishing the tray as if she'd served them chateaubriand with baby asparagus and capers. She lit a Virginia Slim and sat at a table nearby. Mona sprayed down the next window and wiped it clean with a fistful of paper towels. Through the glass the current looked threatening today. The middle of the river had already broken up; small chunks of ice now flowed swiftly between the crust of ice on either side.

The Wissipaw River was wide at this spot, its surface deceptively calm. Far to the north the river was narrow and full of dangerous rapids where it passed through the Lac du Flambeau Indian Reservation. By the time it reached Bassville, a hundred and four miles later, it meandered in a deep and wide path through low-hanging trees and several small lakes. Anyone who swam or boated on the river knew it could quickly carry the strongest swimmer off course. The bayous and cuts made private and hidden spots, and only the locals really knew the extent to which the river became another world. Out-of-towners generally stayed on the widest stretch of the river, between Pigeon Lake and Long Lake. Beyond those points the river twisted itself into dead ends and branched into other less navigable bodies of water.

Bare branches reached the bleak sky above, the water reflecting the somber mood of the day. Early March was slushy. Obstinate. And the residents of Bassville tended to reflect the weather.

Eventually Arlyce stubbed out her cigarette and stood to stretch her lower back. The toes of her sneakers lifted slightly and her long silver earrings jangled against her thin cheeks while she rocked her torso back and forth, easing the kinks out of her spine. "Better get that chicken ready for tonight," she mumbled to nobody in particular and retreated to the kitchen. Mona finished polishing the last window while her next customers took up their spots at the bar.

"Morning, Mr. Trayson, Dad."

Gene Trayson and Loyal Butterfield always met at the Bassville Pub for breakfast after their monthly town council meeting to hash over the latest developments in town politics. They'd served on the board for a cumulative twenty-seven years, giving them an extraordinary aptitude for debating mediocrity like property tax allotments and sewage easement placement.

"Good morning, Mona," Gene replied, straddling his barstool and turning the coffee cup sitting on the paper placemat over with a heavy clunk. His large belly touched the edge of the bar and Gene folded his hands above it. Loyal leaned forward to peer at the chalkboard where the day's specials were posted above the cash register. The specials board was tricky to spot as the walls of the pub were plastered with old photographs, beer signs, posters and flyers advertising local events. Arlyce tended to take the board down to update the specials and rehang it in a different spot each time.

"How's Angie doing?" Mona asked Gene. Everyone who knew Angie, a sweet and shiny-eyed eleven-year-old with a penchant for horses and anything pink, could only ask her parents in a casually practiced manner for any shred of promising news. The aggressive nature of Angie's cancer coupled with the devastating cost of her treatments had been an ugly blow to the Traysons.

"Good. We're bringing her home from Children's Hospital in two weeks," Gene said, his smile belying his private agony. "The chemo's going well so far. Now we just have to find her some bone marrow. And some money to pay for it. Insurance won't cover 'experimental' procedures, but they say it's our best hope."

"Tell her I said hi," Mona said, placing her hand flat on the center of Gene's placemat and holding his gaze for a moment. He acknowledged her sympathy with a sigh. "I will."

"How's that country fried skillet?" Loyal asked.

"You'd like it, Arlyce puts lots of sausage gravy on the biscuits." Mona reached for the coffee pot and started filling their cups. "Sorry I didn't come over for dinner last night, Dad."

Loyal nodded at his daughter. "I missed dinner, too. Belt busted on the tractor. Had to head to Farm and Fleet for the part before last night's meeting."

"Have you talked to Sean?" she asked. Three days had passed since Sean stormed away from the supper table. Mona knew his mind was settled, but clung to the flimsy hope that something might change since the dairy farm wasn't going anywhere and *that* situation couldn't be altered.

"Nope." Loyal took a sudden interest in reading the daily menu.

"Do grandma and grandpa know? They're in the dining room." She wasn't going to be the one to drop Sean's bomb on her grandparents.

"Your mother will talk to them later," Loyal said. "I'll just go say hi to them." He crossed the bar towards the dining room.

Mona heard her father greet her grandparents and could picture him leaning down to give Nancy a peck on the cheek. "I'll be back with your sugar packets," she told Gene and walked back to the kitchen calling, "Arlyce, you got a couple of live ones out there."

"I'm on my way. Fill the salt and pepper shakers." Arlyce set her cigarette in the ashtray by the grill and picked up her order pad and pen. Duly armed, she sashayed out to the bar. "What'll it be today?"

Mona refilled her grandparents' mugs, and retrieved Grandpa Frank's napkin from the floor and set it beside his plate. Gathering salt and pepper shakers, she replayed her brother's words in her mind, trying to find the soft common ground where a peaceable agreement could grow. If only Dad would reconsider her offer to take over the farm—but he was right, she didn't have the training required to manage eighty-odd head of cattle and the county inspectors and the machinery mortgages. Farming was big business, much more involved than just doing chores. Dad had said he wanted a better life for her than the farm, but Mona couldn't imagine what the life might be. She'd started tending bar at the Pub five years ago—right after graduating from high school. But serving drinks was no way to *live* the rest of her life. She wanted something more fulfilling, more purposeful. The door of the pub slammed again and she balanced the tray on one hand before striding back to the bar. "Hey, Spade!"

A short, red-haired man with a bulging forehead and Coke-bottle glasses leered across the bar at her. "What's a guy got to do to get some service around here?"

"Depends on what kind of service you want," Mona returned with a sly wink.

She set the tray down on the far end of the bar, dropped sugar packets in front of Gene, and grabbed a pack of Marlboro Reds from the display rack hanging behind the register. Sliding open a cooler door, she selected a can of Mountain Dew and slapped both the soda and the smokes in front of Spade.

"What? No shake?"

"I didn't forget." Mona reached beneath the bar for the plastic carton holding the "Shake of the Day" money and handed Spade a black leather dice cup. He plopped four quarters in the carton and shook the dice.

"Nothing." He shook again. The dice rattled across the bar's wood surface.

"A pair!" Mona grinned at him encouragingly. "Want to go for it?" For an extra dollar Spade could roll one more time and hope for five of a kind.

"Are you kidding? You know what my luck is like. If it weren't for bad luck, I'd have no luck." He collected the dice back into the cup and slid it towards her. Spade's appetite for gambling sated for the moment, he turned his attention to the two men at the bar. "How are you gentlemen doing today?"

"Not bad, Spade," Loyal answered him.

"Been golfing yet?" Gene asked Spade.

Spade shook his head and got up to plug quarters into the pool table. "Anyone up for a game?"

Spade placed a wager on anything: dice, darts, golf, which direction a bird might land, it didn't matter. On a snowbound afternoon three years ago, Spade suggested betting on how the bar's ceiling fan would stop. The blade pointing toward the river would win the pot. "Oh, and let's make it interesting. I'll put a five-spot on number three." The blades of the ceiling fans above the bar were numbered that day with black magic marker, one, two, three, four. A crew of men had sat there wagering their paychecks on those fan blades for the entire afternoon.

A confirmed bachelor (marriage the only thing Spade wouldn't bet on), Spade wore the same faded combination of T-shirt and jeans every day, Ford Escort and drank tap beer or Mountain Dew. His sole indulgence besides gambling was his annual trip to Las Vegas every January. He offered the same report each year when he returned to Bassville: "The women there are professionals."

Mona refilled the saltshakers while Spade racked the balls on the pool table. "Want to play?" he asked her.

"Let me finish this first. Besides, you need to practice to beat me."

He chuckled and lined up for the break.

Mona and Spade worked in companionable silence for a while, the hum of the coolers, the muffled din of the radio, and Frank and Nancy's laughter drifting through the bar. Loyal and Gene drank their coffee and argued about politics. Arlyce sat down with the *County Post*, pulling an ashtray close to her coffee cup.

"What do you think?" Mona asked, jerking her head to indicate the river.

"Weather man says forties through the week, but we won't see the ice break up anytime soon." Arlyce was obsessed with the weather, her income depended on it as much as any farmer's would. She stared glumly out the windows and Mona set down the tray of salt and pepper shakers in front of her before grabbing a cue stick from a rusty barrel in the corner of the bar.

"Okay, Spade. You have it coming!"

He rubbed his palms together with glee. "Yeah, the day a *woman* beats me ..."

Across the street Snuffy rolled over on the pool table over at Grumpy's Tap. He stretched his beefy arms wide and scratched his head and face in the dusty sunlight, inhaling the lingering smell of stale cigarettes and sour beer. Even if undeterred by the forbidding flicker of the neon Pabst Blue Ribbon sign hanging crookedly in the street side window and the building's peeling red paint and screen door tilting off its hinges, one step across the banged-up threshold onto a sticky concrete floor was as far as the bravest, or drunkest, fisherman made it into Grumpy's. It was local turf. Tough local turf.

Snuffy shrugged off his sleeping bag and kicked it beneath the pool table before reaching for a grey mop and bucket of tepid water with grease glimmering on its surface. He sloshed the mop across the peeling linoleum floor around the bar and replaced the barstools around the bar's edge.

"A little sompin'-sompin' to get me started," he grumbled to himself, reaching for the bottle of Jack Daniels on the shelf behind a wire rack filled with bags of potato chips and pork rinds. He poured a glass half full and tipped his shaggy head back, swallowing the bourbon in a single gulp. He reeked of sweat and booze, his neck creases were permanently black with grime.

He slipped a couple crumpled bills out of his tip jar and found his red plaid quilted jacket behind the trash can. Stepping into the chill of the early spring morning, Snuffy coughed and spat into the street, then stuffed his hands into his pockets. He sidestepped one of fifteen whiskey barrels lined up along the sidewalk down the street. In another month or two the Ladies Auxiliary Club would pack them full of petunias and ivy, but today they only contained dirt, frozen solid and discouraging to look at. He shuffled briskly across the street to the café and paused to notice the ice beginning to break away from the riverbank. "Spring's on her way," he muttered.

Another loud slam announced Snuffy's arrival through the pub's front door.

"Mornin', Snuffy!" Mona greeted him with a wave. "Cold enough for ya?"

"Well, well, well, it's my favorite sexy lady," Snuffy wheezed in reply. He nodded to Loyal and Gene and joined them at the counter, a seat away. Arlyce tipped up the coffee cup on the placemat in front of him and poured it full before topping off the rest of the cups.

"What'll it be, Snuffy? The usual?" Arlyce asked.

"Eggs. Toast. Potatoes."

"Heya there, Snuffy!" Steve Shanski hustled into the bar, his face red with exertion as he carried two cases of liquor bottles through the bar to the storage room behind the register. His high-strung and upbeat nature contrasted sharply against his wife's lackadaisical and pessimistic attitude. When Steve and Arlyce inherited the Bassville Pub ten years ago from Steve's parents, they clashed over every decision, from what size napkins to order to whether to use a new vendor for their pizza sausage. Age and resignation dulled their sharp edges over time and they settled into each other, Arlyce taking over the kitchen and Steve the bar, their natures weaving into the smooth fabric of comfort and warmth that the Pub provided its customers.

"Mornin', you old son of a gun," Snuffy called to Steve.

"What do you know today?" Steve asked, lining up bottles on the shelves and filling the air with a rhythmic clanging of glass.

"Not much more than yesterday."

Steve chuckled and grabbed a box of empty liquor bottles to carry outside.

Snuffy turned his attention to the men sitting beside him, one short and squat, the other tall and broad. Gene and Loyal resumed their conversation.

"This town needs more revenue. We can't raise taxes. If we get new development, people moving to town, that'll increase our tax base.

Plus a man's got a right to sell his property however he sees fit," Gene argued.

Snuffy leaned forward, waiting for an explanation to bring him up to speed.

"You have no idea what can of worms this will open. We'll lose all our peace and quiet, the river will become a speed zone with private docks everywhere, the locals will get priced out. And those are just the obvious problems." Loyal leaned back and exhaled loudly. "I'd love to see you convince Otto Zimm to go along with this. Maybe Vera and Dill will vote for it."

"What are you two bickering about this fine spring morning?" Snuffy asked.

"Money," Loyal told him.

"The root of all evil. Stay away from it," Snuffy joked.

Loyal chuckled but Gene's expression remained frozen. "Come on, Gene."

Gene slapped Loyal's thick shoulder. "Okay. I see the river's finally breaking up."

"Let's head out to the lake and get a little fishing in this afternoon," Loyal suggested.

The men shifted on their barstools, settling in for a good thorough talk about the weather and fishing while Arlyce handed over hot plates of eggs and potatoes, and toast. Spade racked up the balls at the pool table. "Snuffy! You up for a quick game? Mona's all work and no play today."

An hour later the bar was quiet, all the men had left for work.

"Did you hear?" Arlyce asked Mona from her perch in the kitchen.

Mona knew from her tone she had news burning a hole in her mouth. "Hear what?"

"I can't believe your parents haven't mentioned it yet," Arlyce reached for her leather cigarette case. Sliding a fresh smoke free, she lit it, dragging out the moment.

Mona wondered if the "news" referred to Sean. She doubted it. Even though Arlyce and June were childhood friends, that wouldn't be something Mona didn't already know.

Inhaling a second hit, Arlyce leaned forward so she could dangle her cigarette over the ashtray on the counter. "I overheard your father and Gene at the bar. Seems Gene and Dottie talked with a realtor two weeks ago."

"What for?" Mona asked.

"To put the farm up for sale."

"Why would they do that?"

"To pay for Angie's medical bills."

"*That's* what they were arguing about. I heard them getting into it, but I wasn't about to interrupt them. Wow. That's huge."

"I've got more. Did you hear about Jake Paulick?" Arlyce asked Mona while starting to load the dishwasher with egg-smeared plates.

"What?" Mona involuntarily glanced at the little blue cottage across the river from the pub. Jake's dry humor and quiet wit appealed to Mona as much as his good looks. As a freshman, she'd rushed to her locker between classes hoping that she'd see him and he'd talk to her. His locker was three down from hers, and she nursed a galaxy-sized crush on him. But Jake was a senior, captain of the football and baseball teams, Homecoming king, and casually dating a very popular classmate. On a rare and cherished occasion that she dissected and analyzed for weeks afterwards, Jake would smile and say hello to her, before jostling off with a crew of fellow jocks. Mona lived for those moments when he'd *smile* at her. Then, after graduation, Jake went away to college and only visited home on the holidays. Eventually she threw out the newspaper clippings she'd collected about his athletic career, his senior picture and the posters of her other high school crush—Shaun Cassidy. And then T.C. Barlow happened—well, thought Mona, perhaps *took over* would be a better way to put it. T.C. had all the passive force of a tornado; he'd commandeered Mona's life for three years before they broke up. When Jake returned to town a month ago, she had to wonder—karma or coincidence?

"What about Jake Paulick?" Mona asked again, trying to sound casual.

Arlyce smirked and took a long drag off her cigarette before answering. "He has a new job now."

"He does? Where?" Mona knew he wouldn't stay in town forever. He was too smart, too talented to remain in Bassville.

"Still with Beyer's Construction. But Dale Dohill was in here last night talking about how he's up for a promotion, probably to project manager." Arlyce said.

"Really?" Mona tried to picture Jake outfitted in a shirt and tie instead of his faded jeans and sweatshirt.

"Seems there's a big project up in Rice Lake that needs a manager." Arlyce tightened her smug grin while she watched Mona absorb this news. She knew Mona nursed a crush on the town's most eligible bachelor, but she was miffed that Mona didn't share this secret with her. She baited Mona every chance she got.

"Rice Lake? But—that's a hundred miles north of here! He can't take that job!"

"Why not?"

"Because," Mona stuttered. "Because he's too smart to settle for Rice Lake. A smart guy like Jake is better off waiting until something opens up in Northport. Then he's close to home and probably closer to the main office where he'll impress them more than from someplace a hundred miles from here."

"Since when are *you* an expert on how to get promoted?" Arlyce asked, shooting a glance over at Mona's frayed khaki pants and T-shirt sporting the Pub logo.

Mona flushed and turned away. "Need anything from the bar? Your coleslaw's done. I'm going to wipe down the bottles." She stomped out of the kitchen. Arlyce's laughter echoed down the hall behind her, magnified by the standing water by the back door of the kitchen. The Pub's back parking lot started to flood last week and the water still rose towards the building.

"Damn," Mona cursed, picked up a bar rag and worked her way across the rail—whiskey, brandy, vodka, gin. "Stupid construction company," she fumed, straightening the pour spout on a bottle of Wild Turkey. She'd talk to her best friend, Jenny Bender. Jenny would know what was going on. She was the biggest gossip in four counties.

FOUR

"Bassville hotel. how may I help you?" Judi Linske paged through the thick red binder to find the dates in question.

"How many people?" She tapped her pen against the desk and nodded. "We have a room that will sleep five ... No private bath available that weekend. Those rooms are all booked. We do have two bathrooms right down the hall from that particular room, however ... Okay, would you like to reserve that with a credit card? Go ahead." She jotted the numbers on a receipt and read them back to the man on the phone. "Your name as it appears on the card? Expiration date?" She copied the information and read it back to him. "We'll see you on May first."

Hanging up, Judi looked across the desk at the framed black and white photographs hanging on the lobby's walls. She'd discovered the pictures of men in derby caps lined up along the bridge, poles tilted into the river, during the hotel's renovation. Old timers told of white bass runs so thick that people could walk across the river from boat to boat and never touch water. Bassville was originally built around farming, a sawmill and the Dohill family's button factory, but fishing became the predominant industry when wealthy men from big cities yearned for vacations in the northern country at the turn of the century. The button factory closed its doors at the start of World War II and the sawmill cut operations in half, while tiny bait shops, taverns, and rental cottages popped up along the river. Fishing mainly provided locals with service jobs: bartenders, bait salesmen, river guides, waitresses. Every spring the town bustled around its out-of-town guests, serving up their meals and drinks, tidying up their cottages and campsites, selling them bait and gas and beer.

In the Wissipaw River, walleye ran earlier in the spring, right after the ice melted off the lakes and charged dangerously down the river, but walleye never had the same popular appeal as white bass. Bassville locals thought this was strange since walleye cooks up firm and flakey, broiled, baked or fried. White bass, on the other hand, tasted unpalatable unless it was smoked.

Nonetheless, white bass was king. Perhaps walleye fishing didn't appeal to the masses because the weather in March was too risky, still wet and cold. May days were more predictably balmy. After the ice melted slowly at first, and then vanished overnight, the river would rise above the docks and the walleye fishermen started towing their boats to the public landing. When the lilacs began their fragrant bloom, the out-of-state license plates appeared on the highways and people parked their cars, trucks and trailers around the public landing, crowding onto the river, into the cottages and taverns. All in the name of white bass.

Judi filed the receipt and crossed off the remaining room for the first week in May with a triumphant flourish. "Full up, Mom!" Judi hollered into the office down the hall.

"What's that?" Sue Linske appeared in the doorway, pushing her wire-rimmed glasses up her nose.

"We're full up! I just booked the last available room for the first weekend in May!"

Sue whooped and ran over to her daughter and caught her in a hug. "I told you this place would pay off!"

Judi laughed and hugged her mother even tighter. "By the way," she asked, "where's the Dynamic Duo? Haven't seen them around yet."

Sue shrugged. "Scotty called about an hour ago. They have to get lumber over in Northport again."

Sue and Judi had seen a newspaper advertisement for a "vacant hotel with restaurant facilities," arranged to purchase it, and showed up on a fall afternoon in a small truck packed tight with all they possessed. Most of the rooms in the ramshackle three-story building at 316 Main Street were furnished with mice-infested mattresses and battered dressers and the entire place stunk like old lavender and mold. They worked for months from dawn until dusk, scraping filth from each nook and cranny of the old boarding house.

During this time, Judi meticulously saved each old newspaper and photograph she came across, vowing to piece together the entire history of the hotel one day. By the end of that winter the bottom drawer of a file cabinet was full of paraphernalia, including a receipt from a room rented in 1934 for twenty cents a night. She even found a photograph of Joe McCarthy standing at the bar surrounded by the Bassville Town Council; she kept this historic find pressed between the pages of an old guest registry. The signature she later discovered in that registry confirmed that the Bassville Hotel had actually housed Wisconsin's infamous state senator.

Sue and Judi scrubbed the floors, patched and painted the walls. Sue wore out two pairs of rubber gloves every week from February to April, and Judi followed her mother wielding a paintbrush and toolbox. Completely refurbishing the tiny rooms themselves took considerable effort, but by spring they had four rooms ready for the fishing season. Twenty-five dollars rented a room that included clean bedding, electricity, running water in a community bathroom down the hall, and limited use of the lobby's phone. Amenities like color TV and air conditioning could be found at The Bassville Pub.

The Linskes made enough that first spring to contract The Pole and Scott Trayson to begin work on the lobby and front bar. The locals watched with interest and speculation as these rooms took shape with open beamed ceilings and richly varnished wood floors.

By the time Sue and Judi reached the four rooms on the third floor of Bassville's tallest building, they'd used forty bottles of bleach and Windex, twenty-eight pairs of rubber gloves, and Judi begged her mother to hire someone to clean. "I'll cook, I'll do books, anything, but if I smell ammonia one more day, I'll vomit."

Word of the refurbished hotel spread as fast as the springtime ice flow down the river, and fishermen who'd previously booked tiny and primitive resort cottages began calling for reservations. In the local watering holes every man in town grilled The Pole and Scotty about the Linskes that first winter.

"What about Sue? Obviously Judi's got a father. Where is he?" Dale Dohill prodded, a worse gossip than the women attending the weekly Ladies' Auxiliary meetings.

Steve shrugged and gathered empty bottles off the bar. "I hear they're in the witness protection program. Maybe Sue's husband is a mobster or something."

"How old do you figure they are? Judi doesn't look a day over twenty-two," Beau Longwell mused, a lascivious grin on his handsome face. Judi was tall, auburn-haired and stacked.

"Come on, Pole! You never put the moves on either of them?" Maw asked in disbelief.

The Pole and Scotty maintained that both women behaved professionally, above reproach, and no, they never heard nor saw anyone else around the hotel when they were there. This shocked everyone. The Pole always bragged about his exploits with women, fictional and real. The weekend the hotel's bar opened, every bachelor on the fighting side of fifty and a few who were not, plus several married men, showed up to discover a scrawny elderly bachelor with a scraggly moustache behind the bar. This squelched any chance of the hotel's bar becoming a local hot spot. The Bassville Hotel provided a cozy place for locals having a drink at each tavern, a tradition known as a "Death March," to warm up with a fifty-cent tapper between the Riverside Bar and Grumpy's.

Judi had just begun filling out an order for the bar when Maw strolled into the lobby. She greeted him with a puzzled frown. Locals never walked through their doors during the daytime. "Can I help you?"

"Nice place," Maw remarked, nodding at the wall of framed photographs.

"Thanks," Judi said.

Maw continued studying the photographs and Judi waited behind the counter, resting her hands on the glossy varnished surface. Down the hall a door closed and the muffled sound of running water filled the silence. Finally Maw approached the desk and handed her a tin can with a slot cut in the top.

Judi lifted the can and examined its label. "Spare Change for Angie Trayson," she read. "Eleven-year-old Angie Trayson has been diagnosed with leukemia and needs a bone marrow transplant to survive. Please donate your spare change to help keep this beloved angel alive and to help her family pay for her care. Every penny counts!" She looked up at Maw. "Is she related to Scotty?"

39

"His younger sister," Maw said.

"How sad. He never mentioned her."

"Huh. Well, Scotty's not a talker, he's more of a bullshitter."

"That's true," Judi agreed. "How much you want me to donate?"

"Anything you want, but I was really hoping you'd leave this here on your front desk. My wife, Peg, and her friends thought this would be a good way to help the Traysons. Figure with all the fishing traffic, these cans should fill up pretty fast."

"Absolutely. In fact, if you want to bring by another one, we'll put it in the bar."

"That would be eminent of you. Thanks." Maw scratched his beard. "Now for the business end of my visit. Let's say a guy wanted to get a room," he said, leaning one elbow on the counter and looking up at Judi. "What sorts of amenities do you offer?"

"Breakfast, hot water in the shower, clean linen …" Judi trailed off. "You looking for a room, Mr. Cooper?"

"Maw. Call me Maw, my father's Mr. Cooper."

"Maw," Judi repeated. "Did you need a room?"

Maw shook his head. "I might have a friend coming to town and he might want to stay here. What do you charge?"

"Twenty-five a night. Do you know what dates your friend will be in town?"

"No. What if a guy wanted a block of rooms—you get a discount for that?"

"No," Judi chewed on her lower lip for a moment, perplexed by Maw's sudden interest. "We're booked through May, but we've got a couple rooms open in April and again in June."

"Good to know." Maw slapped his hand against the counter twice and started towards the door.

"Is that all?" Judi called after him.

"For now," Maw answered and pushed through the heavy oak door

40

leading to the street. "I'll drop that other can off later this week."

Judi shrugged. Something was afoot, but her life in the hotel was so insulated she figured it probably wouldn't affect her anyway.

Outside on the street Maw got into his car and drove back to the bait shop. The new generation of fishermen wanted convenience, he was convinced of that. His latest brainchild was to sell packaged vacations. He could rent rooms directly from the Linskes at full price, but charge customers a bit extra—a booking fee. For his efforts, he could pad their price of thirty-five bucks a person—charge them forty and pocket the difference. What would it matter to the Linskes, he rationalized, so long as they filled up their hotel? If anything, he decided while easing his car up the gravel driveway to his bait shop, he'd be doing them a favor by booking more rooms for them.

FIVE

THE RIVER ROSE FOUR feet after three days of a steady, relentless rain. The Bassville Pub, built eighty years ago on the lowest point of Bassville's riverbank next to the adjacent boat landing, let the water through its doors.

Mona and Arlyce wore hip waders and sloshed through ankle-deep water to serve their customers. The Shanskis devised a system which left nothing below the 1964 high water mark, three feet off the floor. Boats tied up next to the back door using one of ten dock cleats mounted to the wall facing the river, and the fishermen waded straight from boat to bar. When the dining room was added ten years ago, they'd built it high enough to keep the water at bay. The kitchen kept fairly dry, too. Anyone wanting lunch at the bar left their boots on or risked getting wet feet.

Arlyce was shooing a couple of wayward Mallard ducks out the door and Mona was washing glasses when Steve stepped through the front door, kicking the water ahead of his long stride.

She turned midstream and shoved the door shut against the

indignant ducks' squawking, then followed Steve into the bar. From the pool table, their youngest child cooed and kicked in her car seat.

"What nights do you want off next week, Mona? I have to do the schedule. Cook's sick," Steve said. He rocked the car seat gently and patted the baby's bald head.

While Arlyce ran the kitchen, books, and staff, Steve managed the bar. He preferred to limit his involvement to pouring drinks and ordering cases of whisky. Questions like, "How much chicken do you want to order next week?" and "Do you want potato salad or french fries?" left him shrugging and snapping, "Talk to Arlyce."

"How sick?" Arlyce perched on the edge of the pool table and watched the baby contentedly suck her fingers.

"Chicken pox."

Arlyce and Mona gasped.

"Chicken pox! That's terrible! When did she get them?" Mona asked.

"Last night. The doctor says she'll be laid up at least a week."

"What are you going to do?" Mona stopped wiping a pitcher dry, dreading the answer before Steve uttered it.

The Bassville Pub employed four people, plus an itinerant teenager who helped out in the kitchen doing dishes and slicing potatoes during the busy season. A sick employee meant closing early. They couldn't only keep the bar open, during the spring when business picked up.

"Work more hours," Steve told her.

"How's *that* schedule going to look?" Mona asked. She rubbed the back of her neck and studied the calendar he'd laid on the table.

"We'll have to cook for ourselves. You take the nights and I'll do the days," Arlyce told her. They looked at Steve, who took off his bifocals and polished them on the edge of his polo shirt. Putting them back on, he tugged a frayed spiral memo pad from his jeans' pocket. His thumbs worked through the pages until he came to a blank one. "What else do I have to do?" He gripped a pen in his left hand, tense and ready to copy their commands.

The two women dictated instructions and watched him struggle to get everything down with his chicken-scratch writing.

"We're open all week starting Monday." Steve tapped his pencil against the schedule he'd graphed across his notepad. "I'll open with Arlyce at six and help through the breakfast crowd. Then I'll leave at ten, come back at noon. Mona'll help prep at four and Arlyce leaves at six. Mona finishes the dinner shift alone and she'll close. Arlyce orders all the food, I'll still stock the bar and the Cooper girl starts this weekend in the kitchen so we can stay on top of this mess. Everybody clear?"

"Yes, chief!" Mona saluted with a stern expression.

"Get back to work, then. You still have to batter that fish before you leave."

Mona grunted and hopped off her bar stool with a small splash. "Oh, I was going to ask, do you want me to mop up when I close tomorrow night?"

"Very funny, Mona." Steve rolled his eyes at Arlyce, who raised her thin penciled eyebrows and lit a cigarette. She inhaled sharply and blew the smoke out the side of her mouth away from the baby.

"The kids'll have to come here after school if I'm working until six," Arlyce warned Steve. "They're too young to go home alone."

"Can't your mom watch them?"

"She's got the baby all day and gets the boys off to school. Plus I promised to help plan the benefit for Angie Trayson, and we're meeting every day at two."

Steve sighed heavily. "You can leave at two. All right?"

"Sorry," Arlyce shrugged, her expression anything but apologetic. She looked at Mona, waiting.

"I can handle it, Steve," Mona said, shooting Arlyce a scowl. "Rather bust my ass here alone than trip over your rugrats."

"Get out of here," Steve barked.

"Employee meeting done then?" Mona said, cocking an eyebrow. "I didn't get to ask you about my raise."

"Mona! Got an order here!" Mona jerked herself out of a daydream about Jake rushing through the back door of the pub to rescue her from a life of hard labor.

"Be right there," she called, wiping a strand of hair off her cheek with her forearm since her hands were covered in flour from battering fish. She wiped her hands on a towel and grabbed her order pad. Her waders squeaked while she passed through the bar, smiling at the familiar faces lined up with their Friday night drinks. They'd had a nice steady flow of customers during the last slow weekend before fishing season really got under way. Steve pointed to a table overlooking the river where two couples sat with menus.

"Mona?"

Mona's heart jumped at his voice and she saw Jake at the end of the bar, leaning on his forearms, holding a bottle of beer. He waved her over.

"Yes?" She tried to strike a casual pose. He wanted to order a hamburger, that was all.

"You have a little bit of …" he gestured to his face and then pointed at hers.

"What?" Mona reached up and touched her cheek, feeling the grit of fish batter. "Oh!" Her face flooding red, she nodded and rubbed it away. "Thanks," she mumbled, ducking her head and heading for the table. Of course she'd had something on her face when he saw her. She had no chance of impressing him ever.

On her return trip to the kitchen, Mona avoided looking directly at Jake. She'd just about passed him when he reached out his hand and held her shoulder. "Can I order, too?"

"Sure." She frowned, feeling the blush creep up her neck again like an unwelcome rash. Could he possibly know that she'd been thinking about him? "What'll you have tonight?" She still felt the heat of his touch through her T-shirt.

"The perch special, please. With fries."

"Anything else?"

"A smile would be nice."

She met his gaze and gave him a weak smile. He shook his head.

"I've seen better than that." He lowered his head towards her. "I didn't mean to embarrass you before."

A bubble of hope rose in her chest. "No. Absolutely not. Your fish'll be right up."

The rest of the night Mona smiled easily at Jake each time they made eye contact.

SIX

THE *County Post* HEADLINE created an uproar when it hit newsstands on Monday afternoon.

"A development," Otto Zimm sniffed and blew his nose into a grubby-looking handkerchief. "That's a fancy word for big-city neighborhood, ain't it?" If he didn't like the convenience of plumbing and electricity, Otto would live further off the grid than Bassville. "City stuff." He spat the words with disdain.

"It's a good idea," Dale Dohill argued. "Bring a lot of new business to Bassville—bring this town into the twenty-first century. Imagine, instead of having to drive all the way to Northport, we could get a Farm and Fleet or a Kmart right here."

"Bring a lot of uppity yuppy types if you ask me," Arlyce grumbled, rereading the article. "What's a *Radio Shack*? And why the hell do we need a dry cleaners?"

"Arlyce is right. You know what kind of people build houses like these? The kind that does all their business in Northport—those people won't do anything for businesses here. Those people think country life is swell until the farmer down the road spreads manure on his fields. Or there's a blizzard and they're snowed in for half a day and they're calling and complaining to Town Hall until someone drops everything and plows them out." Loyal Butterfield tore open a sugar packet and drained its contents into his coffee. "That kind is better off staying where they are."

Snuffy dug a forefinger into his ear. "Seems like the kind of city people who'd take the trouble to move here might be country people at heart. You never know."

Otto shot him a skeptical look.

"Maybe, but they'll boost the tax base if they move here," Dale said. "Don't know, but every other town seems to do okay with this kind of thing."

"Bassville isn't every other town. If you want to be every other town, then you should move to one. We've done just fine for a hundred and twenty years and we'll keep doing just fine if we keep outsiders out. Don't need a bunch of city types telling us how to run things." Otto pushed his empty coffee cup forward and knocked it on the bar a few times to let Arlyce know he was ready for a refill. "Next thing you know they'll clog up the river with their jet skis and what-all—scare off all the ducks and fish and destroy the wetlands. I like my peace and quiet."

Jake nodded thoughtfully before speaking up. "You can be smart when you develop, Otto. And we have laws to protect the river."

"Laws are made by special interest groups, not for the good of the environment," Otto groused.

"Maybe," Jake said and paused until Otto looked over at him, "but don't assume that every person who'd move to Bassville is bent on wrecking it. Besides, wouldn't it be nice to pave a few roads around here, improve the parking by the boat landing? Seems like a new development would bring us some perks, too." People hated change, he understood this fact. That's why you had to accentuate the positive when addressing it.

Mona listened to them talk while reading the article over Arlyce's shoulder. April's town board meeting would determine whether to rezone property on the east side of the river from agricultural to residential after a series of scheduled public hearings. Beyer's Construction had submitted the official plan to turn part of the Trayson farm into a subdivision. Mona wondered about Jake's remarks; he seemed to love the river and the quietness of town as much as most people—why else would he buy property on the river? Obviously he appreciated the fishing and the fun and the beauty of it. But on the other hand, construction was his business and that meant building things like subdivisions and it sounded like he was for it.

"This is more than some subdivision going in. Gene's farmed that land his whole life, it was in his family for three generations. I'm sure he didn't make the decision to sell out lightly. Man's gotta do what a man's gotta do," Dale said with a defiant scowl at Otto. He doubted Otto even changed the radio station he listened to. Talk about a man with habits.

"But before Gene's family farmed it, some native tribe was hunting that same land. Change happens," Jake said with a wry smile, easing the building tension around him. "Some folks even might call it progress."

"But it's about his girl more than about farming being tough, isn't it," Otto said.

"Yeah," Loyal nodded and the group at the pub fell silent. Angie needed a bone marrow transplant and nobody's health insurance could cover the cost of keeping her alive. The only way to get that much money was to sell because land was worth much more than all the dairy cattle in the county. If it was his daughter, he'd do the same thing. Loyal looked at Mona and for the first time wondered what she was still doing in Bassville working at the Pub. Why hadn't they pushed Mona more to go to college? His daughter looked suddenly small and frail beneath a baggy sweatshirt. Loyal stared at her until she looked up and smiled at him, her green eyes twinkling as if laughing at some private joke. He returned the smile, feeling somehow he'd missed something important and couldn't for the life of him remember what.

On the other side of the river Maw picked up the bait shop phone on the first ring. "Maw's."

"Hey-hey, it's Chi Town DJ Dave LaMay! How're they biting today?"

"Hey-hey, Dave LaMay. They're biting as good as can be expected with the ice still flowing. I mean, how the hell can you expect a fish to bite when it's getting knocked upside the head with a chunk of ice speeding down the river in the other direction?"

"Not so good then?"

"Did I say not so good? I said *as good as can be expected*. Now if you want to really land the walleye today, there's one thing you can do to improve your chances, outside of fishing the lake and Helmut's Bayou." Maw shut the window to muffle the hoarse cries from the flock of mallards paddling through the ditch near his shop. The weather had warmed up enough to turn off the heat, but the clamor of those *ducks* was impossible.

"What's that?"

"Well, Dave, have I mentioned Maw's Minnows?"

"Now that I think of it, you have." Dave eased straight into Maw's pitch.

"Really? Well I'm here to tell you that I've got three kinds of minnows for sale at my store: Passive-Aggressive, Belligerent and

Cantankerous."

"That so?"

"Yup. Bred 'em, cross-bred 'em, reared and raised 'em. They're ready here at Maw's Bait and Tackle, located off of Rural Route 20. Each breed of minnow here at Maw's is fed a very specific diet to maintain its temperament. Even keep them in different tanks. You mix a Cantankerous with the Passive-Aggressive and you end up with one pissed off minnow surrounded by a bunch of tiny minnow bones. Let me tell you, it's a bitch cleaning those miniscule bones out of the filters. That's a mistake you only make once."

"Really?" Dave laughed.

"Did that back in '76. Took me three weeks to get the tank up and running again and took me another three years to replace my Passive-Aggressive stock."

Dave shook his head and swatted at his manager with a rolled up *Rolling Stone*. "You hear that, Will? Maw, I think you've just sold your listeners on the Cantankerous Minnow."

"If you say so, Dave. It all depends on the weather. Your choice of bait can change on a dime out there. I'd almost tell a guy to use the Passive-Aggressive today for white bass, what with the ice flow and all. I'll let you know tomorrow what they're biting on."

"You heard it here first, folks. Passive-Aggressive and huge chunks of ice in the river. That's the word from Maw's Bait and Tackle in Bassville. And here's *I Want You to Want Me*, by Cheap Trick." Dave punched down the microphone and spun around in his chair. "You hear this guy? He's solid gold, Will. Solid gold."

"He's all that." Will wiped his eyes. "Bones in the filter. What a character."

Maw hung up the phone and raised his coffee cup above his head, sloshing a little down his arm in his enthusiasm. "To Maw's Bait and

Tackle and you Passive-Aggressive little fish!" He walked back to the huge swirling tanks of water and watched the minnows dart beneath the surface, their shadows mixing with the water's current. "Maybe I should have a marketing budget." He gazed at the minnows for another moment lost in thought.

"A new TV set could go over there—I'll take this old clunker and toss her in the trash. Some display cases for reels and tackle. And new beer coolers. Maybe take out the back wall and build on. Could have a whole room devoted just to waders and vests and such. Get ads in the *County Post* and the *Bargain Bulletin*, maybe do some radio spots."

The door slammed, interrupting Maw's bait shop.

"Maw! How's she goin' today?" Dale called.

"Exemplary today. How's it with you two?"

Dale and Dob leaned easily on the front counter, their enormous frames crowding the small space, but they moved with athletic grace. The Dohill brothers could trace their bearish size and providential luck from an early Bassville settler who opened the button factory. Counted among Maw's best customers, the brothers shared a thriving construction business, Dale handled electricity and plumbing, while Dob did the rest of the general contracting work. Nearly every man in Bassville had worked for them in some season of life, doing odd jobs and learning the basics of their trade. Almost every building in Bassville had been built or improved upon by one of the brothers, whether repaired, replaced or renovated.

"It's good. Too wet to work today, so we're gonna fish up in Helmut's Bayou." Dale traced a calloused finger across the dusty glass display case.

"Excellent plan. It's never too wet to fish. That's the great thing about fish, they don't care how wet it gets," Maw said.

"Of course, we could sit in your parking lot and go duck hunting, too." Dale let out a loud, barking laugh.

54

"Go ahead—make my day," Maw told him. "They make me nuts with all their honking."

Dale leaned forward to study the reels laid out in the case beneath his huge hands. "Got anything new?"

Maw scratched his jaw. Dale must have won at cards or something last night. "Got some extra money burning a hole there, Dale?" He didn't have anything new in stock that the Dohills didn't already own, and he wasn't about to sell them what they didn't need. You just didn't do that to the locals.

"Won big last night up at Grumpy's," Dale told him.

"You did?" Maw asked.

"Sure. Playing craps." Dale leaned back, his denim shirt straining across his chest.

"Who was the big loser?"

Dale and Dob grinned and chorused, "Spade."

"No shit! Man, if it weren't for bad luck—" Maw began.

"Yup. He'd have no luck." Dob finished and headed back to fill his cooler with two six-packs of beer and a Styrofoam container of grubs. "Grab some spinner baits, Dale."

"Of course it doesn't help much that Dohills are born with horseshoes up your asses," Maw said admiringly.

"Did we tell you? Dad won a new van."

"He did? When was this?" Maw asked.

"In Northport. He bought some raffle tickets at the Ducks Unlimited banquet. First prize was a new Ford van!" Dale announced this as proudly as if he'd won it himself.

"I'll be damned. Is there no end to your luck?" Maw asked, knowing that Dohill luck never ran out, except with women.

"Not really." Dale flashed his gold tooth with a huge grin. "Not yet anyway. And there's more."

"What's that?" Maw asked. Short of winning the lottery, what else could possibly go right for the Dohills?

"You hear the scuttlebutt around town? Gene Trayson's selling his farm." Dale rubbed his palms together. "He's trying to get zoning to develop it. It's a great time to be in the business of building things."

"Develop it?" Maw asked. "Like build houses?"

"Houses, strip malls, all kinds of development."

"Must be a lot of money in that kind of a deal," Maw mused.

"Sure is," Dob agreed.

"They can't get Angie better without it, can they?"

"Don't think it was an easy choice for Gene and Dottie." Dob headed towards the minnow tanks, bait bucket in his hand.

A brief fantasy of a drive-thru bait shop window flickered through Maw's mind before Dale interrupted him.

"Hey! What's this I hear about some new minnow you're selling?"

"Huh?"

"I was on the phone yesterday with a window company rep in Chicago and this guy asked me about some crazy-sounding minnow he'd heard about on the radio." Dale banged the cooler door shut and strode to the front of the store. "I got a twelve-pack and grubs in here. I'll pay for the spinners and this loser's minnows, too," he added, nodding towards his brother.

"Twenty bucks." Maw punched *No Sale* on the cash register and let the drawer slide open.

Dale pulled out his wallet and handed Maw a fifty. "Sorry," he smirked, "don't have anything smaller than that."

"Does Spade have any of his paycheck left?" Dob and Dale chuckled while Maw counted out the change. "Yeah, the minnows. It's a new marketing approach. Same old minnows, just new and improved packaging. Trying to inveigle the city slickers with some fancy terminology."

"Good luck with that."

"We're going to try our luck at fishing," Dob added. Dale shoved him on their way through the door and Maw cringed as Dob's six-foot, three-hundred pound frame collided with the doorway, the shop shuddering with the impact.

"Get back here, you son of a bitch!" Dob regained his balance and took off running after his brother.

"Hey! Is that any kind of way to talk about our mother?" Dale shouted.

"She gave birth to *you*, so yeah!"

Maw watched the two burly shapes climb into the front of Dob's jacked-up pick up truck. The doors slammed, muffling any further argument from his ears. Every public establishment in Bassville bore the scars of their fighting. Seven years ago Dob took out the bait shop's front window when he pitched Dale through it in the middle of a fracas about losing a bet on a Packer-Bear game. Maw pulled at his beard. "So this minnow thing's taking off. And Bassville's about to get bigger."

"Maw!" Maw jumped at the sudden screech of his wife's voice crackling through the monitor plugged in beside his radio. He reached across the cash register and pushed in the red "talk" button. When Maw opened his bait shop, he and Peg were always yelling across the yard between the shop and the house. She'd picked up an intercom at Sears on a whim and it had improved their communication and saved them from screaming their throats raw every day since they'd hooked it up.

"What, Peg?"

"I need to go to the store. Want anything?"

"What's for dinner?"

"Savory Stew, and yes, I'm picking up frozen pizzas."

"Do we have Mountain Dew?"

"It's on my list."

"We should be good." Maw lifted his finger off the "talk" button and quickly pushed it in again. "On second thought, grab some of those frozen chicken pot pies."

Peg's voice crackled back through the intercom. "Can't I just make homemade?"

"No. Those frozen ones taste better. Sorry."

"Fine. I'm going to pick up the kids from school and I'll be back by four."

Maw pulled his hand back from the intercom. Hot stew, cold Mountain Dew, and maybe there'd be something good on TV tonight. His name getting around Chicago and potentially twice as many people living in Bassville. His future looked providential.

SEVEN

The lull at the pub happened between two and four in the afternoon—after the lunch rush and before the happy hour crowd claimed their spots at the bar. Normally Mona relished the quiet, reading magazines or doing crossword puzzles in the newspaper while Arlyce knitted alongside her, but since Cook's chicken pox, she hadn't time to even flip open *People* magazine.

"I didn't think it would be so exhausting being here every single day." Mona sloshed through the bar and leaned her head onto her arms, the length of her spine curving into a long stretch.

Arlyce flicked ash from her cigarette into the ashtray, bits of it floating gently onto Mona's hair.

"It'll be Memorial Day before you know it." Arlyce inhaled her cigarette and turned around to gaze out the window. The river floated past, more water than ice now, although they could see ice shanties still standing on the frozen bayou on the other bank. "Besides, think of how rich you're getting."

"They're walleye fishermen, Arlyce. Not exactly big spenders."

"Just wait." She stubbed out her Virginia Slim and exhaled. "Supposed to get up to fifty today. Practically a heat wave."

"That'll make the road a mess," Mona grumbled. She sighed and pushed herself upright. She still had coolers to restock.

"You talk to Sean yet?"

Mona looked at her, surprised. Normally Arlyce got family news from her mom. She and Arlyce talked to each other almost every day. "Yeah. We talked a couple days ago. He's not changing his mind. He called the house and I guess Dad refused to talk to him."

"He's a stubborn kid. Still, farming's a tough life. If he doesn't want to do it, he shouldn't have to." Arlyce wound a few ends of yarn into loose knots.

"Maybe. Could you see Mom and Dad selling like the Traysons, though? Retiring to spend their winters in Florida and their summers on the golf course?"

Arlyce laughed and tucked her knitting needles into the ball of yarn. "Remember, dear, Dottie and Gene aren't retiring to Florida. They're fighting cancer. Give me a hand with the coleslaw."

The door swung open and Frank poked his head through the doorway. "Hello? Anybody here?"

"Sure are, Grandpa. Need help?"

"No, no. I've got her."

"Help him, Mona." Arlyce commanded.

"I'm going to." Mona reversed her course and waded back through the bar. "Grandpa, it's pretty deep through here. I'll help you push her around the back way."

"If it's not too much trouble."

"Trouble? Come on. Of course she's trouble!" Mona winked at him and stepped outside, happy to escape the Pub, even if only for a few minutes of fresh air and sunshine.

Grandma Nancy crowed, "Shit!" She cut a glance at her husband. Mona knew he used to tease her like Mona still did.

"How are you today?" Mona asked.

"Shit!"

"I hear that! Arlyce says it's supposed to get up to fifty degrees. That'll make a huge difference, won't it?" Mona grabbed the handles and tipped Nancy's chair back gently, swinging her around. "Down we go. I'm taking you the back way. It's still deep water in there."

"Yeah?"

"Yup. Did you get your hair done? It looks so pretty today." Mona started a flow of conversation while steering Nancy past the dumpsters and through the rear parking lot, Frank tagging along behind them. The alley between the Bassville Pub and Bud's Supermarket didn't see much traffic since it only led to the boat landing and three houses beyond. Mona balanced the wheels of the wheelchair out of the deeper puddles and they slogged through to meet Arlyce standing by the kitchen door. Together they hefted the chair up the five wooden steps. Nancy clutched the armrests with both of her swollen hands and tilted her head back to laugh. Her white hair glowed like a cloud over her face in the midday sunlight.

"No one at the landing today." Frank looked across the parking lot at the lone boat trailer and truck.

"Nope. I told you, this season sucks." Mona stepped back to let him take over.

Frank steered Nancy through the kitchen, around the counter where Arlyce had a freshly lit cigarette resting in the ashtray next to her coffee cup beside a plastic tub of raw chickens. "Want that good table by the window?"

"Yeah." Nancy nodded and they rolled over to their usual spot. Mona checked the bar for customers and seeing none, headed for the first cooler to pull out a bus tub of cabbage heads. On her way to the dining room she grabbed a knife and cutting board.

"Before you know it, we'll have the windows open for the fresh air," she remarked to her grandparents before starting to chop. They fell into their own conversation and Mona was free to keep watch across the river. Jake's truck was still parked outside, unusual for a weekday morning. Mona wondered what was going on. He'd been in the bar for supper last night and then had gone straight home. She knew because she'd turned off the lights in the dining room to watch—he'd parked his truck, let himself into the cottage, turned on the lights and the scene had not changed when she'd headed home at ten o'clock.

"What's going on over there?" Arlyce asked, startling Mona.

"Where?"

Arlcye snorted in disgust. "I have to pick up the boys from school today. Steve's got to check his fish traps this afternoon."

"You coming back?" Mona asked.

Arlyce shook her head. "How long's his truck been there?"

"Since last night," Mona answered.

"Huh. Maybe he's sick," Arlyce suggested. "You should go over with some soup."

"No way. That would be weird."

Mona selected a new head of cabbage and cored it. Maybe he was sick. Maybe she should bring him soup and cough drops, a basket of cold remedies ...

As she finished chopping the last head of cabbage, the cottage door opened and Jake stepped out onto the deck. He carried a cardboard tube to his truck, climbed in and drove out the driveway, around the bend and out of Mona's sight. Was he off to seal the deal on his promotion with the big wigs at Beyer's Construction? Or maybe he'd made blueprints for the Trayson's property. She pictured plans for subdivisions, a strip mall, evenly spaced lines dividing up the pastures and cornfields. He'd never be that disloyal.

Steve relieved Mona a few minutes early and she dumped her tip jar into her purse, not bothering to count it in her rush to leave. "How's Cook?" she asked him.

"Crabby, itchy and scabby." Steve twisted the cap off a fresh bottle of brandy before jamming the pour spout into it.

"Wow. Some gals have all the luck!" Mona winked and slung her purse onto her shoulder. "Have fun tonight."

"You too. Got plans?"

"I'm meeting Jenny at Riverside for a Death March." Mona checked the clock. Jenny Bender became best friend on the first day of kindergarten when she'd grabbed Mona by the hand on the story rug and pointed to her matching pink argyle sweater. "We're twins," Jenny announced and they'd gone through life side by side ever since. Sure, Jenny was kind of demanding sometimes. But, Mona reasoned, she was also a lot of fun. She accepted both the good and the bad with Jenny.

"See you later then."

"In about four hours. When I leave, point me toward home so I make it there all right."

"How about I point you toward the river? You could go for a swim." Steve suggested.

"You're a riot," Mona patted the bar as she passed him. "I'm keeping my waders on tonight. It gets pretty deep around Jenny."

"Good thinking!" Steve said and shook his head while watching Mona walk out the door and down the street towards Riverside. Anywhere but Bassville a young woman wearing a hot pink blouse with olive green hip waders would draw attention. Steve swiped the bar rag across the spotless surface as he made his way around the bar. The customers greeted Steve with enthusiasm. Mona was nice, but

Steve might shake dice for a round, and he always knew a good joke.

"Hear the one about the proctologist who walked into the bar?"

The entire bar waited for the punch line, conversations, drinks and cigarettes paused in mid-air.

"He says to the bartender, 'your job's tougher than mine. I only have to deal with one asshole at a time!'"

The bar erupted with laughter and Steve refolded the bar rag.

"Woman, you're late!" Jenny Bender snapped at Mona as soon as she entered the Riverside Bar.

"I had to wait for Steve. Cook's still pretty sick."

"Nice waders." Jenny looked Mona up and down from her perch on the barstool by the back door of the tavern. They always liked to sit far back wherever they went, better for keeping an eye on the crowd.

"Thanks. Nice skirt." Mona envied Jenny's confidence, and the lavish allowance she had for new clothes. Jenny's denim miniskirt showed off two-thirds of her thighs and in a nod to the harsh spring weather, she wore bright red rubber boots to match her tight red-striped cardigan and the red scrunchie holding her blond curls in place.

"It's old. Check out my new bracelet." Jenny lifted her arm so Mona could admire the sparkling gold chain wrapped around her wrist.

"That's gorgeous. When did you get it?"

"This afternoon. After work I drove up to Northport and stopped in at the mall."

Jenny was such a regular customer at the mall she practically had her own parking spot. And as an impossible size two, her hand-me-downs and never-worns were no use to regular-sized people like Mona, who curdled with jealousy when she thought about Jenny's five overflowing closets. But Jenny was also an only child with divorced parents, Mona was never jealous of that. She'd rather have her mother close by any day than only see her a couple times a year.

"Get anything else?"

"No. It's all old stuff. The new summer fashions won't come out until April."

"Anyone else meeting us tonight?" Mona changed the subject while pulling her tip money from her purse.

"Who the hell knows?" Jenny blew cigarette smoke into the bartender's face. "Rosie, get her a tap. Out of mine." She gestured at her pile of money with a long talon-like finger.

"Thanks."

"You can catch me at the next stop."

"Did you shake yet?" Mona asked.

"No. I've been waiting for you."

"Rosie, we want to shake."

Rosie Isaacson, the heavy-set and jowl-cheeked owner of the Riverside, reached beneath the bar and grabbed a large plastic jar. The girls each dropped quarters through the jagged slit cut across the lid. Rosie set a leather dice cup sticky from beer in front of them. Jenny shook first and tipped the five dice onto the bar. "Nothing!" She shook again and laid the dice out of the cup. "Nothing again."

Mona gathered the dice and thumped the cup twice on the bar, her hand covering the top. She flipped it over and sent the dice rattling against an ashtray. "A pair of fives!" A fizzy rush of luck surged through her and she farmed out the two dice, dropping the rest back into the cup. "Come on," she breathed before covering the cup, thumping twice and spilling the dice across the bar.

"We have a winner," Rosie nodded with satisfaction. She'd rather see that hard-working Mona Butterfield win than that spoiled little Jenny Bender who'd had life served up on a silver platter. Rosie unscrewed the lid of the shake jar and counted out the contents.

"Forty-eight dollars and fifty cents."

"Thanks, Rosie. Catch everyone for me, okay?"

Rosie pulled several cans of beer out of the cooler. That Mona was a right sort, she thought as she set a fresh drink in front of each person sitting at the bar. "It's on Mona, she won the shake," she informed each group, the thick ridges of her fingernails peeling back the aluminum tabs with steady repetition—click-click-pshoow!

"Thanks, Mona!" echoed through the bar as each patron raised their beer in her direction.

A few miles down the river Beau Longwell speared two olives and dropped them into the martini he'd just poured for a customer at the Luau Room. Beau adored women, Pabst Blue Ribbon Beer, and money—but not in that order. Handsome and charming in an earnestly sleazy way with his slicked back auburn mullet and a gold chain hung around his tan neck, women loved Beau in return. An electrician by day, Beau enjoyed one of the few manual trades that didn't require getting dirty. At night he moonlighted as a bartender at the Luau Room. The Luau Room, decorated with tropical posters, fake palm trees and pineapple centerpieces, was a banquet hall and resort that catered to fishermen and boaters alike. On weekends a keyboard player entertained customers by playing old and new favorites from beneath a thatch-roofed tiki hut constructed against the bar's back wall. Beau's theme song was *Turn Me Loose* which he sang every weekend upon request while gyrating his slim hips to the electronic beat. Women ate it up. They ate up every line he served them, while leaning over to display their cleavage and coyly ask when he planned to settle down. But Beau had no intention of settling down—why ruin a perfectly good life by getting married? He could get laid any time he wanted without spending a dime.

Relationships were taboo, but Beau was addicted to sex, and like all addicts, he'd lie, cheat and steal to indulge his addiction.

Tonight his pickings were slim. No wedding receptions this weekend; it was past the season for holiday parties, and the fishermen were starting to arrive in town. He looked around the bar and counted seven females, five accompanied by spouses or significant others. His only options were Jenny and Mona. Jenny glared at him over the rim of her beer glass. Beau didn't make very loyal boyfriend material and two weekends ago Jenny walked in on him and Teresa Barlow. She'd been parked on the edge of the road and watched them stumble into his house together, drunker than a couple of frat boys on spring break, and barged in on them to scream obscenities and throw heavy objects at his back. That was one psychotic scene. Mona was too smart to get tangled up in his sheets. Not that he hadn't tried as soon as T.C. left town. She'd pushed him away and told him "Not in a million years."

He was horny and the only willing prospect in a twenty-mile radius was the line cook with false teeth and protruding varicose veins. Beau would have to make do with Pabst Blue Ribbon and cold, hard cash. Beau checked his watch: ten-thirty. The kitchen was closed and the after-dinner crowd nursed their drinks. Jenny and Mona were halfway through a Death March, so they'd leave soon. He watched them through slitted eyes.

Moments later, Jenny strutted over to the jukebox and punched the buttons for *Heartbreaker, I Will Survive* and *Stop, In the Name of Love*. Beau laughed out loud, pissing her off even more, and leaned over her shoulder to punch in F-7, *Only the Good Die Young*. If only they'd leave so he'd be free to check out the action in town. He itched to find one of the Dohills or Spade.

Beau kept his tip money in mayonnaise jars lined up in rows on top of his dresser in his bedroom next to an advertisement for oceanside rental cottages in the Bahamas for $30 a week. He planned to retire by forty to a Caribbean island where he could live on a sandy beach with a lifetime supply of cold beer. Beau had goals, long and short-term, and for the moment he focused his mind on finding a friendly dice game. Just as well, he reflected. Jenny might stalk him again tonight and God only knows what she'd do to him if she turned up drunk and unreasonable.

The next hour dragged while Beau wiped the bar's surface and straightened the row of top shelf bottles of liquor. The couples ambled out, wishing him good night and leaving their change next to their empty cocktail glasses. The jukebox finished Jenny's songs and Beau launched into *New York, New York* in a loud tenor while switching off a few cobwebbed neon bar signs. Mona and Jenny downed their drinks and headed for the door. "Good night, ladies! Drive carefully now!" Beau called to them.

Mona waved goodbye while Jenny followed her out, slamming the door in a huff.

A slow night took more out of a man than a busy night. Time flew when the bar was busy. Standing around waiting for the last customer to leave was excruciating.

Two hours later, behind the Bassville Pub, Mona hauled Jenny Bender off the ground by the back of her jacket. "Come on, get up."

"I'm fine. Don't rip my jacket." Jenny tugged at the front of her denim jacket and tipped over again.

"Christ! You're so wasted." Mona leaned forward and held out her hand while squinting to see across the river better. She'd hoped to run into Jake somewhere tonight, but no luck.

"Looking over at Jake's?" Jenny brushed Mona's hand aside and stood, leaning against the nearest car.

"His lights are off. He's probably asleep."

"You should go over and wake him up," Jenny encouraged her, untangling her hair from a jacket button. The rings on her fingers glinted. "Bet he doesn't even lock his doors. You could just walk right on in and make your move. Shit—I think I chipped a nail."

"Right. I'll just walk in while he's sleeping and do what? Pass out at the foot of his bed probably." Mona stared at the cottage's dark shape silhouetted against the dim moonlight. The swampy fog of drunkenness made it hard to think clearly.

"I think I'm gonna puke." Jenny braced both hands against the car's hood and retched. The foul soup of tap beer, Alabama Slammers, tequila shooters and stomach acid splattered the front bumper.

Mona choked back the bile in her own throat. A sympathy puker, the sound or smell of vomit made her gag. Backing away from Jenny's puddle, Mona watched her wipe her mouth with the back of her hand.

"Got any gum?" Jenny stumbled towards the bar.

"The Pub's closed. Let's get going. I'm cold."

"I want to see if Beau's in there."

"Jenny," Mona whined, "let's go back to my place. I'm freezing."

"Come with me, if he's not there, we'll go over to Jake's."

"And do what?" Mona was drunk enough to feel intrigued, but sober enough to chicken out.

"I don't know," Jenny snapped. "Come on!" She staggered towards the Pub.

Sighing heavily, Mona tromped around the rear of the bar. "He'll run if he sees you coming anyway, Jenny," she muttered.

Jenny banged on the bar window and stood on her tiptoes to look inside. Dark, except for the glow of the dart machines, and empty. Mona pressed her forehead against the glass and willed herself to feel sober. "No one's here. Let's go."

"I'll drive you to Jake's," Jenny offered, fumbling in her purse for her car keys.

"No thanks, *I'll* drive."

"NO."

"Whatever. Good night, Jenny." Mona crossed the deck and flung her legs over the railing, dropping to the ground below with a thud. Four more blocks and she'd be home where she'd mist her windowsill garden before burrowing under the covers in her nice warm bed. With a final glance across the river, she jogged up the street, her footsteps bouncing off the pavement and ringing in her ears.

A block away from her house headlights temporarily blinded her and she froze mid-stride on the sidewalk. A pickup truck slowed down and the driver leaned over to roll down the window and call to her, "You all right?"

She had hoped she'd run into him tonight. Overjoyed at her luck, Mona stepped towards Jake's truck. They'd probably been just missing each other all night, she realized. He'd probably walked into the Pub while she and Jenny were upriver at the Luau Room. "I'm good. What are you doing out so late?"

"Hot date over in Northport," he told her. "Need a lift somewhere?"

"No, I live right there," she said and pointed, trying to ignore the scorching disappointment in her chest. A hot date. She'd spent the night hoping to find him. Of course Jake wouldn't hang around a stagnant backwater like Bassville. He was looking for someone smart, sophisticated—not a small-town bartender. She felt stupid and sick and fought the urge to curl up right there on the road and cry.

"You sure?" He looked past her at her house.

Mona nodded. "I'm good."

"All right then. Take care." He waved and drove off while she watched his taillights shrink, then disappear around the bend.

A hot date, those were his words. It made sense. He worked in Northport; Bassville was probably just a stepping stone alone his way to a bigger city. Jake would probably lose his down-home charm and start wearing ties and dress pants soon. He'd become one of those guys who wore flannel a couple weekends a year to hunt or fish, using a place like Bassville for a vacation. That type, Mona reflected, traded in all the wild beauty of nature for convenience—drive through windows and parking lots and air-conditioned shopping centers. If Jake became that person, she decided she wouldn't like him much at all anymore.

EIGHT

"Five thousand, all black." Maw scratched the back of his neck with the sharpened point of his pencil. "I want the shop logo on the back, the minnow stuff on the front. How many weeks is this gonna take?" Grunting, he scribbled the date and sales code on the box top of a Remington Ultra-Lite reel. "Send it," he barked and hung up.

Maw turned to look at his wife who stood in the doorway holding a box full of notebooks, receipts and envelopes. "The T-shirts are on their way. Now we just need that extra something. Any ideas, Peg?"

"Swimsuit models," Peg suggested sarcastically. "You get after last month's paperwork before anymore ideas."

"But—"

"No buts. You know the drill."

"Can I get a sandwich first?"

"I'll slide it under the door. Get in there." Peg shoved the box of papers into Maw's arms and pushed him toward the door. Maw shuffled out of the bait shop, up the wooden steps into his house, across the scuffed brown and orange kitchen linoleum and into a closet beneath the staircase.

"Calculator in here?" Maw ducked his head to get through the low doorway. A folding chair and small table created a sort of office space beneath the bare bulb hanging from the slanting closet ceiling.

Peg crossed her arms. "Quit stalling and get started."

"All right, all right," Maw grumbled, easing himself onto the floor and dropping the box in front of his legs. "Bring me a sandwich. Please."

"I will in an hour." Peg shut the door and turned the lock before pocketing the key and returning to her pile of ironing.

Every month they went through the same routine: Peg would lock Maw in the closet under the stairs with the month's paperwork. Left unsupervised, Maw wouldn't pay a bill, organize his receipts or balance the checkbook, so his family put him under house arrest to do it, usually on the third Monday of the month.

"Swimsuit models," Maw mused, tearing open the electric bill. "That's not a bad idea." He glanced at the total while opening the checkbook. "The Minnow Swim Team. No, The Bikini Regatta. I'll think of something. Get the Fisher girl, Jenny Bender, maybe Mona—they could do a calendar shoot." The electric bill fluttered to the floor while Maw slumped back against the wall, his mind racing full speed ahead.

Otto Zimm slowly eased back down the boat ramp, his neck craned around to see his trailer and boat pop up suddenly before gliding down to the river. His raw-knuckled hands shifted the steering wheel to the right and corrected his course. He accelerated once more and the boat slid into the water. Throwing the parking brake, Otto jumped out to release the winch. The boat separated from the trailer and he walked along the dock next to it, grasping the ropes firmly with his right hand. Rex, his black lab, leaped from the truck bed to the boat and stood alert, ears back until the boat finally reached the end of the dock. Otto tied it off with a loose knot before he walked back to the truck and drove to a parking spot on the east edge of the lot.

Rod and tackle box in hand, he loped back to Rex and his boat. Otto didn't own anything new or fancy, but he had impeccable habits, so his fifteen-year-old boat looked just as new as the one coming across the bridge that instant. He recognized the eighteen-foot bass boat from the marina where he'd stopped two days ago to pick up spark plugs. Otto gazed at the fine machine while it passed overhead and tried to imagine spending a year's salary on a boat. That was city people for you, he thought. They had all the best and latest gear, clogging up the river with their giant boats and buying up the cottages along the shores. He knew for a fact that they'd mow down every foot of riverbank and plant grass, consequently wrecking the habitat for fish, birds and critters. He'd seen the destruction on the Wisconsin River, the Fox River and the Rock River. All those buildings and roads and businesses turned the rivers into dead slime pits. If that happened in Bassville, he'd cash it all in and move to Canada. Like some damn draft dodger. If the Trayson development went through, there'd be no peace on the river. Otto's gut snarled at the idea while he stepped aboard "Reel Good Dreams," the name his wife had come up with when he'd bought it from his cousin over in Rhinelander. It crossed his mind that maybe he'd understand Gene's decision better if he and his wife had ever had kids of their own.

The motor roared to a start and Otto pushed the throttle forward an inch before reversing his course. "Buhdada buhdada buhdada," the motor growled, the boat drifting backwards into the river's current. Otto knew it wouldn't take long to get over to Big Eddy to fish today. The current was still swift. The river had swollen to its peak after the thaw and a solid week of rain. The return trip would be bitter business, however. Especially if no fish were biting. Driving at a snail's pace against the current since no-wake laws stayed in effect until the river receded below flood stage, he always felt frozen to the marrow by the time he reached the shore. Rex curled up at his feet, looking equally miserable despite his fur coat.

"Before we know it, it'll be May and you'll be sweating all the way back, old buddy."

Rex whimpered a reply before scrambling to his post at the front of the boat. Two in the afternoon and the sun shone bright. It might reach fifty today like the weatherman said. They puttered downstream past the woods and wetlands interspersed with tiny summer cottages, the Pine Acres Resort & Campground, and an occasional cluster of ice shanties tucked back in a bayou. The sharp smell of clear spring air filled Otto's nostrils and he leaned his head back to inhale the end of March.

Below Otto and Rex, the dark shadows swirled in the muddy water. A prehistoric looking eight-foot long sturgeon glided silently through the weeds. A group of walleyes swam out of its path and into a sunny patch of water by the shore. The river floor swarmed with life and bubbles rose from the layers of silt.

June Butterfield drove over the bridge, noticing more boat traffic on the river for the first time in five months. Until the past weekend, it was too dangerous for anyone to take a boat out with the ice crashing its way down the current. June opened her car window a few inches to enjoy the breeze on her face. Fifty degrees today! Boats on the river! Spring had finally kicked winter out the back door.

She began a mental list of spring housecleaning chores while turning off the highway. Clean the wastebaskets, wash windows and light fixtures, air out the bedding and curtains. If it held to fifty through the weekend, it would be perfect weather to get after the stale air in her house. June parked behind the Bassville Pub and stepped out of her car, boots sinking into the mud but her jeans staying clean tucked carefully inside them. She didn't see Dottie's Suburban yet, but Dottie always ran late and always managed to have some excuse. "The UPS man showed up as I was leaving." "My mother called from Scranton, I had to take it."

Arlyce was standing at the kitchen door tossing cracked corn to the flock of mallards. "I was about to wonder where you were."

June squeezed her friend's shoulders and sat down at the first dining room table closest to the kitchen. "I went shopping in Northport this morning."

"Anything good?" Arlyce asked.

"Two new shirts, shorts and a spring jacket," June told her.

"Good for you! Any big sales?"

"Not really. The winter racks are really picked over and the spring stuff's still full price. But I was in the mood to shop and I'm getting too damn old to wait for sales. If I like it, I'll buy it—that's my new philosophy anyway," June said.

Arlyce nodded approval. "Can I get you a coffee?"

"And cherry pie?"

"I'm having the same." Arlyce started the coffee maker with a click and a whoosh and pulled the cherry pie out of the cooler behind the counter. She bent over the carrier to check on the baby before slicing the pie. "Still working on that cable-knit for Sean?"

"Can't wait to finish it. I've got a new pattern for a crewneck sweater I'm dying to make Mona. If hers turns out good, I'll make myself one. In a different color, of course."

"Of course." Arlyce placed the two mugs and plates of pie on a tray and returned to the table with their refreshments. She reached below the booth to grab a bright yellow paisley knitting bag and unwound a forest green and burgundy striped Christmas stocking from her needles. "Speaking of Sean, have you talked to him since …"

"He called yesterday. He's doing well. The selfish part of me wants him to toss in this school business and come home to the farm. But I know that wouldn't make him happy. He's got to find his own way." June held the cable hook aside with her thumb and worked the stitches behind it. "Loyal will understand eventually." He had to, he was a reasonable man.

"He will," Arlyce agreed. "He's got to see past his disappointment first."

"The weekly Stitch and Bitch has now come to order!" Dottie rushed in, cheeks and nose glowing bright pink and coat unbuttoned. "Sorry I'm late."

Arlyce and June exchanged knowing smiles and waited to hear her excuse.

"I was on my way out the door when I realized I hadn't put anything on for supper tonight. Had to run to the basement freezer for a bag of chili to dump into the crock pot. Anyhow, here I am!"

"Sit down. We're having cherry pie." Arlyce set down her Christmas stocking.

"Sounds wonderful! Where's that sweet baby girl?"

"On the kitchen counter in the carrier," Arlyce told her.

Dottie walked over to peek at the sleeping child. "You have the easiest babies, Arl. Mine were always colicky." She peeled off her wool coat and hung it on the back of a chair before picking up her bag. She eased her stout frame into the chair across from June and dug around until she produced a bright pink cardigan. "There. I want to get this done for Angie before her birthday next month." She held it up and slid her glasses up her nose. "Do you think it looks the right size? Girls wear everything so baggy and loose these days."

"Should fit her fine, I'd think. Lovely color."

"Thanks. I tore apart an old afghan for this yarn. It's knitting up like new, isn't it?"

"I wouldn't have known if you hadn't told me," June assured her.

Arlyce brought another mug and plate of pie and set it down in front of Dottie before settling into her chair once more. "How's Angie doing these days, Dottie?" she asked, her voice somber.

Dottie laid her knitting needles in her lap and looked up at her two friends, worry creasing her forehead. "She's tired and keeps getting headaches and now she's not keeping food down. She can't go to school anymore, so the teachers sent some workbooks for us to do at home when she's up to it. My mom's sitting with her today just to give me a little bit of a break, we have to be so careful about who's around her with germs and everything." She took a shaky breath. "And the doctor's appointments and the tests have us going to Milwaukee every week. Gene's brother took over the morning milking at the farm when Scotty has to be at work." She shook her head. "I don't know what we're going to do in May when it's time to plant. We've exhausted all our options, so the only thing to try is this bone marrow transplant. If she can't get it soon, it doesn't look good." Dottie's voice broke.

June reached across to hold Dottie's hand. "I know. Loyal told me you've got a realtor to help you sell the farm."

"Well, if Gene and Dottie can sell their acreage and make a small fortune that's terrific. It's their land—and lucky for them it's worth something," Arlyce declared.

"I know, and of course more business would help you and Steve," June said before pausing to choose her next words carefully. "It's just—well, Loyal thinks that if we open the doors to development, Bassville will change forever. Change in ways we can't even imagine. But if it looks anything like Northport, oh, I can't imagine ... And I think Loyal's scared because of the business with Sean."

"You'd think differently if it was Mona instead of Angie, June," Dottie said, her voice quavering and her spine straight. "Just the hospital room costs us hundreds of dollars every night. We got charged $2,000 just to meet with a specialist. Sure, the insurance company pays for some things, but anything 'experimental' is all on us. And then there's the time."

Dottie pounded the table and cursed. June flinched and pulled her hand back.

"A round of chemotherapy takes six hours out of a day. I have to be there for her, which puts all the burden back at the farm and house on Gene. And then there's the time I spend fighting with the hospital, the insurance agency, the goddamn doctors and the teachers at school who expect her to do homework even though she's throwing up and exhausted. Try and imagine *that*, June."

"I can't. I'm sorry." June looked down at the slubby carpet beneath their table. She felt horrible for her friend, she really did. Cancer was too expensive for regular people to bear, she thought.

There was a long silence while the three women reflected on what the future of their town boiled down to: strip malls and suburbs to pay for Angie's medical bills.

"Rumor has it Jake Paulick's working on the plans for a subdivision. Have you and Gene looked at it?" Arlyce asked.

Dottie nodded. "It made more sense to plan how the land would be sold ahead of time. We'll have to spend a little upfront—surveying and assessing it, but with a planned development we'll make more money in the long run. Plain old farmland only sells for eighteen-hundred an acre. Divide the same land into lots and you can sell each lot—say two half-acre lots, you can make over forty-thousand an acre."

June let out a low whistle. "I had no idea."

"I know. For what you can make on a development, I wonder why anyone would bother farming it anymore," Dottie said.

"That's loads of money." Arlyce agreed. "Almost makes me wish Steve was a farmer. You two could afford to move on a permanent vacation in the Bahamas with all that."

"Have you and Gene considered only selling part of your property and farming the rest?" June asked.

"The realtor we've talked to doesn't recommend that. Farmers and strip malls don't make good neighbors I guess." Dottie shot an apologetic glance at June. "But we'll find something else to do if it comes to that. At the very least we'll keep our house and the big barn. And they said they can even name the whole development after us—'Trayson's Crossings.'"

"My goodness," June murmured.

"I hear there was another domestic disturbance down the road from you last week Sunday." Arlyce's needles clicked against each other as rhythmically as a clock's ticking while she looked up at Dottie.

"You heard right," Dottie confirmed. "You'd think Joann would up and leave that son of a bitch one of these times."

"Saw her at the grocery store on Tuesday. Her face was swollen and she had a doozy of a shiner," June said. She clucked her tongue.

"Somebody ought to give that overgrown beast a taste of his own," Dottie said, jerking yarn across her needles. "Nuts. I dropped a stitch." She began unraveling the sweater on her lap while clenching her jaw tighter.

"How does a woman survive all that and stay whole?" Arlyce asked. "I'd snap."

"If she's not crazy from all his nonsense, then she's crazy because he's punched her too many times." Dottie turned the sweater over to knit back across the other side.

"If she's not careful, it'll be the end of her," Arlyce said.

Their needles clicked faster.

Dottie took a bite of pie and spoke around it. "Great pie, Arl. Remind me to take a piece home for Gene when I go."

"Sure thing," Arlyce replied.

They knitted companionably before Dottie broke in again. "Did you hear about Maw being on some Chicago radio station?"

"When?" June asked.

"All this past week. Every morning. Some big shot disc jockey called him up for a fishing report and Maw's practically a regular on his show now."

"No kidding."

"Peg told me he went over to Northport and talked to some ad agency. Spent a bucket of money on some posters and signs and matchbooks." Arlyce shook her head. "Don't know the point in advertising, either you need bait or you don't, and Maw doesn't have much competition." Arlyce never took out an advertisement in her life, despite the monthly sales call from Ed at the *Bargain Bulletin*. She claimed word of mouth was all she needed. If a person wanted breakfast, lunch or supper, well, they knew where to go.

"How on earth does one create an ad campaign for fishing bait anyway?" June mused, abandoning her knitting to start in on the cherry pie.

"Don't know. Peg went wild. Seems *she* felt a new Kenmore washer and dryer were in order before a bunch of posters about minnows."

"Can't say that I blame her. Loyal pulled any business like that, well, I'd smack him in the head with a fry pan."

Dottie laughed. "Smack him in the head? June, you two are such a couple of old sweethearts, you don't even raise your voice at him."

June considered this and licked her fork before setting it on her empty plate. "Perhaps. But Loyal's a good husband. I'm not saying Maw isn't, but you have to put your family's needs first."

"Peg's got her hands full with that one." Arlyce set down her needles and cracked her knuckles, the rhythmic popping startling June.

"I hate it when you do that! It's a worse habit than your smoking." June told her.

"Oh, smoking, knuckle cracking, a gimlet every Friday after work—I'm a woman of many vices," Arlyce bragged.

"How's poor Cook doing?" Dottie asked suddenly.

"Better, but still miserable. Just *covered* in pox. I brought over some soup two nights ago. Steve's worked every night since the first of March and it's not looking to get better any time soon." Arlyce shrugged. "There's no one to hire; the only people needing a part-time job are high school kids and they're too young to work behind the bar."

"It'll get worse before it gets better. It's almost April, and before you know it, this place will be packed. Mona's exhausted—she came over yesterday afternoon, fell over on the couch and *napped*." June shook her head in amazement, "Mona hasn't taken a nap since she was three years old."

"All in the name of white bass," the three ladies said in chorus, looked at each other and laughed.

NINE

Mona shoved the cooler door open with her hip and hauled a tub of fruit salad over to the stainless steel countertop. The only job worse than washing spider web-covered windows was filling the salad bar. She had to top off every bowl and make sure nothing smelled or tasted bad—straining to reach things beneath the sneeze guard, inevitably spilling something sloppy and greasy like ranch dressing or cottage cheese.

"Mona, someone at the bar wants to order."

Of course. She set down the tub and grabbed her pad and pen. She put her hand on her hip and glowered at Steve.

"The couple by the door."

Mona greeted the various locals on her way to the farthest table by the windows where the couple sat. They wore coordinating Izod V-neck sweaters and held hands across the table. "What can I get you?"

"Is the Danny Boom-Boom any good?"

What the hell did they expect her to say? *No, the food on the menu is terrible, I wouldn't order any of it. Go down the street for supper.* She mustered a weary smile. "It's one of our most popular sandwiches."

The woman looked at the menu again and sighed. "You go ahead and order first, Babe."

"I'll have your Bassville Special. That comes with fries, right?"

Can you read the menu, dumbass? Right where it says, 'Sandwiches come with fries and pickle spear?' "It sure does."

"Great."

Mona looked at the woman and waited. Her legs ached. Her lower back throbbed. She didn't care about these two yuppie sandwich eaters and the two-dollar tip they'd leave her.

"I'll have the Danny Boom-Boom. But can you hold the bacon? And the mayonnaise? And only add lettuce if it's Romaine, not iceberg. Is it extra if I order a side salad instead of fries—never mind. He'll eat my fries."

Why didn't you just ask for turkey breast on a croissant? "Of course." One more week, two at the most, and fishermen would pack the place, ordering burgers without stupid requests, and leave behind five- and ten-dollar tips. She'd read the weekend forecast in the newspaper, the temperature held steady in the fifties every day now and rain would start on Tuesday. She'd read her horoscope too, which told her she was coming into a sum of money very soon. On her return to the kitchen, Mona felt the palpable shift in mood at the bar. Everybody was leaning forward, voices hushed, expressions tight or concerned. She noticed Jake among them, sitting beside Scotty.

"Oh my God," Steve said, his eyes wide. "How did it happen?"

Mona hurried over to hear what had stunned the locals into a somber silence.

"What's going on?" she asked.

"Vera Schmidt died today."

When Vera Schmidt first ran for town council, she was fifty-seven years old and an imposing figure of a woman. Despite being five feet tall, her ramrod posture and commanding voice left the impression of great height. Her high school English students often remarked, "You're so short!" when standing next to her for the first time, since her presence at the front of the classroom suggested otherwise.

No one could recall seeing Vera without carefully applied "Parisian Rouge" lipstick, pearl earrings, and seldom, if ever, did anyone see her wearing slacks. While everybody else living in the Midwest donned blue jeans, Vera Schmidt still favored skirts and pumps with matching handbags. She ran uncontested for town council twenty years ago to replace Earl Dohill and she'd missed only three meetings in those twenty years. Her votes were a stark contrast to her conservative clothing. She held a liberal, expansive view of Bassville, embracing opportunities to change the town. For seven years she'd been lobbying unsuccessfully to pave Main Street and build a wastewater treatment plant.

Thursday morning Vera Schmidt had sat upright in bed and reached for her glasses when, before sliding her feet into her bedroom slippers and walking into her kitchen to brew a pot of tea, she slumped back against the pillow, death the only force strong enough to make her slouch.

At eight-thirty when Vera didn't show up for the monthly Ladies' Auxiliary Club meeting, Peg Cooper volunteered to check in on her. By eleven o'clock Joe the Cop was summoned when Peg's knocks on Vera's front door went unanswered and fifteen minutes later Joe, Peg and Vera's next door neighbor, who kept the emergency house key, discovered her body.

"Thank God she died before the elections," Doris Lobermeyer, the stout and stolid town clerk said, wiping her eyes dry with a Kleenex when the news reached Town Hall. "We can probably get somebody on the ballot yet before the fourth."

"Didn't think she'd ever die," Scotty said, shuffling his feet. "She seemed invincible when I had her for English class."

"Hell, Scotty, everybody in this bar had her for English." Steve fell silent before adding quietly, "Never imagined she could die, though."

Snuffy thought of all the times Vera left a cottage cheese container full of soup or casserole on the bar at Grumpy's. She was never a customer, Lord no. But she'd regularly walk through the door as proper as you please and deposit that offering in front of him with a stern look before turning on her heel and striding out. "She was kind."

"She was an amazing person," Jake said. "She challenged all of us to grow so we could realize our potential. That's what I'll never forget about her. She was never content with the status quo." And, he thought, she would've voted to rezone the Trayson property. No question about it.

Mona bowed her head out of respect for Miss Schmidt, and wondered what this might mean for the Trayson's land deal next month. Everyone knew she'd have voted for the rezoning. Vera Schmidt believed in progress. And, she knew for certain, so did Jake.

TEN

Loyal's face was red from the sun and the heat of the argument about the Trayson's cornfields taking place over coffee at the Pub. He clenched his jaw shut and took a deep breath before continuing his rant.

"Damn it, Maw, you don't understand anything about zoning. You think a bunch of city folk will appreciate country living come spring when we're planting—fall when we're harvesting—combines and tractors clogging up their highway going ten miles an hour? Think they'll appreciate the fresh country *air* when they smell us spreading manure? They all love the *idea* of farms—until reality kicks in. You have any idea how many ordinances have been passed in other counties because of subdivisions butting up against farms? And then can you even imagine how much money a farmer has to spend to stay in business while upgrading to new codes? There's a reason you don't see a single farm a mile out of Northport."

"So we make it known to people before they buy a lot and build a house. We get a lawyer to lock down existing ordinances to protect your farm."

Loyal grunted and took a swallow of coffee. "You think it's so easy. Hell, you can't even sell bait without pissing people off."

Maw glared at Loyal while Arlyce walked over to top off their coffee cups. "I have to agree that some new business would be good," she said. The rain all week had doused business—even Otto wouldn't fish in the torrential rainfall that started four days ago and finally let up last night. Arlyce squinted out the window, feeling almost happy when she looked at the bright sky. The rain had washed the remnants of ice and snow and winter filth down the river—she'd noticed tiny shoots of new grass sprouting up on the lawn that'd been caked for months with mud and cigarette butts.

"Exactly," Maw said, nodding at Arlyce. "Think of the boost our tax base would get with fifty new families moving in." He couldn't fathom any downside to this equation. But he knew farmers were notoriously averse to change, old-fashioned and set in their ways.

"It's not that simple," Loyal told him. "Fifty new families require new services too—garbage and recycling pick up, sewer and water mains, sidewalks, streets and gutters."

"Fifty new families to clog up the intersections—but hey—what's more fun than waiting at a stoplight," Dob added.

"Would new people move here anyway?" Mona asked, startling everyone with her contribution. She cleared her throat. "I mean, the mall and all those new stores went in on the west side of Northport, the towns between here and there are all growing—you see those subdivisions going in alongside the highway. Would people want to live this far away? Maybe they would. Although maybe it's better if we know they're coming and then we can plan ahead—even contain it somehow."

"Mona's right!" Dale smacked his hand on the bar and gave her a wink. "If we don't plan for them now and they come anyway, won't there be a whole lot more trouble?"

"They'll move here, whether we want them to or not," Arlyce muttered with a sour face.

"But if we *invite* that growth and make it work for us—" Maw said.

"Then we can have all the benefits with none of the problems?" Loyal asked.

"And Angie gets her treatment paid for so she can grow up healthy and strong," Maw added.

"Something like that," Dale said around a bite of sausage.

"Or," Loyal said, shooting his daughter a fierce look, "we keep it out and don't deal with it at all."

"Spoken like a traditionalist, Dad," Mona gave him an affectionate pat on his hand.

"Hell, if they rezone, maybe I should get on the bandwagon and sell *my* farm," Loyal said, surprising even himself with the thought. "It's not like I've got family lining up to take it over from me."

"Hey, I *offered* to help you out," Mona reminded him.

"It'll be interesting to see what the new board member has to say on the subject," Arlyce said. "Speaking of which, any word on when Vera's funeral will be?"

"Friday morning. The wake's Thursday night," Dale said.

"It'll be packed," Loyal predicted while he stood and pulled his wallet out of his back pocket. "I got crops to plant and fish to catch—not necessarily in that order." He nodded to Arlyce. "Keep the change."

"I better get going too," Maw said, pushing his plate forward. "I got the missus tending the shop right now and she'll be ticked if she finds out I spent my morning here yakking instead of taking care of the tax stuff."

Arlyce stubbed out her cigarette and collected Loyal and Maw's plates. "I better check on Frank and Nancy. Don't forget to core and cut up that lettuce the salad bar, Mona."

"You should run for Vera's seat, Mona," Dale said to Mona. He met her astonished expression with a thoughtful gaze. Here was a way to get his viewpoint on the council.

"You know, he's right," Loyal agreed. He zipped up his coat and nodded to Mona. "You have more sense than a dozen of us old men."

Mona blushed and started wiping down the bar. "Politics isn't my thing."

"Maybe not," Dob said, "but common sense and hearing people out isn't politics. It's good leadership."

"You think?" Mona asked, the idea planting itself in her mind.

"Sure," Dale chuckled. "Think of it, Mona, you and Loyal here serving on the town board together—like a—what's that called again?"

"Monarchy," Dob answered.

"Monarchy," Dale said, chuckling. "Listen to Mr. Encyclopedia here—thinks he's Maw."

"Shut up, asshole."

"Shut up yourself, smartass."

"Both of you shut up or I'll make you take it outside," Mona chimed in. "Jackasses," she muttered, clearing plates off the bar.

They laughed and stood, pulling out their wallets. "Have a good one," Dob told her, pushing in his barstool.

"Thanks, guys." Mona raised her hand to wave and turned to her father, waiting for him to speak again.

He looked at her for a moment and then shook his head. "I'll see your grandparents before heading back," he told her. "You only need thirty signatures to get on the ballot, you know."

Her mind reverberated with those words for the rest of the day as the considered: could she do this?

92

ELEVEN

GLOWERING AT THE SHINY bass boats with Illinois registrations, Otto threw the throttle on his bass boat and sped away leaving a spray of water. Two idiots had anchored just off the boat launch, creating a traffic jam and the Wissipaw was choppy with wake. When the white bass run started, he'd head further up the river to find the secret spots even some locals didn't know about. One year Otto pulled a fallen tree across the opening of Cooper's Bayou, nearly burned out his motor in the effort, but managed to make it look impassable so he could fish back there alone. That lasted three weeks before he floated around the bend to find Scotty Trayson and The Pole cutting the tree into sections with chainsaws.

"Hey! What're you two doing?" Otto had hollered over the whine of the saws.

Scotty and The Pole killed the motors and dropped their saws. Scotty hauled a giant branch into the back of his boat and wiped his brow. "Storm last week must've knocked this tree across the river here."

Otto snorted and spat into the river. "And you're a couple of helpful Boy Scouts clearing it out of the way." He watched a bluegill flutter to the surface to nip at the thick phlegm, breaking it apart with its open mouth.

"There's good fishing back in this bayou," The Pole said. "Can't get back there with this tree in the way."

Otto continued up to Partridge Point where he'd only seen five other boats, stewing the entire way there.

Yes, Otto Zimm hated sharing the river and judging by the boat traffic this morning, he might be better off going to work. The mill would probably be more relaxing, he thought. But with a cooler full of bait, a tank full of gas and only ten vacation days left, he might as well continue scoping the shoreline for a decent spot to drop anchor.

Judi Linske stared mournfully out the window at the muddy street and wished for the sultry heat of summer so hard that her head ached. At least the sun broke through today; there'd been nothing but grey sheets of rain all week. All but one room was booked this week, but a dry weekend forecast meant no cleaning up after the fishermen who tromped in and out with their muddy boots and sodden clothes. The smothering odor of wet wool was everywhere. She'd change sheets and lay out new towels and end up spending an extra half hour mopping the dirt-streaked floors and cracking open windows. Maybe they should start a laundry service for their guests. Muddy wet fishermen definitely needed it.

"Come and give me a hand!" Sue called to her daughter from down the hall in the bar. Judi arched her back and held the stretch for a moment before standing. She switched off the radio and headed toward her mother.

"I picked this up wholesale. We have to store it somewhere." Sue stood behind the bar surrounded by several large cardboard boxes.

"What is it?"

"Snacks. We can sell 'em in the bar at night when the kitchen's closed."

Judi leaned over and lifted the flap of one box and peeked inside. Colorful foil packages of chips and pretzels nearly burst out of the box. "How many are in here?"

"Five hundred assorted bags. Chips, pretzels, nuts, and candy bars."

"How much did you pay for this?"

"Came out to about a quarter apiece. We'll sell them for fifty cents and double our money."

"Did you hear Mona might run for town council?" Sue asked her daughter. "I ran into Arlyce at the gas station and she told me. Guess they need that seat filled before any decision on the Trayson property."

"I wonder what her take on it would be. I bet she'd be for it, if only to help that little girl. Oh, that reminds me, Scotty dropped off a couple more cans to collect donations for Angie's treatment. I put them on the bar."

Judi watched her mother pile the bags into baskets along the back of the bar. "Take the rest of the boxes to the store room," her mother directed. Judi bent down and reached around one of the large boxes. They were light, but awkward in size. Unable to see over it or around it, Judi edged down the hall using her right shoulder to guide her along the wall. She'd nearly crossed the lobby when the front door blew open and two men barged in, the first colliding with Judi and the box, ramming the box into her face and scattering red bags of ruffled potato chips everywhere.

"Damn it!" She dropped the box and rubbed her nose and upper lip, her eyes watering and her nose flaring red with pain.

"I'm so sorry." The man bent over, scooping up the bags of chips and trying to stuff them back into the box. "I didn't see you."

"It's okay. I'm fine." Judi clenched her eyes shut to clear the tears.

She opened them and slowly focused on the bright blue eyes staring at her from behind wire-rimmed glasses.

"We're here to see about a room," he said.

Judi studied him. These were no fishermen, not in those clothes. Even the most apathetic city kid didn't come to Bassville wearing a denim jacket over a concert T-shirt and carrying a black leather backpack. The man behind him was taller and wore a silk shirt, gold chains and dress pants. They were lost, she decided.

"Lucky for you, we have one left." She knelt on the floor to retrieve the rest of the chips and stuffed them into the box, folded the lid down and hefted it behind the reception desk.

"Wow, that's really great." He walked closer to the desk, staring at the photographs on the wall beside her. "Are these of the river here?"

"Yeah. That's turn of the century white bass fishing you're looking at."

"No shit. Hey, check this out, Dave."

"You have a bar?"

"It's down the hall." Judi pointed the way.

The man called Dave sized her up over the rim of his sunglasses before sauntering out of the lobby.

"I'll take care of the room." The first man stepped up to the desk and dropped his backpack on the floor. "We're up from Chicago to check out your fishing scene."

"You're a little early for white bass."

"I know, Maw said it won't start for a couple of weeks. We'll be back then."

"Maw Cooper?" Are you friends of his? Judi pulled out a registration form. "Cash or charge?"

"Charge." He pulled out a black wallet. Thumbing through a rainbow of credit cards, he selected a card with a flourish and set it on the desk. "Aren't you going to ask if we want smoking or nonsmoking, poolside, river view?"

"Nope. Only got one room left."

"Excuse me?"

She sighed and set down the credit card she was about to run through the machine. "We have one room left, then we're booked solid."

"One room? We're *sharing* a room?"

"Yup. And a bathroom."

"Obviously, if we're sharing a room."

"I better clear this up, too. Your room doesn't have its own bathroom. You and two other rooms all use the bathroom at the end of the hall."

The man gawped at her. "You mean this is like an old-time boarding house or something?"

"Something like that."

He frowned at her. "Dave's not going to be happy."

"Listen," Judi glanced down at his Visa, "William Donne, I don't know what you're looking for in Bassville, but if it's not a boat, beer or bait, you probably want to keep driving east. In Northport they've got a Holiday Inn and all that other stuff you're used to having in Chicago."

"No, no, no. We've got to have the Bassville experience. Boss's orders. There's nowhere else to stay around here?" His eyes were pleading and Judi felt a twinge of pity; this guy wasn't a jerk. He just didn't understand that he'd entered a completely different world.

"You can rent a cottage at a resort. Only you'll have to walk outside to use the bathroom. Unless they have a deluxe model available, which I doubt since we're nearly booked. But I can call over to Gala or Pine Acres if you want."

"No, this will be fine."

Judi pushed the roller across his credit card and the carbon receipts before handing the receipt to William Donne. "Sign here."

He peered over his glasses. "Is this for one night?"

"Uh-huh."

"It would cost less to stay here a whole month than to pay my rent on Michigan Avenue." He grinned at her, surprising Judi when his face transformed. The flash of his white teeth and the way his eyes crinkled made him look kind of cute. Flustered by the thought, she dropped her pen. She reached below the desk and took the remaining set of room keys from a drawer.

"You're in room five. Up the stairs and to your left. It's got four beds, two queen-sized and one bunk. The bathroom's at the end of the hall." Judi slid the keys across the desk until they touched his fingertips. "You have a nice view of the river from that room," she added.

"You're too kind. I don't suppose you have a bellhop to carry our luggage?"

"No, and before you get any ideas, we don't offer room service either." Judi looked up again, feeling a warm flush rising up her cheeks.

"I'm afraid I'm going to have to give this place a two-star rating," William Donne teased.

"That's one star above our Triple-A rating."

Judi watched William Donne round the corner before hauling the box of chips back to the storeroom. After making room for the boxes of snacks, she returned to the bar to see her mother pointedly ignoring her only customer. She sat at the far end of the bar doing a crossword puzzle from the daily newspaper. Dave sat alone nursing a martini and delicately eating a bag of cashews, one nut at a time.

"I'm back for the rest of the boxes," Judi announced to her mother, raising her eyebrows in silent acknowledgement of their shiny, silky guest.

Sue rolled her eyes and grimaced. "Need any help?"

"No."

"I insist." Sue followed her daughter behind the bar to lift a box labeled "Fancy Stick Pretzels" and carry it out of the bar.

Once in the storeroom, Sue unleashed her annoyance. "You get a load of City Boy? Wanted to know why we didn't pour Absolut as our rail vodka, what time room service closed, and *told* me to change the radio station."

Judi smirked. Most fishermen had a general idea of what they'd find in this neck of the woods. In fact, the only complaint she regularly heard was about the lack of an ATM. That came up every year, but since no one in Bassville used anything but cash and most places took credit cards, it wasn't much of an issue. Most of the Chicago crowd soon realized that food, drink and lodging cost a fraction of what they were used to paying back home, so they never needed to get more cash anyway, unless they got caught playing cards or dice against a Dohill. And even then a personal check sufficed.

"Somehow I get the impression those two aren't here to fish."

"What else is there to do around here?"

Sue frowned and shrugged. "I hope they're not a couple of deviants."

"They're probably lost or something. They're paid up, so what's to worry about?"

From the lobby phone, Will placed a call back to the station. "We're here. You want the good news or the bad news?" He paused and nodded grimly. "Our expenses will be way low this trip. The bad news is Dave's about to learn we're staying in the same hotel room— and sharing the bathroom down the hall with at least seven other guys." He chuckled while tossing his backpack onto the floor. "No TV either. But we have a river view." Will lifted the plaid curtain to the side and looked out. "It's a nice view anyway."

"Want another drink?" Sue asked her lone customer when she returned to the bar.

Dave LaMay stared at her for a moment, his eyes bleary behind his sunglasses. Last night he'd stayed out until four in the morning. A new club had opened downtown and he'd been on the *very* selective list of people invited—he'd spent half the night dancing with two supermodels who bared enough cleavage to keep him popping wood every time they ground their hips against his. Today he sat alone in a bar half the size of his bedroom with a middle-aged woman wearing a pilled "I Love Branson" sweatshirt and smudged eyeglasses. He exhaled and shook his head, pulling his cigarette back to his mouth. If he looked busy smoking, this broad would leave him the hell alone.

"Dave," Will walked into the bar, his boots heavy on the wooden floor. "I brought our bags up to the room. You want to find Maw's or have dinner first?"

"Let's find Maw first."

"Maw as in 'Maw's Bait and Tackle?'" Sue looked up from her newspaper.

"Know him?" Dave asked her.

"Everyone knows Maw. Bassville's a small town. Everybody knows everybody."

"Great. Can you give us directions to his store?" Will sat down on the barstool next to Dave. "We're supposed to meet him sometime today."

Sue frowned. "How do you know Maw?"

"From the radio," said the sunglasses man. "I'm Dave LaMay. Maw's been a regular guest on my radio show down in Chicago. This is my manager, Will."

"No fooling? I didn't know Maw was on a radio show." Sue looked impressed by this piece of information.

"He's been providing the Chicago area with a daily fishing report

100

for two weeks now." Dave got a thrill being famous in front of any audience.

"Can you tell us anything about those minnows he sells?" Will leaned forward on his elbows and squinted to read the beer bottles displayed on a shelf above the cash register.

"What are you drinking?" Sue asked him.

"Do you have Heineken?"

"Nope."

"I'll take a bottle of Genuine Draft." Will glanced at Dave's glass, empty except for the discarded plastic cocktail pick. "Fill him up too, while you're at it."

"Maw sells the same minnows everybody else sells. Golden shiners you can catch right over here in the lake. Although he probably buys his from a breeder." Sue paused to find a bottle opener. "Why do you ask?"

"He's been telling us he's got special minnows. Ones that go after the fish for you." Dave fished out his cocktail pick and tossed it on the floor. "Passive-aggressive, belligerent and what's the other kind called?"

"Cantankerous," Will supplied.

"I'm sure they are. I'd be cantankerous too if someone stuck a fishing hook through my guts and laid me out there for some fish to eat." Sue rattled the cocktail shaker and poured its contents into Dave's glass.

Dave raised his fresh martini to toast Sue and Will before draining half of it in a single swallow. Sue shrugged her shoulders at Will.

"That your daughter out front?" Will asked her.

"Yep."

"How long have you been in the hotel business?"

"This one or total?" Sue asked.

"Either. Both."

"Three years." Sue reached below the cash register and pulled out a heavy leather-bound photo album. She set it on the bar in front of Will and opened the cover with a loud crack. Will looked down at the fuzzy black and white photographs of men standing along a bridge, their fishing poles raised above the water, the lines hanging below them. He waited until she turned the page to reveal a yellow and creased receipt. 'Bassville Hotel and Boarding House. One week lodging--$2.00 Supper .25 extra.'

"This is something else." Will pulled the album closer to study the next picture, a shot of the boats lined up in the river as thick as seagulls scavenging at Navy Pier in August. He turned the page to see two men sitting on upturned buckets cleaning a small mountain of fish.

"You know you can get your fish cleaned about anywhere in town. Lots of the young boys do it for extra money."

"I saw some kids placing a sign that said they'd clean fish for a dollar a dozen."

"That's the going rate." Sue nodded.

"Interesting." Will studied the rest of the photo album before returning it to Sue. "You have quite a history here."

"We do."

Dave yawned and stretched. "Let's find Maw and get some supper."

Will added to the pile of change on the bar to leave a proper tip, he stood and pulled his car keys out of his pocket. "As you wish, boss."

TWELVE

THE YARD AROUND THE bait shop was littered with toys and trash, including a deflated basketball, several upended bicycles, a rusty metal barrel and two busted-up marquee signs. Dave and Will surveyed the scene before leaving the parked car and crunching across the gravel drive.

"Not exactly Cabella's," Dave muttered.

"Not exactly *anything* I've seen before," Will replied.

"You first." Dave braced open the screen door to the shop with his foot and waited for Will to walk through.

Maw looked up from a tattered ledger. "Afternoon, men. What can I do you for?"

Dave sauntered over to the display of rods and reels. Will noticed the sharp smell of dirt mixed with cigarette smoke.

"Are you Maw?" Dave finally asked.

"Does a snake crawl on its belly? Maw Cooper at your service." Maw dropped the ledger on the counter and walked around to personally greet his customers.

"I'm Dave LaMay, the—"

"Dave LaMay!" Maw interrupted and grabbed Dave's right hand, shaking it hard while clapping his left hand on Dave's back. "Good to finally meet you. Shit, I've been wondering when you'd show up, and look! Here you are! My most famous customer."

"This is Will Dunne, my manager." Dave pulled back to straighten his leather jacket.

"Good to meet you, Will." Maw extended the same warm greeting to Will and sighed happily. "Can I get you boys a beer?"

"How about we begin with a tour of your shop?" Will asked before Dave could suggest getting a ride out of town. "And then we can get drinks and dinner. Sue from the hotel told us the Bassville Pub would be a good spot for dinner."

"She's absolutely right. They've got great burgers and pizza. Or we could head over to Pine Tree for a steak." Maw rubbed his hands together, anticipating the weekend ahead. His marketing blitz would pay off huge dividends. He'd buy Peg *five* new washers and dryers.

"You son of a bitch!" Otto's voice echoed through the cut, the fog carrying it clear to the mouth of Rat Creek.

"Otto, the river isn't your private property."

"You got nerve bringing *tourists* to *this* spot!" Otto cut his motor and drifted closer to the lone boat anchored along the shore.

"Calm down," Maw stood up in the boat, his legs wide to keep his balance. He held hands out in front of his chest. "Be reasonable, Otto."

Otto glared at Maw and the two men sitting behind Maw holding their poles straight out. One of the bobbers disappeared beneath the water and Otto could hear the high whine of the line as it spun out of the reel.

"Son of a bitch! I think I got one!" In a swift motion the tall man stood, raised the tip of the pole and began turning the reel. Seconds later a frantically twisting silver fish surfaced.

"Holy shit, pull her in! Pull her in! She's gotta be about thirteen inches!" Maw dipped a net into the water and scooped the fish against the boat and lifted it high in the air. Flipping and arching in the green nylon net, the fish strained toward the river. Maw braced himself and leaned the net's handle on the side of the boat for leverage. With a push, he brought the walleye thumping onto the floor of the boat.

"That's a beauty! Can you get the hook out yourself?" Maw asked, dropping the net handle and wiping his chin with the sleeve of his sweatshirt.

Nodding, the tall man knelt to grab the fish.

"First time out and you bring them *here*." Otto spat in the water. Disgust snarled his eyebrows and mouth.

"There's a lot of fish in the river, Otto. This isn't the only spot. You fish here, too. You know as well as I do there's plenty for the taking. Need bait? I got plenty. Help yourself." Maw pulled the lid back and looked down. The minnows swam in a tight, frenzied circle, startled by the sudden light.

Torn between the offer of free bait and his fury at Maw for bringing two strangers to where he considered to be a secret locals-only fishing spot, Otto hesitated. "Keep your bait," he muttered.

"Let me introduce you. Otto, Dave LaMay, radio DJ and his manager, Will Donne. Guys, meet Otto Zimm. Dave's doing a piece on the fishing season here for his radio station," Maw explained.

"Great. 'Cuz what we need, Maw, is *more* people coming here to fish." Otto watched the tall man finally jerk the hook free from the fish and dry his hands on his jeans.

"I brought them here because Dave's a radio celebrity and if we fished in the middle of the river, people would recognize him and bug him all day for autographs and stuff. You know I wouldn't bring total strangers down this far."

Otto felt pretty certain that Maw would do anything if he could make money out of it, but he didn't say so. Instead he looked up the river and saw another boat drifting ahead.

Maw broke the silence. "How about taking some bait? Or I've got some extra three-way rigs in my tackle box."

"Nope. I'm heading further upstream." Otto pulled the cord and his motor roared to life. "And I'll get my bait from the gas station from now on," he yelled before heading out of the bayou.

Will slipped another shiner onto his empty hook and flinched when it poked into his forefinger. "Are all the locals this ornery?" he asked Maw.

"Just Otto." Maw told him. "The rest are fun. Wait until tonight when I introduce you around."

"Sounds great." Dave stretched out along the front cushions of the boat and leaned his head against the boat's windshield. "Hope you're taking us someplace with some action, Maw. Fishing is boring."

"How can you say that? I just caught one and we've only been here ten minutes," Will protested.

"No music, no babes, hell, the beer's even lukewarm."

"Let's fish here a little while longer and then I'll take you guys to the Pub. You gotta keep that bait moving, Dave. That's the trick." Maw cast his line into the center of the river. He wanted Dave to like him and have such a good time fishing that he'd keep him on the air forever.

"Fine. Meanwhile, I'm taking a nap." Dave pulled his new fishing cap low over his sunglasses and folded his arms across his chest. Maw shrugged and slowly drew his line back, the reel buzzing as he turned the handle in tiny circles.

"You'll miss all the fun," Will warned. "Hey!" The tip of his pole bent toward the water. "I think I got another bite!"

At the Pub, Mona struggled to keep her face straight. The weather finally turned a corner, the lilac bushes next to the Lutheran church morphed overnight from bare branches to clusters of tight purple buds. Three young men, fresh out of their cars, stood at the bar. Their fishing vests bore store creases and their Timberland boots had no scuff marks. She guessed the only terrain their outdoor wear experienced to date was paved parking lots and sidewalks.

"My God! Look at that view!" the first one through the door cried.

"I want to move up here. Wouldn't this be a great place to live? You could fish every day." Mona could both see and hear the family resemblance while she placed napkins on the bar. Definitely brothers, she guessed.

"We saw a deer on our way over. A deer. Right by the side of the road," the youngest one told Mona. She nodded and tried to look interested.

"Hey, look at the ducks over there!"

Mona passed a pitcher of light beer and three glasses across the bar to them. "That'll be four-fifty."

"Four-fifty?" The duck enthusiast looked incredulous.

"Um, yeah?" Mona chewed on her lower lip.

"Hear that, boys? Four-fifty for a pitcher! Cheap beer, gorgeous view, hell, I bet a guy could buy a house right on the river for less than a hundred thou."

"Man, I want to move here," the youngest repeated. "This is the life. Smell that fresh air. Look, there's nobody around. It's not all crowded and crazy like in the city."

Mona grinned, amused by them. She'd seen this child-like excitement out of city boys before. They loved Bassville—for the first twelve hours or so. But the city must be a powerful force because none of these guys ever came back to live permanently. Occasionally a family would buy a cottage downriver. Most of the time a week out of the city was enough rustic living to last them a year or longer.

After advising where to buy bait (Maw's, of course) and the best spot to get breakfast (right here at the Pub), she handed them menus. Off they went to sit by the window to gawk at the river rushing past and comment on the wildlife. Mona looked beyond them to Jake's cottage where he'd propped cane poles along his deck, the lines dragging in the river below. He'd come home after work to find a fish or two caught, enough for his supper, and set new lines with fresh bait overnight. Mona stood on the dock last night after work and watched him do this. The ducks, frogs, turtles and fish swam below her feet and the air hummed with the early noises of young insects—lake flies and mosquitoes. In the chilly spring wind, the light shining from Jake's cottage windows looked cozy and inviting. What would he say if she showed up one evening with a hot pizza and a six-pack of beer? She'd never have the courage to do it, though. Maybe Jenny Bender would do something like that, but not Mona. But if she became a town councilwoman, then that might be a different story.

She climbed onto a barstool to switch the channel on the TV and jumped lightly to the floor. She had no stomach for soap operas and despised the local evening newscast—that smug little redhead reported every story in the same perky voice whether talking about how to keep your cholesterol low or a house fire killing four. Thank God for sports, she thought, at least *something* could fill the void.

"Mona!"

She started at the sudden shout from the back door and waved as Maw crossed the bar, two strangers in his wake.

"Heya, Maw. What's up with you?"

"Not a whole hell of a lot," Maw said, pulling out his wallet with one hand and slapping one of the men on the back with the other. "My good friend Dave LaMay from Chicago is in town this weekend to party with me."

Mona nodded at the thin man in a leather jacket who scoped out the room from behind his sunglasses. "Nice to meet you," she offered.

"Mona's the best bartender around. She's been working here for—what's it been, Mona? About five years now?" Maw asked.

"About that," Mona answered, turning her attention to the man behind Maw.

"This is Will Donne, Dave's manager and right-hand man," Maw said, grabbing Will by the sleeve and dragging him forward. "Will, this is Mona. I've known her since she was in diapers."

"Nice to meet you," Will said, smiling pleasantly and offering a hand.

"Pleasure's mine," Mona told him, shaking his hand. "I'm glad to report the diapers are part of my past these days." Screw the DJ, she thought when Will laughed, the manager's cute.

"Ever been to Chicago?" Will asked her.

"No. But someday I'd like to go there," Mona said, glancing at Dave. He looked bored, flicking his cigarette onto the bar, ignoring the ashtray just past his reach. Mona pulled it right in front of him. "Where are you staying?"

"The hotel," Will answered.

"That's nice." Mona tried to think of something else to add, but came up dry.

"This round's on me, boys," Maw announced. "What'll you have?"

"Can you make me a martini?" Dave asked Mona, sounding doubtful. "Absolut, just a drop of vermouth?"

"Absolut martini, dry," Mona repeated in a brisk voice. "How about you?" she asked Will.

"Sam Adams," he told her, the expression on his face apologetic.

"I'll have the same," Maw said. "Nothing like a Sam Adams to whet your whistle after a good day of fishing."

"Really?" Mona couldn't help asking. "You usually drink light beer on tap." Maw scowled at her as she headed into the walk-in for the beers.

When she returned, she watched the DJ visibly relax after downing his martini in four swallows and push his glass forward, signaling at her to refill it. She emptied the shaker into his glass. "Want some menus?"

"Yeah," Dave said, appraising her over the tops of his sunglasses. "Mona, right?"

"That's right." Mona grabbed three menus off the stack by the register. "Special tonight's the Bridge Burger."

"What's a Bridge Burger?" Will asked, opening his menu as she handed it to him, a sure sign he was hungry.

"Half-pound burger with the works, topped with our special sauce. Comes with fries and a pickle," Mona explained.

"Sounds good," Will said, snapping the menu shut.

"I'll have the same, Sweetheart," Dave said.

"Triple it, Mona," Maw instructed her. "You boys wanna grab a table by the window? The view's terrific."

"I'm doing fine right here," Dave said, staring at Mona through half-closed eyes.

"Okay," Maw said, aware that Dave's attention had strayed. "If you want, I can tell you about my next promotion I'll be running in a couple weeks …"

"Enough business," Dave interrupted him. "It's after four. Time for fun."

Two hours later, in the middle of the dinner rush and happy hour crowd, Mona's hair had grown damp with perspiration. She paused by the storage room to peel off her sweatshirt. When she walked back into the bar she was conscious of Dave's eyes following her and she wished she'd left the sweatshirt on.

"Mona," he called to her while she loaded a tray with water glasses. Mona walked over and leaned forward to hear him over the loud voices and the jukebox. "You're not wearing underwear, are you?"

She blushed at the brazenness of his comment. "Of course I am," she snapped.

"Doesn't look like it from here," he told her. "You have a nice ass."

Mona glared before grabbing the tray of waters and carrying it into the safety of the dining room. *The absolute nerve of that guy! If T.C. were here he'd have knocked him out cold for saying that to me.* It was the first time she felt unprotected without him around. No one ever gave her grief when they were together.

The happy hour crowd provided a fresh audience for Maw to play to and he introduced Dave and Will to every person who walked through the door. And, Mona noticed, Maw was mixing business with politics. She watched him pull a piece of paper out of his jeans pocket and unfold it. "Don't know if you've heard, but I'm running for that town council seat. I promise no new taxes because development will pay for things like new roads and a library. I think the Traysons selling their land is a wonderful idea because it's win-win for the town and their daughter. All I need is 30 signatures on this form here …"

Mona narrowed her eyes. She hadn't counted on Maw running for the seat.

"I want you to meet my old buddy, Dob Dohill. This here's his brother Dale. They've been buying minnows from me for as long as I can remember, haven't you boys? And of course we've hit all the best fishing spots together over the years. Remember when we landed that seventy-four pound sturgeon in Cooper's Bayou? By the way, boys, would you mind signing my paperwork so I can run for that seat on the town board?"

She hadn't decided for certain whether to run, but watching Maw easily collect his thirty signatures right under her nose did not make the prospect encouraging. On the other hand, her determination kicked in. The town didn't need someone as self-serving as Maw on the council. He'd be for rezoning and people really needed someone more thoughtful than him making decisions for the town's future.

"I want you boys to meet my good buddy, Spade. Spade's not much for fishing, but he's all right for drinking and playing cards, aren't you Spade? And signing your name on this line right here?"

Everyone signed his paperwork, Mona observed while she refilled drink after drink. But that didn't mean they'd vote for him if given a choice.

The combination of spring fever and a celebrity in town packed the Pub to overflowing. Jenny elbowed her tiny frame through the crowd, a know-it-all grin on her face.

"Guess who just walked in?" Jenny shouted.

"Who?" It seemed to Mona the whole town was in the bar.

"Jake!" Jenny shrieked. "He's sitting back by us. Come over when you have a chance."

"Right. I'll do that," Mona hollered back, waving to Jenny before she grabbed an empty pitcher from the guy standing in front of her. "Regular or light?" There were over two hundred people in the Pub, the odds that she'd get to leave her post behind the bar and talk to Jake were about as slim as getting a chance to pee before she closed.

Mona was right. She glimpsed Jake through the crowd, but by the time it thinned out so she could walk back to clear empty glasses into a bus tub, he was gone. What would he think of her running for town council? She saw Jenny perched on Maw's knee, reigning queen of the corner where Dave was holding court now. Mona's ears hurt from the volume of the jukebox and her feet throbbed. She finished filling the bus tub and stacked it with the others. Dale had yelled at her for pouring his whiskey and coke into a plastic cup, but every glass the Pub owned needed washing and she didn't have time to start scrubbing. The bright side, however, was the pile of crumpled bills and loose change overflowing from the beer pitcher serving as her tip jar. Even though she'd be too tired to count it tonight, she knew she probably set a record for March. "You know, you have four-diamond legs," the smooth, low voice she'd come to hate was now purring in her ear.

"And what's that mean?" Mona asked wearily. She opened a cooler and started to restack and sort the beer cans.

"When a woman wears high heels, you see diamonds of light between her legs. Four diamonds means you have perfect legs for modeling. You ever consider becoming a model?" Dave asked.

"No."

"You should. I know some agents—next time I'm in town I'll bring you their cards. A lot of girls get modeling work in Chicago."

"Is that a fact." Mona looked at the clock and then at Dave.

"You don't like me, do you?"

Mona gave him a level stare. "I like you fine. We've just been very busy tonight and I'm tired."

"I'm staying at the hotel if you want a nightcap later."

She closed her eyes and tried to bury her disgust. What the hell did everybody see in this clown? Famous or not, he was a slime bag. "My boyfriend probably wouldn't like to hear you say that," she lied, imagining T. C. perched at the end of the bar waiting for her to get done with work. "Spade! Need a refill?" Mona grabbed a can and moved across the bar towards Spade, grateful for any excuse to avoid Dave and Maw—both loathsome in their cloying, fake flattery.

THIRTEEN

"Mom, I need to talk to you about something." Mona leaned forward on her elbows and clasped her hands. The cozy chaos of her mom's kitchen made it her favorite spot for confessions and seeking advice. From the rattling hum of the refrigerator, covered in layers of newspaper clippings and photographs to the row of geraniums crowding the windowsill, June Butterfield's kitchen pulsed with life.

June set her mug of tea down on the kitchen table and looked across at her daughter. The sun was bright through the window above the sink and caught the red highlights in Mona's hair. Her expression was serious—even the dash of freckles on Mona's nose seemed subdued.

"What is it?" June's heart picked up pace as she imagined what Mona might say. Seldom did her daughter require her services as confidante these days.

"I'm thinking about running for Miss Schmidt's seat on the town board." Mona's mouth felt dry. She hadn't told anyone—there was no one she could trust with such an idea. Jenny wouldn't understand,

Arlyce would laugh, and the guys at the bar—well, even though they'd put the thought in her head in the first place, most of them had signed off supporting Maw last night.

"Really?" June's eyes brightened with pride mixed with relief. "That's wonderful, Mona! Whatever gave you the idea?"

"Some of the guys at the bar the other day. Dob and Dale were talking to Dad and Maw about the zoning changes. They said I should run for the board because I listen to everything before talking. I've been thinking about it ever since. I think I might be good at it."

"You'd be more than good at it, Mona," June said, reaching for her daughter's hands. "You'd be amazing."

"You think, Mom? You think I could do it?"

"Why on earth not? Plenty of stubborn old men set in their ways— old women too, for that matter—have held seats. You're young, with fresh perspective, and you understand Bassville since you've always lived here. You have so much to offer, honey. You can do much more than pour drinks at the Pub."

"Maw Cooper's running."

June waved her hand dismissively. "Big deal. This town doesn't need another old windbag on the board. You've got youth and fresh insight to offer."

"What about Dad?"

"What about him? He'd be proud of you, too. He's always saying you could do more than tend bar. Besides, it's not his seat you're running for."

"But what if I vote against him on something?" Mona glanced out the window toward the barn where she knew her father was busy repairing an engine with the same singleness of mind he applied to political decisions.

"What if you do?" June returned. "You think Loyal and Gene have always voted alike all these years? Your father's a reasonable man. He can see more than one side of an issue."

"I guess that's true." Mona shifted in her seat. "Except in Sean's case."

"That's different, honey. Loyal's proud of this farm—it's his legacy—his family's legacy. He's having a hard time accepting that it might end with him."

"I miss Sean." If her mother knew the truth of it, Mona thought. She missed the pressure he applied to her. He always pushed her to consider other possibilities, alternate endings for her life outside Bassville. She missed their regular cribbage games, she even missed the way he'd swipe the last Pop Tart and leave the empty box in the cupboard. Last week she deliberately left an empty Pop Tart box in her own kitchen cupboard as a sort of tribute to him.

"I know," June's eyes softened. "He loves his work at school. And your dad will accept that. Eventually."

"I hope so. Will you be my first official supporter?" Mona pulled the campaign papers out of her backpack, the edges still flat and crisp. She'd picked them up yesterday on her way to work. Handing the petition portion to her mother, she watched her mother sign it, sealing the commitment she'd made to herself.

Instead of riding her bike straight home, Mona headed for Bunker Hill and its exhilarating dirt trails. After a couple hours she could gather the rest of her signatures, first she'd enjoy the afternoon. At the top of the run she tilted her face to the sunshine and felt all the promise of spring, bright and warm. Spring is about new beginnings, she thought. Maybe I'll be really good at this. *What could I accomplish if I got elected?*

Mona stood up on the pedals of her bicycle, straining to climb Bunker Hill. The rough terrain was cut up by ATVs and dirt bikes, and Mona loved the thrill of careening downhill through the ruts and gullies on her mountain bike. Enjoying her freedom from the bar, she grunted, sweaty and muddy, and reached the top of the hill again. The view below her flushed away the jelly-like exhaustion out of her legs. The treetops, the buildings of Bassville, farm fields and glint of the river spread before her and she marveled at the sight while panting for air.

"What a town," she said aloud. A blue jay sailed into a tree beside her, and perched on a branch overhead. Fresh green clouds of budding leaves covered the trees, reminding Mona of why she loved spring better than any other season. Frogs and fish and turtles swarmed in and around the water, the birds filled the air, the quiet town came to life after shedding the stillness of winter. Would there be any quiet season if the town grew, Mona wondered. Or would the noise of more people drown out the natural sounds?

To the west she could see her dad plowing up a field on the farm, crawling slowly across the earth in his tractor. At the Trayson farm another tractor rumbled across the field, plowing the soil because no matter what happened this week, a crop would be planted and harvested at least one more time. Mona wondered whether Angie would live to see fall, and the beginning of her 5th grade year. It must be so scary for her to wait for a transplant, getting sicker each day. A bitter taste filled Mona's mouth when she thought about the possibility that next spring the farm field would be dotted with the poured basements of future homes of strangers moving to the town she'd always known. *But that wouldn't be the worst outcome, would it?* She stared for a long time before kicking her foot back and tilting full speed down the hill, her thumbs poised against the handlebar brake levers.

Back on the road she felt the tightness of mud drying on her legs, coated brown as though they'd been painted. Her shoes were caked from when she'd wiped out on the second turn. She pedaled faster towards home and the garden hose that she'd use to rinse herself clean.

At the highway she stopped, waiting for a lull in traffic. She leaned her weight on her right leg and bounced her left foot impatiently on the pedal. A truck pulled up alongside her, and she peeked over her shoulder to see who it was.

Jake Paulick looked down at her from the truck cab. "Is that you, Mona?" he asked, leaning across empty passenger side.

Mona ducked her head and wished she was anything but muddy, sweaty, and beet red beneath a bike helmet. "Hi, Jake," she answered in a choked voice.

"You look like you've been through hell. Want a lift?"

"Um, no. I'm good. I'm headed home now."

"It's no trouble. We can toss your bike in back." He waved his hand toward the truck bed behind him.

Mona inhaled the leather and motor oil smell of Jake's truck—the most intimate place in his world besides his house—perhaps even more so when she thought about the time he spent in it. He really only slept at his house. She'd be sitting right next to him ...

Jake threw the truck into park and started to open the door.

"It's really not necessary. I kind of planned on getting my miles in today."

He looked at her with a strange expression. "Don't you think you should get that bandaged up before it gets infected or something?"

Mona followed his gaze to her left leg. Her shin had a five-inch gash and blood was draining steadily out of it and dripping onto the road.

"Oh my God. I didn't even notice ..." She climbed off her bike.

Jake jumped out of his truck and lifted her bike in an easy movement, setting it gently next to a metal toolbox in the bed.

"Door's unlocked," he said over his shoulder. "Climb in."

Now aware of the throbbing pain from the cut on her leg, Mona slid herself onto the seat and bent forward to study it closer. She'd probably ripped it on a tree branch or the edge of her bike pedal, but the cold mud kept her from noticing it until now. She lightly touched the torn skin and grimaced.

Jake climbed in the cab and pulled onto the highway. "Maybe I should take you to the emergency room," he said, glancing at the blood dripping on the floor mat. "You might need stitches."

"No, I think it just needs to be cleaned up and bandaged." Mona inhaled the faint soapy smell of Jake. His arm brushed hers when he reached across to the glove compartment and opened it. His faded blue sweatshirt felt soft on her skin.

"Look in there for a napkin or something," he told her.

She did and found some from a fast food restaurant, along with a collection of ketchup packets, straws and the owner's manual to the truck. A stack of maps slid forward and Mona grabbed them to keep them from falling out.

"You have a lot of maps," she said.

"Yeah. Beyer's sends me all over the state. You sure you want to go home?"

"Yes. Thanks a lot for the ride."

"No problem. I'm done for the day anyway. Just finished up a job over by Eagle River—three days ahead of schedule. Earned myself a few hours to fish." He smiled at her and she wished so hard to kiss him and call him hers she could feel it in the pit of her stomach.

He pulled in front of her house and got out, striding around the front of the truck to the passenger side. "I'll get your bike," he told her, holding the door. "Where should I put it?"

"The porch is good." She hobbled up the steps to her house.

Jake followed her with the bike and leaned it next to the front door. She turned around and looked up at him while she toed off her shoes. "Thanks again. I really appreciate it."

He nodded and she turned to head inside. She dropped her bike helmet on the floor and realized that Jake was following her through the door.

"I'll get you an ice pack," he said, heading for the refrigerator. "Where do you keep your dish towels?"

"In the drawer by the stove." She limped to the bathroom and grabbed a washcloth. In the mirror she saw her hair was matted down from the helmet and mud splattered across her nose and eyebrows. She cleaned her face first before working on her leg. Vainly she reached up to fix her hair. *Of all the times to get so close to Jake*, she thought in despair.

Jake appeared in her bathroom doorway holding a towel filled with ice. His head almost touched the top of the door frame.

"That's some garden you got growing in there."

"It's gotten out of hand I guess," Mona said. "I didn't expect *all* the seeds to grow."

"Must have your dad's farming gene. Sit down," he said. Taking the washcloth from her, he dabbed at her leg. She winced and involuntarily jerked back.

"Sorry," he said.

Mona concentrated on the part in his blonde hair, the sun-browned tips of his ears.

He sighed and leaned back on the heels of his work boots. "Mona, I really think you need to see a doctor." He opened the washcloth with both hands and held it up for her to see. "That's a lot of blood."

She nodded.

"Come on," he stood and reached out his hand, pulling her up from the edge of the bathtub where she'd sat.

He held the door again for her.

Two hours and fourteen stitches later Mona and Jake emerged from the emergency room at Northport Memorial Hospital.

"I have to call Steve and tell him I'm going to be late," she told him.

"You're not tending bar on that leg. Doctor said to take it easy until tomorrow at least. You're going home and putting it up. Steve can manage one night without you."

"It's the middle of—"

"I know, I know. Fishing season. You have fourteen stitches, Mona. Fish or no fish, you're out until tomorrow."

"But—" she began and he interrupted her again.

"We're going to call Steve, get some supper, and set you on your favorite chair back at home." Jake held the truck door open for her. Seeing her expression he smiled. "You know, you should take advantage of this situation and just get drunk."

Mona laughed and rubbed her arm; the tetanus booster hurt more than her leg. "It's a funny thing, Jake. More you're in the bar sober, the less you like to get drunk."

He pulled out of the parking lot. "What are you hungry for?"

"Sorry?"

"Supper. What do you want to eat? We can get Mexican, Chinese, pizza, hamburgers. What do you like?"

"Chinese sounds good."

"There's a good place a couple blocks from here."

"You know Northport pretty well," Mona said.

"Our main office is on this end of town."

"Ah. I guess you get to eat out a lot then."

He laughed. "Guess so." He pulled in front of a small storefront with a green striped awning. 'Chinese Restaurant No. 1' was painted on the front window. "There's a pay phone inside you can use to call Steve."

Inside the restaurant Mona looked for something familiar on the menu board after calling Steve and cringing at the frustration in his voice. "Stitches?" He'd asked in disbelief. "Fine," he sighed, the noise of the bar loud in Mona's ear. "You'll be back tomorrow, right?"

"Yes," Mona said. "You can leave as soon as it slows down."

"Damn right I will."

"I'm a big fan of the Kung Pao Chicken," Jake told her when she joined him at the table.

Mona found it on the menu, marked with three asterisks to describe the heat and spice factor. "I'll pass," she said, deciding on Orange Chicken.

Mona felt so at ease with Jake at dinner that it surprised her. Their conversation flowed from fishing to the subdivision debate raging in town.

"I know people don't like change," Jake said. He skillfully picked up a pepper with chopsticks. "I love Bassville, too. But there's a lot about the town that could be improved."

"Like what? What's bad about Bassville now?" Mona asked. She set down her fork and to give him her full attention.

"The public library needs money, the fire station needs upgrades; Main Street needs paving; the pilings by the boat landing need replacing," Jake rattled off a list so fast that Mona suspected he'd given this argument before.

"Some of that makes Bassville what it is—like Main Street being muddy."

"Some of that makes people move away from Bassville, turning it into a ghost town given enough time."

"Changes like that'll make it more like Northport or any other big city."

"Not if you do it right." Jake cracked open his fortune cookie and tossed the thin strip of white paper to the side of his plate. "If we plan well, we can control how the town changes. If we ignore it, the town will change anyway, but we won't be in control."

Mona shook her head. "I don't know. I hear you talk and your argument sounds right. Then I hear Otto and my dad and some of the others, and they make a lot of sense, too." She pulled her nomination papers out of her backpack. "Because I'm in the middle of this, like most people in Bassville, I've decided to run for the open seat on our town board. I need thirty signatures to get my name on this month's ballot. Will you sign it for me?" She crossed her fingers, praying he hadn't signed Maw's papers already.

"Absolutely," Jake held out his hand for the petition. "But before I sign, what is your position on increasing taxes?"

"Ummm, I don't *want* to."

"Will you push to get Main Street paved?"

"I haven't really thought about it," Mona confessed.

"What is your position on garbage collection?"

"I'm for it," she said, relieved to have an easy question.

"I'm teasing you. Don't look so worried." Jake scribbled his name and handed back the clipboard.

She flushed. "Thanks."

"Do you need a campaign contribution?"

"No." Her surprise turned to understanding. "You're still teasing me, aren't you?"

"You're quick—just what the board needs." Jake gave her a wink. "You can count on my vote, Mona Butterfield."

The waitress laid their bill on the table. "I got it," Jake said, pulling it over to his side of the table.

"Let me leave the tip," Mona said, pleased that Jake Paulick was buying her dinner. This was almost a real date.

"Nope." Jake peeled a couple of bills out of his pocket and dropped them in the center of the table.

"Let me get something. You've really gone out of your way for me and I appreciate it." She opened her fortune cookie and read *Tiny changes will create big results.* Big changes for her, Mona wondered, or for Bassville, or Angie?

"Catch me a beer next time I'm at the Pub," Jake said.

"That's no big deal," Mona argued.

"It is to me," he insisted and stood.

"Did you read your fortune?" she asked, pointing to the strip of paper by his plate.

"Huh? No. I make my own fortune." He pushed his chair towards the table.

Mona slid his fortune into her pocket when he turned to walk towards the register.

On their drive back to Bassville, Mona mentally phrased and rephrased her request to invite Jake in when they got to her house. He parked and helped her out of his truck.

"Want to come in for a while?" she blurted.

"I'd love to, but ..." He stopped in front of her front door and looked back at his truck. "I'm already running late."

She waited in painful silence.

"I wish I could," he began again, shoving his hands into his jeans pockets. "But I'm meeting someone in Northport later tonight."

Mona felt the heat bloom from her neck and up her cheeks. "Oh. Thanks for bringing me to the hospital and to dinner." She fumbled with her backpack straps.

"Sorry, Mona. I wish I could stay."

"You've got plans. No big deal." She forced a smile and shrugged. "Have a good night."

"Thanks." Jake turned to go and halfway to the road he stopped and looked up at her. "Call if you need anything, okay?"

"I'll be fine. Thanks." Mona waved and shut the door before the tears welled. Her leg throbbed, but it was nothing compared to the pain in her gut. She pulled Jake's fortune out of her purse and read it. *True happiness stands before you.*

On her way to work the next day, Mona collected her remaining signatures from her grandparents, Rosie and her customers at Riverside, and Beau who was filling up at the gas station. She sealed the paperwork in an envelope when she returned home and nestled it between two boxes of sprouting zucchini plants, anxious to drop it off Monday morning and officially begin her foray into town politics. Pulling a glass out of the red-painted cupboard, she studied the view outside her kitchen window. In another month it would be time to till up the yard and install wire fencing to keep the rabbits out. Mona filled the glass at the kitchen sink and drank half of it, before pouring the rest over the zucchinis.

Looking at the garden growing all over her kitchen brought her an unexpected surge of pride and, she realized, peace. Maybe there's some truth to the zen of gardening, she mused, the balance of elements—earth, water, air and sunlight for fire. A small seed planted in the right balance of things grows well, Mona thought while taping her fortune from the Chinese restaurant to the window above her kitchen sink.

FOURTEEN

On the second tuesday in April the voters trickled in all day—most of them elderly. Some civic-minded people made it to the polls, like Peg Cooper, who volunteered her time with the Ladies' Auxiliary, and Loyal, who'd wrapped up eight years of service on the school board to turn around and run for the town board. A few people registered for the first time, notably Spade, Scotty and Jenny.

"Mona's why the younger people are coming in to vote," Frank remarked to Nancy. Frank volunteered to register voters and Nancy sat parked in her chair beside him. He nodded at Jenny before she disappeared behind the short green curtain of the second voting booth while Nancy crowed, "Oh shit!" Her voice echoed in the silence of the town hall and the two ladies checking addresses and assigning voter numbers paused to smile in their direction. Mona served customers all day at the Pub, trying to convince herself that the outcome of the election didn't matter, it was the active participation in a democracy and the people's final decision that she was celebrating.

Steve came in early to wash the windows, telling Mona "you've put in enough extra work around here—I can do the windows this week." Even Arlyce, usually cranky and terse, wrote the day's special on the board with unusual flourish: All-American Cheeseburger, French Fries and Apple Pie. She bought a package of miniature flags attached to toothpicks at Bud's Supermarket and stuck them into each sandwich that left the kitchen.

At seven-forty that evening, the volunteers at town hall struggled to their feet, bleary-eyed and numb-fingered. The last person had walked through at six-forty, but by law they had to keep the polls open until eight no matter *how* slow the traffic. Frank collected empty Styrofoam coffee cups and wadded up napkins, and shuffled across the room to drop them in the wastebasket before locking the door. "We ready to count them up?" he asked.

By nine the Town of Bassville called in the results of their election to the news stations. Mona Butterfield had 142 votes to lock in her seat on the town board, beating out Maw Cooper for the seat by sixty votes. The same number of people voted for a resolution limiting state legislature terms to twelve consecutive years and 240 people voted for Ron Stadler to remain as County Clerk of Courts. Jenny Bender didn't vote for Ron because her nail chipped when she pushed down the metal tab to vote for Mona. Furious that she'd messed up a manicure applied at the Best Little Hair House only hours earlier, she yanked back the lever opening the curtain and left in a huff. Dale didn't vote for Ron because he never forgave Ron for cutting ahead in line at the Mini Mart years ago and buying a lottery ticket that won five thousand dollars.

It was unusual for Frank and Nancy to wheel into the Pub late at night, but they wanted to share the good news with Mona in person. Nancy grunted in her effort to lean forward and push on the door.

"Hey, you two!" Scotty held the door open for them.

"Where's our granddaughter?" Frank asked him. He'd never felt prouder.

"Behind the bar. Got some good news?" Scotty leaned forward to peck Nancy's cheek.

"Mona!" Frank yelled.

"Oh shit!" Nancy chuckled and patted Scotty's hand.

Mona hurried to the end of the bar, her stomach flipping in anticipation of their news. She geared herself up for bad news; she knew losing would feel devastating.

"Want to be the first to congratulate our new town board member," Frank told her, holding out his hand.

"I really won, Grandpa?" Mona gasped, pulling him in for a hug instead. "Thank you." She leaned down to give Grandma Nancy a squeeze. "What was the final vote?"

"One-forty-two to eighty."

"No kidding?" Mona shook her head, amazed to win by such a margin. They chose her over Maw. Amazing. "Well, news like this calls for a celebration. Next round is on me, everybody!"

Bassville's future now lay partially in her hands. She imagined how it could change while she drove home past the Best Little Hair House and Riverside. She tried to see past the chipped paint on the town hall and familiar muddy street. What did an outsider think of this place?

After closing she went home too keyed up to sleep, so she lined up a dozen plastic tubs on her kitchen table and scooped a combination of peat moss, compost and potting soil into the bottom of each. The dirt sprinkled across the yellow checked tablecloth and onto the colorful rag rug beneath her feet. What would it be like to have fifty new houses where the Trayson's farm now stood? It looked square, she realized, square houses on square lots with boring grass lawns dotted by the occasional swingset. The image changed and she saw cows placidly standing behind the houses, chewing the sod yards.

Then she recalled the latest picture of Angie plastered all over town— her frail-looking body propped in a hospital bed, a baseball cap covering her bald head. She thought about Scotty's words to her in the bar tonight, "I know you'll do right by Angie." So many people's lives at stake in different ways, from her dad and his farm to Angie and Arlyce and Maw.

Gently she tapped a set of squash seedlings out of a pot and separated them with surgical precision. She repotted each one into its own plastic tub and watered it before relocating them to the front window in her living room. What didn't fit on the deep window sill went onto Grandma's old oak dresser positioned nearby to catch the most afternoon sunlight. She replaced her vision of Bassville's development with one more pleasing—the vegetable garden that would transform the space behind her house next month.

FIFTEEN

THE WARM AIR AND sunshine had lured people away from work, making the Pub unusually full for a Wednesday afternoon. Mona cracked open a soda for Beau who was walking in through the back door.

"What the hell, Mona? All those trucks in the parking lot, I figured you were tending bar naked or giving away free beer!" Beau sat next to Jake and nodded greetings all around.

"It's spring fever," Spade told him. "Nobody can work on a day like this. I'm going fishing."

"And if it was raining, you'd take off work to play cards," Mona said, trying to ignore the heat that crept up her cheeks whenever Jake looked at her. She hoped he didn't sense how much the other night had gotten her hopes up.

The back door swung open and three strangers stumbled over the threshold, men in their early twenties, and already half-crocked if the redness of their eyes and their unsteady gait were any indication. Two wore T-shirts emblazoned with Maw's Bait Shop and the third wore a baseball cap with Maw's logo, the price tag dangling over his left ear. Mona eyed them cautiously while they approached the end of the bar. She saw them notice Steve's sign by the door—"Vote Against Change in Bassville."

"Maw says this is the place to come to eat. You serving out on by the docks?" The tallest one, ruddy and whiskered, asked Mona.

"No, but you can take drinks out there if you'd like." An electric tingling ran through her feet and up her legs. She felt like she did when she came home from middle school one day and found the family dog dead in the driveway. Tyke, their beloved collie, had taken his final nap beside the front tire of Loyal's pickup and Mona's loud wails had brought her parents running out of the house. Ignoring the warning vibe, she waked toward them. "What can I get you?"

"Three Miller Lites." The shortest one asked her from beneath a White Sox baseball cap pulled so low that Mona couldn't see his eyes.

"You got IDs?" she asked.

They dug around in their back pockets and produced wallets. Mona waited while they flipped them open in turn and she examined the birthdates and the metallic Wisconsin state seal. "Okay, you're good." Mona passed three menus across the bar and turned to grab three cans of beer.

"Can we put the drinks on our lunch tab?"

She knew better, but it was slow, so she nodded and passed them their beers. She made her way around the bar and checked each person's drink, digging fresh cans out of the coolers for those nearly empty.

"Mona, get us a dice cup," Dob told her while she slipped a five-dollar bill out of his pile of money resting on the edge of the bar.

"You bet."

"Can I change the channel?" Spade was balanced on a bar stool, about to switch the TV station to something other than *Guiding*

Light.

"Thought you didn't like change in this town. That's what your sign says." The tallest stranger jutted his chin at Steve's sign before elbowing his way through the door.

"I suppose Maw's indoctrinating them down at the bait shop," Spade quipped while he found a basketball game and returned to his seat.

"I like *spare* change just fine," Mona said and rattled her tip jar. Dob laughed and flipped a quarter at her. "Keep the change."

"Speaking of change, any word on Angie?" Beau asked Scotty.

"Mom talked to Dottie last night. She's staying at the hospital for now. Guess she's on an IV because she's so dehydrated. They started testing family members to see if there's a match for a transplant." Mona rubbed her thumb across the quarter before dropping it in the can on the bar marked "Donate to Our Angel Angie."

"How'd she get dehydrated?" Jake asked. He leaned back on his barstool and hooked one hand beneath the strap of his Carhartt overalls.

"Guess the chemotherapy makes her throw up so much," Mona told him.

"That's awful. And it probably doesn't take much for a kid who weighs what? Seventy pounds soaking wet?" Dob remarked.

"It's really taking its toll on her little body," Mona said.

The first startling *thud* against the front windows of the bar made everyone jump.

"What?" Mona looked up from pouring Dob another rum and coke.

Thud!

She turned to watch a can of beer hit the window and explode, the amber liquid catching the sunlight while it dripped down the glass. Outside, the three strangers had started an impromptu snowball fight scraped from the melting pile on the edge of the yard—and now began tossing the pieces of lumber Steve had stacked outside for repairing some benches.

Mona's mouth turned dry. She slid Dob's rum and coke across to him before running toward the door. Slamming the door open she yelled to the men, "Hey! What the hell do you think you're doing?"

A half-full can of beer whizzed toward her and landed against her right thigh, soaking her jeans. For a long moment Mona watched the can roll across the wooden boards of the dock, leaking beer until it finally stopped beside a bench.

"Go lie down in your corner, bitch," the tallest one snarled.

"That's not your wood. Put it back." Unabated, adrenaline coursed through her arms and her hands trembled.

"Fuck you," the tallest guy retorted. He held the board gripped in his hand.

She lowered her voice, trying to keep calm. "You need to clean this up."

The shortest one fired a snowball at her, forcing her to duck behind the door.

"What the hell's going on out there?" Jake and Dob had reached the door, the rest of the customers stood at the windows, their expressions ranging from curious to menacing.

"They're trashing the yard out there. These clowns are totally bombed." Mona told them. "Where's Arlyce?" Then she remembered Arlyce had gone home to dislodge matchbox cars from their VCR and feed the baby.

"Call Steve," Jake commanded her. "I'm going out there."

Mona ran inside and dialed Steve's number, the phone's receiver rattling against her ear. She tried to take a deep breath while it rang.

"Hello?"

"Steve!" Her voice shook and she gulped. "There's a bunch of guys, three of them, on the docks. They're trashing our place."

"Call the cops!"

Steve slammed the phone down. Mona dialed 911 and waited. The rest of the bar filed out the back door and circled around the three men on the deck. "Come on, come on," she muttered.

Dob threw the first punch, hitting the tallest one square on his jaw, sending him crashing into one of the front windows. Mona flinched at the sudden noise, and out of the corner of her eye saw movement on the edge of the yard. The other two were jumping the railing that separated the Pub's property from the road.

"Emergency. How can I help you?"

"This is Mona over at Bassville Pub. We need somebody here right away. There's a group of guys trashing our deck." Mona hung up the phone after the dispatcher repeated the information back to her, and walked to the side window. Outside Dob and the tall guy took turns punching each other. The dock bowed slightly with each hit.

Jake's head popped up suddenly next to the railing and he sprinted down the road. Mona ran to the window overlooking the street.

In the middle of the muddy road, the bar's customers chased the two remaining strangers. Sinking to their ankles in the slick muck, they plodded on and before anyone reached the intersection, Steve Shanksi cut around the corner in his jeep, two wheels on the sidewalk, a flurry of mud splattering behind him.

Steve jumped out and grabbed the shorter man by the front of his sweatshirt, lifting him fully off the ground and slamming his body onto the jeep's sidewall. A frenzy of fists flew at him while the locals gathered around. Even Spade got a shot in to the guy's jaw. The remaining man staggered toward the center of the road and in a swift movement dropped his pants around his ankles. He yelled something, his mouth wide open, pants sinking in the mud below him. Dob and Dale stopped in their tracks ten feet away from him.

The wail of the police sirens broke up the battles on the street and a dog began to howl in the distance. Jake backed up a few steps. Spade and the Dohill brothers retreated back to the bar. Steve paused still holding the short stranger a moment before dropping him on the ground beside his jeep.

Joe rounded the corner and got out of the squad car with his new deputy following on his heels. Mona opened the door and walked out to the street to hear what they'd say.

"What's going on here, men?" Joe asked as casually as if they were socializing around the bar on a Friday night. He hitched his thumbs through the loops of his pants and rocked back on his heels.

"Seems these fellows were busy trashing my place, Joe," Steve replied.

"They were?" Joe looked at the man in the middle of the road. "There a reason you're running around with no pants on?"

"These guys here were about to beat the shit out of me—"

"Tell you what," Joe interrupted, "Let's take down one statement at a time and sort it out from there." He looked at the short man whose face was smeared with blood and beginning to swell. "Looks like you need some ice."

"These fuckers were punching—"

"Take him back in the car and I'll start here with Steve." Joe whipped out a pad of paper and a pen while his deputy escorted the short man over to the back seat of the squad car.

Mona turned back toward the bar. Beau and the Dohills followed her.

"Mona, can I have an ice pack?" Beau asked.

"What's wrong?"

"Think I busted my hand." He held up his left hand to show the swelling.

"Shit, Beau, that looks pretty rough," Dob commented.

Mona scooped some cubes into a clean bar rag and wound it tight. "Here you go. It figures that as soon as the floodwater recedes, the rats show up."

Beau set the ice pack on his wrist and winced.

Mona pulled shot glasses down and lined them up along the bar.

"What're you doing?" Beau asked.

"Pouring you something to calm your nerves." She reached for the bottle of Wild Turkey and held it up.

"You want to calm my nerves, you better not pour any of that," Beau grumbled.

"What, then?"

"Doctor," Beau answered.

"Dob?" Mona asked.

"Doctor," Dob nodded.

Mona set the bottle of whiskey down with a clank. She opened the walk-in cooler and seized the frosted bottle of Doctor McGillicuddy's. She poured it into all five shot glasses in one long motion, pulling the bottle across the glasses and turning it up at the end with a flourish.

"To your heroic protection," Mona proposed, raising her glass.

"To Bassville," Dob added.

"To Bassville," Beau agreed. They toasted, swallowed, and their shot glasses landed on the bar with a solid thud.

"Mona?" The barstools swiveled as they watched Joe enter the bar behind Jake, a sheet of paper in his hand.

"Yeah?"

"You need to fill out this police report. Be as thorough as you can. Try to include everything you remember."

"Okay." Mona took the sheet from him and studied it.

"I'll have to ask you some questions, too." Joe looked at the men seated at the bar.

"What do you want to know?" Dob asked.

"The gentlemen outside are saying they were beat up by a bunch of guys. Know anything about that?"

"You know, we'd just walked outside when you pulled up. All I saw was them chucking lumber and beer around outside. We followed them to make sure they didn't run away, right Dob?" Dale looked at Dob.

"That's right, Joe. Can't imagine who would've beat them up." Dob shook his head and looked at Beau.

"Is that blood on your coat, Beau?" Joe's expression didn't change.

"Could be. Wore this last week when I was butchering a turkey," Beau answered.

"Think anyone else might have seen anything?" Joe asked.

"What's Steve saying?" Dale asked Joe.

"Pretty much sticking to the same story you all told me right now."

"Must be the truth then," Dob remarked.

"Must be. About done there, Mona?" Joe tapped the bar with his walkie-talkie.

"Just about." Mona was trying to write and watch the street outside where the short man stood holding up his hands linked with the silver metal cuffs. He was yelling, but Mona couldn't make out what he was saying. The other guy sat motionless in the squad car. She flipped the sheet over and finished writing on the back. *I watched them run away from the front windows. Some customers were chasing them. Then the police car pulled up.*

"Where's the guy who was on the dock?" Mona asked, passing the paper across the bar.

"He's out in the back parking lot. He needs some medical attention. Did you see him slip on the ice out there, Mona?" Joe took the police report from her and folded it in half. Then he looked into her face, his dark eyes unblinking.

"Not really."

"Funny, everyone else says they did. That's all for now. Stay out of trouble." Joe hooked his right thumb into his holster and winked at Mona.

"Bye, Joe. Thanks for coming down."

After the door closed behind Joe, Mona walked back to the window to see the squad car parked alongside the sidewalk, its doors wide open. The deputy eased the tall man into the back seat next to his friend without any resistance. She watched until they drove away.

Back in the bar, Steve walked in with Spade trailing behind.

"What'd you say, Steve?" Beau asked.

"I told him the lie closest to the truth. I came down the road and seen two guys running, right after Mona called me over. I blocked their path with the jeep and grabbed the one who'd fallen down in the mud." Steve gestured to his filthy T-shirt.

"What did they say? The jerks from out of town, I mean," Mona asked.

"Said they were just trying to order some lunch when a bunch of fellows came out on the deck and started attacking them," Steve said.

"They said *what*?" Mona gaped.

"Funny thing is," Steve added, "no one here saw anything like that. Can't figure out who did it. Goddamn I hate out of towners."

"You see that moron in the street with his pants down?" Dale asked.

"Yeah—what was up with that?" Mona asked.

"All of a sudden me and Dob are heading toward him and he knows we're gonna beat the shit out of him so he stops and pulls his pants down and starts yelling, 'You wouldn't hit a guy with his pants down, would ya?' He kept yelling that and pointing to his legs." Dale shook his head while the rest started chuckling.

"It worked, though, didn't it?" Steve pointed out.

"Yeah, I guess it did."

They fell silent a moment and Beau shifted the ice pack on his wrist. Mona looked at Jake out of the corner of her eye, wondering what version he'd told Joe. He'd said nothing since returning to the bar, but had pocketed his change after extracting a dollar to leave her as a tip. She wanted to ask him about his statement to the police, but she didn't want to seem nosy. "Can I get you something else, Jake?" she asked, hoping he'd stay.

"No thanks." He slapped Dob on the back. "Boys, that's enough excitement for me for today. See you around." Jake headed for the door and Mona could only chime in with the rest of the crowd, "Bye, Jake."

"Think I'm going to wait here a while." Steve sat down next to Spade at the bar. "Get me a Pepsi, Mona."

The door slammed open and The Pole walked in with Snuffy at his heels. "Hear there was a fracas in the street today," Snuffy said with an eager grin. "Any of you boys know about it?"

"How did you hear already?" Dob asked him.

"Gals at the Hair House saw it from their front window and came down to the hotel to tell us." The Pole chuckled. "Sorry we missed all the action. I've been itching for a good fight."

"It didn't last that long," Dale frowned. "Practically over before it started."

"What sparked it?" Snuffy asked from the door where he stood keeping an eye on Grumpy's across the street. "I saw you all come running down the road and next thing I know there's Steve in his jeep and the cops and some guy's taking off his pants in the middle of Main Street."

Their voices climbed over each other in their excitement to tell a willing audience, the first good fight of the fishing season became history, legend and lore the same afternoon it occurred. While the tale kept mutating from the truth, Mona reflected on all the disruption outsiders could bring to a quiet little town.

140

SIXTEEN

Beau sat next to Otto at the Bassville Pub and eyed Otto's plate of biscuits and gravy with disgust. "Scrambled eggs, Arlyce."

"Coming right up. What's wrong? You look pretty down in the dumps there, Beau." She reached below the bar for fresh silverware and set it on the bar next to his placemat. "Coffee?"

"Coke, please."

"So why the sad face?" Arlyce returned to slicing the banana cream pie she'd just pulled from the cooler.

"Got fired this morning."

"Already?" Arlyce looked at the clock in surprise. "It's not even nine-thirty. How can you lose your job in less than two hours?"

"Broke my wrist yesterday in a fight and tried to blame it on an accident at work so I could collect workman's comp for it. They didn't believe me."

"Isn't that illegal?" Otto asked.

"Who were you fighting?" Arlyce eased the first slice of pie out of the pan and onto a plate.

Beau chose to answer Arlyce and ignore Otto. "Those three guys who showed up here yesterday and started busting up stuff. Bunch of us went out to stop them and it got a little crazy."

"Sounds like spring fever to me. Did you see the doctor yet?"

"No." Beau shifted his arm on the counter and turned his soda can in small circles with his good hand. "He'll just tell me it's broke and tell me to go home after charging me fifty bucks. I can tell you it's broke for free."

"Three guys?" Otto asked, leaning towards him in his excitement. "One of them tall, wearing a baseball cap?"

"Yeah," Beau looked at Otto. "What do you know about them?"

"They stopped at Riverside yesterday afternoon, ordered burgers and ate and left without paying their bill."

"No shit?" Beau cheered up at this news.

"Yeah, after Maw gave them the red carpet treatment. He's a sucker, giving free stuff to people—then they expect everyone in town to hand stuff out for free. No wonder they thought they could skip out on Rosie." Otto snorted. "Thank God Mona beat him in the election. Him on the board? What a disaster. He'd let every farmer in the county make subdivisions out of their cornfields."

"I heard about those guys," Arlyce said. "They stole some gas from the Mini Mart, too. June Butterfield was through this morning and told me all about it. They filled their tank and drove off. Of course not without walking through and filling their pockets with cigarettes and candy bars."

"This town is crazy," Otto declared. Maybe he should look into a move further north. The fishing wasn't as good, but land was cheap and there were fewer people up there.

"Oh, you haven't heard the worst of it," Arlyce warned. "Hear about Maw's latest scheme?"

His wife's purse flew past his head and Maw ducked behind the cash register.

"You stupid son of a bitch!" Peg shrieked. She scanned the room for something else to throw at her husband, something heavy, but not too expensive. Her eyes settled on the back cooler.

"Peg—don't!"

Banging the door aside, Peg reached for two Styrofoam cups of grubs and hurled them one at a time. They exploded in a slimy, writhing mess against the display case.

"A bikini fishing team?"

"It's a marketing tool!" Maw bellowed.

"It's asinine!" Peg returned. "I don't want a bunch of bimbos in swimsuits parading their stuff all over my front yard."

"It's only this Saturday. One time." Maw protested and ducked again to avoid a fresh assault of grubs.

"N. O. No way. Not at my house."

"Peg," Maw pleaded, "It's only a calendar shoot. You already know the girls. They'll be in the boat most of the time anyway."

"A calendar shoot!" Peg reached for a fishing net from the wall above display racks of spinners and jigs. "Over YOUR dead body!"

The phone rang, interrupting the melee. "I'll get it," Peg fumed, stomping across the shop. "Maw's Bait and Tackle. Peg here."

As she listened to the voice on the other end, her face softened and the net slowly lowered to her side. "Oh. Tomorrow's fine." She hung up and turned to Maw. "You ordered a new washer and dryer," she said.

"It's all part of the plan." He eyed her warily from behind the register before deciding it was safe to come out and explain his blueprint for financial success.

When Beau returned to the Pub it was packed. Steve stood behind the bar regaling his customers with the story of the brawl for the fifteenth time.

"Then Joe calls me to tell me they impounded their car and threw them in a jail cell for processing. He's throwing the book at them—drunk and disorderly, broken taillight, expired registration. Hell, I wouldn't be surprised if he invented a few charges," Steve added with a chuckle.

"Did you tell them about the Riverside?" Beau interrupted.

"Oh yeah, they dined and ditched there, then headed to the gas station and filled up for free. These assholes were having a hell of a time in Bassville yesterday after leaving Maw's."

"We showed them not to mess with a small town," Dob boasted.

"Think they'll press any charges against anyone here?" Beau looked at Dob and Dale. He knew for certain they'd done some damage to the guy on the dock.

Steve shrugged. "Seems no one saw anything. Not even Snuffy who had a front row seat across the street. Kind of strange, three guys all insisting people from this town beat them up, but nobody can find a witness." He shook his head in mock amazement.

"How's your wrist?" Spade asked Beau.

"Shit, I forgot all about that. How is it? What happened at work?" Steve looked at Beau's arm.

"I went to the job site and started working, pretended I dropped a board on my wrist and went to the foreman. He told me to go home and don't come back." Beau slumped onto a stool.

"Maybe if you didn't use all your grace points by showing up late all the time you'd still have a job," Dale pointed out.

"Maybe if you like having all your teeth you'd shut the hell up." Beau glared at him, in no mood for anyone's smartass comments—between the shooting pain in his arm and the fact that he'd lost his day job.

"What'll you do, Beau?" Steve tried changing the subject. Both Beau and the Dohills had a tendency to punch first and sort the truth later. His place had seen enough excitement for a while.

"Don't know," Beau answered through gritted teeth. "Maybe ask my uncle if he's hiring."

"I hear Gene needs someone at the farm. You could make some money and really help them out since Dottie's been down in Milwaukee with Angie and won't be coming home any time soon." Steve nodded at him. "Yeah, that would help you both out."

"I'm no good with farm work. I don't like getting my hands dirty. Unless you guys are looking for anyone?" Beau looked over at Dob and Dale.

"No, not now anyway. We'll let you know if anything comes up," Dale lied. Worse than Beau's work ethic was the risk of his girlfriends showing up on the job site. Jenny Bender was notorious for making an appearance for the sole purpose of screaming her lungs out at Beau about his infidelity—real or imagined. Once she'd climbed into a backhoe and drove it through a pallet of shingles during a tantrum of epic proportions. He'd heard they weren't together anymore these days, but the *thought* of that girl's screeching voice made his head start aching.

"Figures." Beau reached for his wallet. He'd have to earn a living the hard way now. "Anyone up for a game of dice?"

The phone rang all morning. First the beer distributor, then several calls about rooms, and just when she nearly had the ledger balanced, it rang again. "Damn it!" Judi slammed the calculator down in frustration. Her balance was off fifty-three dollars and she could not figure out why. "Bassville Hotel," she barked into the receiver.

"Is this Judi?"

"Yes," she answered, hesitating while she tried to place the man's voice.

"This is Will Donne. From Chicago? Dave LaMay's manager?"

"Right. What can I do for you?"

"I need to book another room."

Her irritation vanished as Judi flipped open the reservation book. "When are you coming to town?"

"First week of May. Got anything?" Will held his breath. He knew Dave would rather drive the distance to the next town and stay in a regular hotel.

"Well …." Judi looked at the list of names. Thanks to Maw booking most of their rooms as part of an outfitters package, they were full. Still, she wanted to see William Donne again. And they were Maw's friends, so it would be returning the favor in a way. "Give me your number and I'll call you back."

"If it's not too much trouble."

"No trouble at all." Judi jotted down the number on a pad of paper. She hadn't felt this silly about knowing someone's phone number since middle school. "I'll get back to you in just a few minutes."

"Mom?" Judi found her mother in the bar busy folding drink price cards into Plexiglas holders on each table. "I just got a call about a room for the third of May and we're full. Maybe we could rent out my room and I could sleep in yours, on the couch or something."

Sue looked over her glasses at her daughter's face. "That's an interesting suggestion." She centered the drinks menu on the table and walked to the next one.

"It's for William Donne and that Dave LaMay."

"Aha."

"They want to come up again," Judi said, sounding sheepish.

"Will it be your habit to book your room when we're full?" Sue

146

struggled to keep the teasing note from her voice.

Judi shook her head. "It's just for two nights. I thought it would be nice of us. Maybe they'd mention us on the radio show."

"Sure, free publicity. Great idea. Especially since we're booked all month." Sue snapped another Plexiglas holder together. Her daughter was impressed by Dave LaMay's fame or attracted to him. But that didn't matter as long as they could charge whatever they wanted for Judi's room.

SEVENTEEN

"M<small>AW!</small>" <small>PEG'S VOICE</small> screeched down the stairs after her husband. "Did you pack clean underwear?"

"Woman, I'm going to Chicago—not Siberia. If I forget to pack something, I think I'll be able to find it down there." Maw shook his head and stuffed his arms into the sleeves of his windbreaker. Dave had invited him to Chicago for a weekend media blitz. He'd arranged a half-dozen appearances and interviews with assorted sister stations and newspapers. Maw had been a bundle of energy, packing boxes of T-shirts emblazoned with 'Maw's Minnows' and telling anyone who'd listen about the celebrities he was sure he'd meet.

"You'll call when you get there, right?" Peg followed Maw down the hall and tugged his collar straight.

"I'll call, I'll call." Maw hoisted his suitcase and leaned forward to kiss her lips. "Don't forget to change the filter on the tanks tomorrow morning," he said before planting his lips on hers.

"I won't."

"And call in the order to Remington. We're low on sinkers. And stock the bait coolers …"

"And stock the beer coolers and set up the new display behind the register," Peg finished. "I know, I know."

"This is our big chance, Peg." Maw straightened his shoulders and grinned at his wife. "We're gonna put Maw's Bait and Tackle on the map."

"Be careful." Peg's forehead wrinkled with concern. "Don't do anything stupid."

"How stupid can I be, Peg?" Maw kissed her again and headed out the door. She stood in the doorway waving goodbye, watching their kids race the car down the gravel driveway. "Famous last words," she muttered.

Exhaling in frustration, Mona slumped across the ream of papers on her kitchen table. Half the words in last month's meeting minutes didn't make any sense to her. *Motion by Butterfield/Dohill to approve vouchers #20178 thru #20208 (with exception of #20206 & 20207) and direct deposits #849 – #876 for a total amount of $52,168.71. 5 Yes 0 No.* She read it again out loud. It still didn't make any sense.

She'd spent most of the afternoon looking over old meeting minutes to prepare for her debut board meeting. It was an uphill battle unraveling the legal terminology. She had pages of notes she'd taken trying to decode the numbers and complicated phrases. Nothing she tried made budgets and reports easy to understand.

Shoving her chair back, she retreated to the tangle of leaves overtaking her kitchen countertops. She'd spent an hour pinching back the tiny sprouts, thinning the zucchini plants she'd transplanted into margarine containers. According to what she'd read in the Farmer's Almanac it was still five degrees too cold to transplant them, but she worried that she'd started them too early and they'd get root rot or something. She'd already thrown out five squash plants that faded from bright green to a putrid brown and crumpled back to the soil.

"Plants are simple," she muttered. "Vouchers, parcels, motions—this means nothing to me." She squared her shoulders and returned to the table. Still, she had to admit, it felt nice to have a challenge. Nothing at the Pub was this tough to figure out—except constructing intelligent sentences when Jake was around.

She started when she heard the rapping on her back door. "Mona? Are you home?" her mom's voice called.

Mona opened the door and greeted her mom with a kiss. "This is a surprise!"

"I was at Mom and Pop's place helping with the laundry and saw your light on when I drove past. Look at that!" June shrugged off her jacket and crossed over to the small jungle on Mona's kitchen counters. "Mona!" She turned to look at her daughter with admiration. "This is really something."

"Thanks. I found the seeds in that old dresser of grandma's that you gave me. Remember the great gardens she used to grow?"

"I do. Look—you even have those striped cucumber plants. I recognize the leaves." June picked up one of the pots and inhaled.

"Yeah. So I found a book at the library that explained how to set the seeds in wet newspapers. I planted them then, but I didn't count on all of them making it. Turns out their survival rate is pretty good." She felt proud of her green thumb, but other than Jake no one else had seen proof of it yet.

"You'll need to till up your entire back yard to plant them all."

"I know."

"And then you'll need to set up a farm stand to sell all the produce."

"What do you mean?"

"Sweetie, you're going to have bushels, I mean *bushels* of tomatoes and cucumbers and peppers. Each of the pepper plants will give you at least five peppers. What do you have growing here? About twenty pepper plants?"

"The grand total's closer to thirty. I had to move some to the bathroom. They were taking up too much space in here." Mona gestured to the chair across from her at the table and sat down.

"Thirty. That's a lot of pepper plants."

"I guess I've been having so much fun watching them grow I haven't thought about what would happen next."

"Come July you'll be up to your armpits in vegetables, which isn't a bad thing, but how will you deal with it?"

Mona shrugged and picked at chip in the table top. "I don't know."

"At the very least you ought to try selling some to Arlyce. She could use them on the salad bar."

"Maybe I could set up a pick-your-own pumpkin patch in my back yard this fall," Mona said. How much could she make on this? Enough to scale back her hours at the Pub?

June laughed and covered Mona's hand with her own. "Whatever you decide to do, I'll tell everyone I know about it."

"Have you heard from Sean?" Mona asked, switching topics. She'd tried calling him once last week, but got no answer.

"I spoke with him briefly last night. I gave him updates on Angie— you probably heard they're testing Scotty to see if he's a donor match for her. Sean's doing well. Cramming for a big exam in chemistry. Still single."

"Want me to make some tea? Can you stay for a while?"

"Please do," June told her and kicked off her shoes.

Mona pushed back her chair and began rummaging in her kitchen for teabags. While she filled the kettle at the sink, she told her mom, "I feel awfully grown up right now, having you visit me."

"Mona, you *are* grown up," June said, "and you make me so proud.

Maw was not a man easily shaken. He'd endured an IRS audit, his mother's open heart surgery and several near-death encounters involving the Dohills and alcohol, including one that left him floating in Lake Michigan for eight hours before the Coast Guard pulled him to safety. None of these experiences made his heart palpitate like driving on the Chicago Tollway.

Sweat spread in rank circles under his arms and beaded on his forehead. Every time he tapped the brakes he was rewarded with the blare of a horn or an obscene hand gesture—often both. Traffic zoomed past both sides of his car, and Maw, who'd never driven on anything wider than a four-lane highway, suddenly felt a great affinity for those elderly drivers he'd previously dismissed as idiots when they puttered down Rural Route 20, eight cars tailgating in their wake. Now the red speedometer arrow was hovering at 90 MPH, the fastest he'd ever driven. Cars passed him, their passengers sneering in disgust at his Wisconsin license plates, and Maw felt his throat constrict while he swallowed back the terrible thought that he might never get off this interstate alive.

"That lady in the Pinto lookes as old as Peg's mother," he said to the mirror. "If *she* can handle driving on this, *I* can."

Green highway signs appeared and disappeared before his mind could register them. The only thing Maw was able to comprehend for the past hour was the sign that appeared on each exit he passed: Toll 40 C.

"Forty cents? Dave didn't mention forty cents. He scrabbled for change in his pants pocket. Nothing but lint and a foil gum wrapper. Another green sign appeared and he tried to slow down to read it.

Blooooohhhhhnk. The baritone warning of an eighteen-wheeler changed his mind and he accelerated, urging the Buick to keep pace with the rush of traffic. Another semi screamed past on his left and the Buick shuddered. Gripping the steering wheel with one clammy, white-knuckled fist, he reached across the car and popped open the glove compartment. A flurry of paper spilled to the floor—two maps, the driver's manual, various licenses for fishing and hunting and registrations stuffed there for safekeeping. Among the wreckage he found a broken pencil, two pennies and a quarter. He set them on the passenger seat and clawed his fingers across the floor beneath his legs.

"Oh fuck, what did that say?" he yelled as he raced past another sign. Trucks filed aside into the lane to his right and he noticed a highway patrol car parked alongside the next tollbooth. "Will they pull me over if I go through without paying?" His fingers pried up two dried out wads of gum and several junk food wrappers, but no spare change.

At the next exit he saw the $1.00 lane option, but after rifling through his wallet, Maw found nothing smaller than a twenty. "Shit!"

For mile after mindless mile Maw searched, the panic pooling in his chest while he tried to find a way off the tollway. "If I had never gotten on in the first place," he moaned, passing another exit and wishing he were lined up with the drivers who had the correct change to pay their way to safety. "Twenty-seven cents. I just need twelve more. Does a tollbooth even take pennies?"

The sun hovered above the horizon, long shadows dimming the highway. Headlights switched on around him. He was two hours late to meet Dave. His breath came in fast and shallow pants, drying out his mouth.

The fuel gauge light flickered its bright orange admonition. "E means 'enough' my grampa said. But what's 'enough' now?" Maw asked the Buick while pressing his foot against the gas pedal and praying for a miraculous rescue off the interstate. Maybe the tollbooths shut down after rush hour, he thought between heavenward pleas for deliverance.

Maybe there won't be anyone at the next exit and I'll just pull off and drive away. But what if I drive through without paying? Do they arrest you? Ticket you? Let you pass because you have out of state plates?

The desolation of the eight-lane interstate circling Chicago put Maw in mind of a family vacation years ago to the Badlands. No one and nothing as far as the eye could see—except traffic and blacktop swimming in his blurry vision.

Before the next exit, before Maw could execute his master plan to speed off the tollway and into the next truck stop for fuel, the Buick sputtered. He steered it through an opening between two trucks and a car to the shoulder and stared at the gas gauge in disbelief. He climbed out of the car and looked around, wheezing for breath and grabbing his chest.

"Oh God," he moaned, and then collapsed into blackness.

The brightness of the room entered Maw's consciousness first, followed by the clamor of voices and brisk footsteps. A faint electronic beeping sounded close to his ear. He raised heavy eyelids and gradually focused on a grey tiled ceiling. He moved hands, arms, feet and legs successfully to his pleasure. Then he strained to sit up.

A blue flowered hospital gown covered his torso—and running from his chest were a series of red and white wires connected to the source of the beeping. For a fleeting moment he thought of little Angie Trayson who was lying in a hospital room that probably looked and smelled similar. What parent in their right mind wouldn't do anything possible to get their kid well and back home? Even if back home looked a little different after selling off most of the property.

"Hello?" he croaked out.

A behemoth of a woman wearing aqua-colored scrubs wedged

herself through the door. "Well. I'll go tell the doctor you've woken up." She reached for a chart at the end of his bed and scratched a few notes on it with pencil.

"Where am I? What's happened?"

"You're at Northside Memorial. Sir, do you know your name?"

"Maw Cooper," he told her, brushing off her question with his hand. "Why am I in a hospital? What happened to me?"

She appraised him over the top of the clipboard in her meaty hands. "You've suffered a panic attack. We'll have you on your feet in no time."

Instinctively Maw's hands clutched at his chest. "A panic attack? Okay, that's fine." He exhaled and closed his eyes tightly. "I need to get a hold of Dave LaMay."

"Who?"

"Dave LaMay. The DJ from the radio?" He searched the nurse's face for recognition.

"Huh." She looked unimpressed.

"Where's my clothes?"

She retrieved a plastic bag out of the closet by the door and handed it to him.

"I need a phone book." He looked around the room, feeling hysteria wrap around his thoughts so that no matter how hard he tried, he couldn't think. "What day is it?"

"Didn't your mama teach you manners?"

"What?"

"You say 'please' when you ask for something."

"Please. I. Need. A. Phone. Book." Struggling to retain his composure, Maw took a deep breath while she handed him a thick, ragged-edged book. He stared at it, realizing that Chicago has a much larger population than Bassville, so of course the phone book's size would reflect that. No matter. He thumbed through to the L's and ran his finger down the page. There were hundreds of LaMays listed in the Chicago phone directory, none of them named Dave and about a dozen sharing "D" as a first initial. He cursed and grabbed the phone.

"You need to dial nine before calling out," the woman told him, before leaving the room.

His first three tries went unanswered. The next two never heard of a Dave or any variation of 'David.' After the twelfth call he hung up and stared at the thick phone book feeling very alone.

After a moment he looked up the radio station in the yellow pages.

"WLUP. How can I help you?"

"I need to speak with Dave LaMay," Maw said.

"One moment."

Maw kicked the covers off his legs while he waited for Dave to pick up. He still didn't know what day it was, whether he'd missed any of the scheduled appearances or interviews.

"Hey, hey, it's Dave LaMay."

"Dave! It's Maw."

"Where the fuck are you?" Irritation coated Dave's voice and Maw rushed to explain.

"I'm at Northside Memorial. I had a, er, a heart attack—but it's only a mild one. I'll tough it out. Look, I'm on my way, just tell me how to get there. By the way, do you know what day it is?"

"You had a what? Never mind. Look, I'll send a cab for you. You've already missed *The Chicago Sun*, but we've got two news shows and *The Tribune* so just get your ass here, okay?"

"I'm on it. Don't worry." The phone went dead in Maw's hand and a tall man in a white lab coat entered the room.

"Dr. Jeffries," he said, extending his hand.

"Maw Cooper."

"We've got good and bad news for you, Mr. Cooper," the doctor began, stroking his grey beard while he looked over Maw's chart.

"Look, I need to get dressed. A cab is coming to pick me up—I have to be at the studio for a very important interview." Maw began pulling his pants out of the plastic bag and froze when the sharp smell of piss reached his nose. "Aw shit," he exclaimed.

Dr. Jeffries nodded sympathetically. "A common and little-known side effect of the anxiety attack is a loss of bodily functions. Do you have a spouse or family member who can bring you some clean clothes?"

"No. I'm really sorry, but I'm just going to have to—" Maw stood up and the wires attached to his chest pulled him back. "Listen, can you just unhook me here?"

"Sir, we'd prefer to keep you here for further tests. The EKG shows signs of ischemia and we'd like to keep you here for twelve hours or at least until your cardiac enzymes come back."

Maw reached over and grabbed the pen out of the doctor's lapel pocket. He scrawled his name, address and phone number on the front of the phone book. "Send me the bill." He ripped the leads from his chest, pulled on his shoes and, holding the hospital gown closed with one hand, grabbing his plastic bag of soiled clothes with the other, stumbled out the door and down the hall.

Dave surveyed Maw and handed the cab driver a twenty-dollar bill. "Marshall Field's. And step on it." He slid into the backseat next to Maw. "If the station doesn't pick up the tab on your clothes, you'll owe me."

Maw nodded happily. A new outfit—a big-city outfit. He imagined himself in a suit and tie, sharp creases in the trousers—pinstriped trousers. Although anything was an improvement over the flimsy hospital gown barely covering his ass crack.

Maw followed Dave through the glass doors of the department store, marveling at the displays of cashmere gloves and perfume bottles and jewelry. The carpeted aisles muffled their footsteps and in response to soft music playing, he slowed his pace while he looked around, forgetting to hold closed the back of his hospital gown until the titters of two salesclerks behind a register reached his ears. Marshall Field's was paradise, nothing at all like shopping at Fleet Farm or J.C. Penney's.

"Come on," Dave urged with an impatient edge to his voice and Maw looked up to find the DJ halfway to the next floor on an escalator. Maw hastened to join him, one hand securing the hospital gown modestly across his pale, hairy buttocks.

When they reached the fifth floor, Dave led them past the suits and sportswear and even, to Maw's dismay, past Finer Men's Leisurewear.

"I'm guessing you wear a Large. Try these on," Dave instructed him, throwing a plaid flannel shirt and a pair of blue jeans into Maw's arms.

"But," Maw protested, "these are just like the clothes in my bag."

"Yeah?" Dave looked at him, an eyebrow raised.

"Well, since we're here and all, wouldn't it be nice for me to wear something like that?" Maw motioned to a mannequin wearing a royal blue satin jogging suit with orange piping and an ostentatious logo across the chest.

"That?" Dave shook his head. "No way. You're a small town fisherman-slash-bait salesman. People are expecting to see Mr. Up North wearing plaid flannel and blue jeans, maybe even suspenders. Come on man, let's get going." He turned Maw around and led him by the shoulders to a dressing room.

Maw came out, his shoulders slumped in defeat. His reflection in the mirror looked just like it did any other day of his life. He noticed no discernible difference between his twelve-dollar flannel shirt from

Fleet Farm and the hundred-dollar one by, he read the tag again, Ralph Lauren.

"Really, Dave, couldn't we jazz this up a little? Maybe with a hat?"

Dave shook his head and tore the tags free from the shirt and pants. He grabbed a pair of socks from a table nearby and headed for the register. Maw sighed and gazed longingly one last time at the shiny jogging suit before following Dave.

An hour later Maw perched on the edge of a couch next to World Wrestling Federation star Sergeant Slaughter, waiting for his television interview for *Chicago Today!*. The camera lights felt hot on his face, but emboldened by the attention, the make up on his face and the crisp feel of new clothes on his back, Maw took a swig of his Mountain Dew and sat up straighter, ready to make his prime time debut. Okay, maybe not quite prime time, but lots of people in the Chicago viewing area tuned in to watch TV at ten-thirty at night.

Dave leaned forward and whispered to him, "After this is done, we'll catch a bite downtown at this restaurant Michael Jordan is going to buy."

Maw beamed and rubbed his hands together, mentally rehearsing his pitch for the host of *Chicago Today!*. The stylishly dressed young host took his seat across from Maw and Sergeant Slaughter, paused while a middle-aged woman in an apron dusted powder across his face and then faced the cameras with an ingratiating grin.

"Good evening, Chicago! We're back tonight with Dave LaMay, the voice guiding us through the hits on the loop weekday mornings on WLUP. He's brought along his newest sensation, the man famous for his minnows and fishing advice, Maw Cooper from The White Bass Capital of the World, Bassville, Wisconsin. Welcome, Maw."

"Good evening. It's a real pleasure to be here in the Windy City. The wind blows through Bassville, but nothing like this I tell you."

Maw felt a trickle of sweat form at his temples.

"Why don't you tell our viewers a little about your hometown, Maw?"

"Well, it's a lot like Chicago. We've got culture, great restaurants and bars, and of course, we've got recreation galore. Fishing, hunting, you name it. Not only is it the White Bass Capitol of the World, Bassville's got plenty else besides."

"I had no idea Bassville was a bastion of high culture. What do you offer besides outdoor sports?" the host pressed.

"If you want fine dining, the burgers at the Bassville Pub are second to none. And if fish or steak's more to your liking, Pine Acres or the Luau Room have 'em both. The Luau Room's got live music every weekend and I promise you, I've never been to Grumpy's Pub and *not* been entertained. And then there's gambling and snowmobiling on the river in the winter. The only thing we don't have is a professional basketball team—but our girls' varsity volleyball team took conference this last year."

To Maw's surprise, everyone in the room, from the host to the scraggly-looking fellow in the AC/DC T-shirt, erupted with laughter. Warming to the task at hand, he launched into a description of some of the local color, starting with Snuffy.

"Maw, you son of a bitch, you sure nailed it this time." Dave slapped him on the shoulder and pushed the door to the restaurant open. "Whatever you want, my man, order up because tonight's on me."

Buoyed by his success in the TV studio, Maw shook his head emphatically. "No, sir. I would not be here tonight if it weren't for you, Dave. This is *my* treat." He waved the bartender over. "Table for eight," he gestured to Will and the rest of Dave's entourage following them to the bar. "And get out a bottle of your best champagne. The tab's on me!"

The carousing and laughter continued around Maw while he gaped at the bill the waiter had discreetly left in a black leather folder next to his elbow five minutes earlier. Peg's going to kill me, he thought. His next realization was equally gut-wrenching. What if my credit card gets rejected?

"Maw? What's wrong, man? You look like your best friend just died," Will said, noticing Maw's pale face and stricken expression. "You all right?"

Maw nodded and pushed his chair back. "Fine—I'm fine. Maybe the lobster didn't agree with me. Shellfish allergy or something." He hurried to the men's room where he vomited up eighty dollars' worth of steak and lobster into the nicest porcelain toilet he'd ever seen.

Even the toilet paper was soft and plush on his skin as he wiped his mouth. "Doesn't matter now," he said to himself. "I'm here and the damage is done. Nothing left but to enjoy it."

Rinsing his face and noting how blue his new shirt made his eyes shine, Maw squared his shoulders and returned to his seat of honor in the dining room. He'd make this up in the next month at the bait shop—you have to spend money to make money, he reminded himself.

"I'm there, Maw. Not this spring, but next year. I'm coming to Bassville and you and I will catch a thousand fish with those minnows next spring," Sargeant Slaughter told him.

"I'm holding you to that," Maw answered and raised his glass.

EIGHTEEN

A FEW HUNDRED MILES north of where Maw was living large on Michigan Avenue, Mona and Jenny squeezed through the crowd to perch on freshly vacated barstools at a corner table in the Luau Room.

"Look at this place." Jenny said. "Even *you* could catch someone in here tonight, Mona." Jenny sipped her drink and scanned the room, mostly men since the fishing rush was in full swing. She'd pointedly ignored Beau when they walked in, concentrating her efforts on fresh blood.

"Catch what? VD?" Mona asked. Her night began on a sour note two hours ago when Sean called to congratulate her on winning the town board election. At least he started the call by congratulating her—before reminding her that she was now "entrenched in dead-end Bassville until the end of a four-year term." "When are you going to shake the dust off your heels and give life a chance?" he'd asked, cajoling her again to join him in Ohio or enroll at the tech in Northport. Her irritation led to tears welling at the edges of her eyes. Why couldn't Sean see that living in Bassville wasn't so bad? It wasn't so bad, was it? It was one thing to decide it wasn't for him, but Sean didn't have to be so critical of *her* choices.

Jenny kicked her feet in beat to the music in the bar and then hopped off her barstool. "I'm going up to the bar. You coming?"

"No. Go ahead." Mona watched Jenny slither between two of the younger, more handsome specimens in the bar. She sipped her beer and tried to get in a party mood. It was dumb to stay hung up on Jake, he probably wasn't staying in town much longer anyway.

"Why the long face, sweetheart?"

Mona looked up at a face with rugged whiskers and piercing dark eyes. "Nothing. Just tired, that's all."

"Can I get you a drink?" The man gestured at Mona's bottle.

She held up her beer and looked at it. It was still half full. "No thanks, I'm good."

He paused. "Mind if I join you?"

"I don't care." Mona recrossed her legs and returned her attention to Jenny who now leaned back against the bar, swinging her long hair behind her shoulders and rubbing her hand along the broad shoulder of her selected prey.

"Friend of yours?" The man followed her gaze.

"Yeah. She's a piece of work."

"I'm Tom, by the way." He held out his hand.

"Mona," she answered, shaking it.

"So, Mona, you from around here?"

"Oh my God! He's totally hitting on you!" Jenny squealed in a voice two octaves higher than normal. "Mona! You should go for it!" She punched Mona's arm and leaned closer the ladies' room mirror to check her lipstick.

"He is not," Mona protested. "Let's get out of here."

"No way, babe. It's hopping here tonight and I'm not leaving. Quit being a poop." Jenny turned and dug her talons into Mona's wrist. "You're staying." She opened the bathroom door and dragged Mona back into the loud heat of the Luau Room's main bar.

Mona hung behind Jenny long enough for introductions to two new men with thick south Chicago accents before she backed unnoticed toward the door. Then she saw Jake across the bar, sitting with the Dohills and Scotty Trayson, talking to Beau. *Don't be a coward*, she thought. *Let him notice you.*

"Mona, are you ready for that drink?" Tom stood next to her suddenly and Mona smiled brightly.

"I am. How about a shot?"

"A shot—that's my girl," he grinned and nodded. "What'll you have?"

"Beau!" Mona hollered across the bar and waved. "Need some shots over here!"

The keyboard player switched keys and started into a rendition of something by Johnny Cash. Beau bounded up in front of her, wiping his hands on a bar rag and giving her a wink. "A shot? For Mona Butterfield?" he smirked.

Mona jutted her chin up and shook her head. "Just having a good time, Beau. It's fishing season! We'll have a couple of Blow Jobs— Tom wants to celebrate his first fishing trip to Bassville."

"Two Blow Jobs, coming right up." Beau plunked two shot glasses in front of them and began pouring the Irish whiskey and Kahlúa. He reached below the bar and pulled up a can of whipped cream with a flourish and topped the shots off.

"You know the rules, right, Tom?" Mona asked. "No hands, just your mouth." She clasped her hands behind her back and before bending over the bar to take the glass in her mouth, she glanced at Jake. He was watching them with a bemused expression. Mona bit the shot glass between her teeth and tipped her head back.

"You do that like a pro," Tom complemented her.

"Let's see how you do," Mona returned, dabbing whipped cream from her lips with her thumb.

He bent over and halfway back up he sputtered, the glass clattering on to the bar.

"Must be his first time, Mona. Look at the mess he made." Beau wiped the bar clean. "It's okay, man, happens to the best of us." He poured a shot of tequila and slid it in front of him. "Here, drown your sorrows."

"Thanks." Tom lifted the glass towards Beau before downing the shot. Leaning in to Mona, his breath hot on her ear he whispered, "That was embarrassing. But I'm glad to know you're better at blow jobs than I am."

Mona blushed and looked past Tom's head at Jake who was now focused on a card game. She might as well be invisible to him. She stepped away from the bar to put a more comfortable distance between her and Tom. She had to get in the card game, that's where Jake was, not over here where she sat flirting like an idiot with some fisherman.

"Thanks for the drink. I need to stop by the ladies' room," she said.

He leaned in to whisper, "I'll be right here."

Mona edged through the crowd of Carhartt jackets and flannel shirts. As one of only five women in the room she couldn't disappear into the card game and Tom made her feel uneasy. She glanced over her shoulder to see him lean his back against the bar and lift up a fresh bottle of beer.

"Hey, leaker!" Jenny squeezed past the pool table and grabbed Mona's sleeve.

"What?"

"You leaving? Jake's over there," Jenny pointed across the room and shoved Mona in that direction.

166

"Yeah, I know."

"Well?"

"I'm going over there. In a minute."

"You're going over there right now." Jenny dragged Mona around the bar, through the crowd to stand between Scotty and Jake. Jenny threw her arm around Scotty's shoulders and rubbed her hand across his scruffy whiskers. "What's a bunch of local guys doing in a place like this tonight?" Scotty kissed her cheek while still holding his cards propped against his chest. "What's a good-looking girl like you doing in a bar full of fishermen? Or need I ask?"

"What are you playing?" Jenny asked.

"Sheephead," Dob told her.

"Will you deal us in?" Jenny asked.

"After this hand," Scotty promised. "First I have to try to get my paycheck back from Dale. I don't know where he gets his luck."

Dale laughed and drew a card off the deck. "Scotty, you want that paycheck back, you'll be sittin' here all night long. I told the wife I'd be home an hour ago."

Mona watched Jake out of the corner of her eye. He studied his cards, then sighed and discarded two. He must have come straight from work, she guessed, because his sunglasses were dangling from his front shirt pocket along with a lanyard strap.

"Who's your friend, Mona?" Scotty asked, jutting his thumb in Tom's direction.

"Some fisherman from Chicago way. I was showing him a little Bassville hospitality."

"Don't show him too much hospitality," Dob teased.

Mona blushed and looked away. She should go home now. Jake knew she was an idiot and now that Tom guy was staring at her from across the bar, creeping her out. The whole night was a disaster.

"Okay, boys, baby needs a new pair of shoes," Dale tossed his cards onto the bar with a flourish.

"Looks like he's getting them," Scotty said, dropping his cards on Dale's and digging in his jeans pocket.

"I'm done buying shoes for your kid, Dale. I gotta get going." Jake set his cards on top of Scotty's and stood, stretching his arms wide and yawning. "Jenny, you can have my spot in this game. I'm going home."

"Already? It's only eleven," Jenny said, hopping onto his barstool.

"Past my bedtime. See you later," Jake nodded at them and pulled a few crumpled bills out of his jeans pocket and tossed them onto the bar. He was tired, too tired for this scene. "Beau, catch these kids on me, all right?"

"You leaving already, Jake?" Beau called.

"Yep. See you tomorrow."

Mona stood by silently watching Jake head for the door, his blonde head inches above most of the crowd. Invisible and lonely, she considered making an exit herself when she heard Tom's voice in her left ear.

"Thought you were coming back," he murmured, his breath searing her neck.

"I was—am. I needed to say hi to these guys." Mona looked back, catching a glimpse of the back of Jake's faded red sweatshirt before the door slammed shut behind him. She closed her eyes for a moment and then opened them. "Need a beer?"

"No." Tom snaked his hand around her waist. "I don't need a beer."

Scotty glanced up at Mona and frowned. "You okay there, Mona?" he asked in a loud voice.

"Yeah, I'm good."

Scotty eyed Tom warily. "Okay then."

Hours later the crowd in the Luau Room had thinned out and Mona leaned on her elbows watching the Dohills take another ten dollars off of Scotty. It had slowed down so much that even Beau got in the game. Jenny was long gone—headed back to town with two brothers, one who looked like Val Kilmar.

Tom stumbled and slurred incomprehensibly and Mona yawned. He kept groping her around the waist and nuzzling her neck, and she evaded him playfully at first but now felt the pressure of his expectations.

"I'll be back," he said, running his hand down her back and standing.

"Okay," she told him, preparing for a quick exit while he went to the men's room.

He stumbled across the room and Mona bent over to grab her purse. Swinging her purse over her shoulder, she stood, called goodnight to the card players and made a beeline for the door. The bathroom door opened and Mona froze mid-stride.

An old man wearing a blue wool fedora walked out. She rushed past him and towards the exit.

Pushing the heavy wood door open, the cold air a shock after the heat of the bar, Mona scanned the parking lot. It was dumb to think Tom would follow her out of the bar, even if he did he wouldn't know which car was hers and how to find her. Still …

She ran towards her car. Her shoes thudded against the pavement and her heart kept a frantic pace in her chest. She yanked her car door open. Sliding in, eyes on the Luau Room's main entrance the whole time, she started the engine and backed out.

The door opened and a dark figure stood silhouetted against the light of the bar.

Mona didn't waste time to see who it was. She gunned it, and sped down the road. Headlights followed her towards town and she tried to steady her breathing. Crossing the river, she noticed that Jake's cottage was dark, and she couldn't see his truck. Mona watched the headlights follow her down Main Street, at a distance, though.

She decided to park behind her house and turned onto a side street to come around the back way. On the outside chance Tom was following her, he'd never find her. Locking her doors, she made her way toward the front door. A beam of light swung across her path and she broke into a run.

"It's okay!" Mona heard a man's voice shout. "It's me, Jake!"

She spun around to see him sitting in his truck across the street from her house, shining a flashlight on himself. "You scared me!" she gasped and clutched at her chest. Was she having a panic attack? Her heart never beat so hard.

"Sorry. I just wanted to make sure you got home all right, that's all. You're good, right?" Her skin looked white beneath his flashlight beam.

Mona nodded.

"You sure?"

"I'm fine," Mona said again, raising both arms to demonstrate.

"Okay. Take care." He switched off the flashlight and his truck rumbled down the street.

Mona let herself in, deadbolting the door behind her. Jake had followed her home—why? Worried that she'd brought Tom home with her? Or concerned for her safety? Either way it showed he cared about her in some small way. She tossed her purse on the kitchen counter.

In her bedroom she shoved aside a pile of clean laundry and pulled back the green and pink patchwork quilt her grandma had made for her when she turned sixteen. She curled up beneath it and shivered, her arms tightly wrapped around her knees. The dark shadows from the tree outside her window moved in the breeze and she felt no comfort from the pale, harsh glow from the moonlight. *I need to do better than this. It changes now. I'm on the town board, for God's sake.* An ache spread through her chest and leaked into her stomach. It was a long time before she finally fell asleep, worn out by rationalizing her behavior and knowing she'd behaved badly.

NINETEEN

During the predicted mid-morning lull on Friday, Maw barked out instructions from his post in the center of the bait shop.

"Hold up your fishing rods and say, 'Cheese!'"

Maw paced back and forth behind the photographer, holding a clipboard in both hands. "Let's get the next shot with them on the boat, Ed."

Ed Lyons photographed weddings, high school seniors, and the occasional family portrait when he wasn't writing ad copy for the *Bargain Bulletin*. Four and a half feet tall with a goatee and receding hairline, Ed dressed in black and collected record albums which he piled on the shelves lining his studio. This was his first photo shoot involving swimsuit models—and fishing equipment.

"Okay, girls, you heard Maw." He took a few more pictures before setting his camera on the counter by the cash register. "Grab your gear and head to the boat."

"Are you nuts?" Jenny Bender narrowed her eyes at Maw. "It's like forty degrees out there today."

"It'll only take a few minutes. By the time we're done you'll hardly have a goosebump," Maw said, holding the door open and letting the other girls pass. "Besides, Jenny, this is the chance of a lifetime!"

"That's what you keep saying," Jenny muttered, following the crowd outside to a new bass boat parked on a trailer. She hugged her arms around her chest, regretting her decision to wear her tiger striped thong bikini.

"Climb up!" Ed was giving each woman a hand up to the brand new Tracker boat on loan from Smith's Marina down the river for the occasion. Three women in bikinis, all carrying fishing poles and wearing assorted fishing hats and vests, swiveled sideways to narrow their waistlines, pop their hips and purse their lips.

"That's great, ladies. Just great," Maw enthused from behind Ed. "Let's pull that cap down a little more there, Lottie. I want the logo to show."

The women had agreed to Maw's swimsuit calendar in exchange for fifty dollars and unlimited fame and fortune when their modeling talents were discovered. Maw promised each girl her own page in addition to the group shots. The photo shoot caused a stir around town and traffic past his store had been steady all day.

"Hey, Maw!"

Maw looked over his shoulder to see Beau and Spade pulling into the parking lot. Spade had never fished a day in his life as far as Maw knew, but then even a few locals who dug up their own nightcrawlers had showed up this morning to buy a carton of slugs. Yes sir, this publicity stunt was paying off and the Chicago money was just beginning to roll in.

"What can I do for you?" Maw asked, leaving Ed to set up his tripod and start shooting.

"Heard you had some nice scenery out here at the bait shop," Spade said, leering over Maw's shoulder. "Looking good, ladies!"

"As you can tell, we've got the calendar shoot today," Maw told them.

"Man," Beau nodded at the flow of traffic in the parking lot. "You should have girls in swimsuits out here every weekend to help you sell bait."

Maw stared at Beau. That wasn't a bad idea. Peg had been wild when he'd asked her to man the shop while they did the shoot. He had no choice, though. Sex sold stuff—new cars, bottles of booze, even fish bait. His mind churning like an outboard motor, he left Beau and Spade and hustled back to the boat.

"Girls, I've got a proposition for you," Maw said.

"What's that, Maw?" They asked, tugging at their swimsuit straps.

"I'll pay you to come out here every Saturday. You can pose for pictures with the customers, sign autographs—help sell T-shirts and stuff. I'll get tables set up here by the road." The ideas rushed into focus as he spoke.

"What'll you pay?" Jenny asked while clutching her goose-pimpled arms around her. Even her hair, stiff with mousse and hairspray, vibrated. "I'm freezing my ass off today. Name a price that would make it worth my while."

Calculating the cost, Maw scratched behind his neck and wrote a few numbers on his clipboard. "Hundred bucks apiece. Come out here ten to three."

"I'm in," one sang out, tossing long dark hair. "You never know when some talent scout comes up here to fish. And I'll never make twenty bucks an hour at the Mini Mart."

"Count me, too," another told Maw. "Can we go back inside now? I can see my breath it's so freaking cold." She stamped her feet for emphasis.

"Yeah," Maw said and waved them back to the store.

"What shots do you want to do next?" Ed asked. "I was thinking we could have them form a pyramid, you know, on their hands and knees in front of the minnow tanks."

"Sure, sure. Whatever. I gotta call a guy about a sign," Maw said. "You in?" he called after Jenny.

"I'm in," Jenny yelled back, climbing out of the boat and scurrying across the yard to the warmth of the bait shop.

Maw rubbed his hands together and whistled, his bearded face alight with joy. He could hardly wait for Dave to call him Monday morning for the fishing report. Flinging the store door open with a bang, he rushed inside and grabbed Peg to swing her around and kiss her on the lips.

"Maw, what the—"

"Peg, my good woman, we're on our way to fame and fortune," he announced. "We don't have to wait for the Traysons to sell their property because this bait shop is moving to the big time."

Peg stood back and appraised her husband. "Have you been drinking?"

"No," Maw smiled.

"Good. When are Ed and the bikini bimbos getting out of here? He's got them draped all over the minnow tanks."

"They're almost done. Listen, I've got the most brilliant idea ..."

"Wonderful. Hold that thought. I'm going to the store."

"Don't you want to hear my idea?" Maw asked.

"Sure." Peg reached up and tugged Maw's beard. "But if it involves more girls in swimsuits, then you keep it to yourself. I'll be back in a half hour."

Maw's shoulders slumped as Peg walked out of the bait shop. But the idea of five bikini-clad girls holding T-shirts emblazoned with "Maw's Bait and Tackle" in the middle of his jam-packed parking lot zipped him out of his funk. "Ed! How's it looking?" he shouted.

TWENTY

THURSDAY NIGHT MONA WAS working at the Pub and trying not to fret about her first board meeting in less than a week. The lilacs had begun to bloom, the first tiny flowers letting loose their heavy fragrance and the white bass run had started. Spade and Dob sat at the front corner of the bar—dice clattering between them. A couple of Italian Mafiosi on their annual trip from Chicago enjoyed a friendly beer after trolling the river all day. Some elderly fishermen nursed their Manhattans at a table by the window. Two Army officers on leave sat at the bar with a young woman one of the men introduced as his sister. The girl didn't speak English and Mona could only remember, "Cerveza, por favor," from her one year of high school Spanish, so they exchanged silent, sympathetic smiles. Scotty and The Pole had walked in ten minutes ago fresh off a day of work, and they split a pitcher of beer while waiting for a pizza. Mona looked again at the clock with a weary sigh. Only three hours to go before she could close. She wanted to get home early so she could read over a fresh stack of various ordinances and bylaws her dad had handed her Sunday at dinner.

She picked up a bar rag and began wiping down bottles. "You two heading out early tomorrow?" she asked the Mafiosi.

"We'll probably sleep in," one answered. He ran his hands through his thick white hair and leaned back in his seat. "We caught eighty today—that's hard work."

"Who's cleaning them?" Mona asked.

"We left 'em with Steve's oldest. We're paying him ten cents a fish," he said.

"Nice," Mona nodded.

"Pretty busy for a Thursday in April," he said, looking around the bar while his partner headed for the bathroom. They had come to Bassville every spring as long as anyone could remember and always stayed three weeks at Pine Acres.

"It is," Mona agreed. "Figured I'd be in bed early tonight. But no matter." She shrugged and lifted a bottle of rum out of the rail. "There's nothing on TV so what am I missing, right?"

"That's the truth," the man said, turning his cocktail glass on the bar, the dim lights glittering on his diamond-studded watch and the heavy rings on his fingers. "Who's the kid?" He asked, jabbing his thumb at the can with Angie's picture.

"Angie Trayson, Scotty's little sister," Mona explained. "She's got leukemia and needs a bone marrow transplant. We're trying to raise money to help out. Her dad's a farmer and their insurance is crap."

"Poor thing. How's long's she been sick?"

"Last fall is when her mom first brought her to see a doctor. They didn't figure out it was leukemia until this winter." Mona spun the can around to look again at the photograph of Angie in a hospital bed hugging a pink teddy bear. She still had most of her blonde hair when Dottie took the picture. Now she was totally bald and wore a baseball cap all the time. "I used to babysit her when I was in high school."

"They test Scotty to see if he's a match?" the man asked.

"I think so. I know they tested her parents already."

He reached across and stuffed a hundred dollar bill into the can.

"Thanks."

"Forget about it."

He nodded at his partner who'd returned from the men's room and pointed to the can. He also reached for his own wallet, peeled off a few bills and folded them before adding his contribution.

"Appreciate it," Mona told him.

"This town's like family to us. We look forward to coming here every year and you people treat us good. You never come to Chicago where we can return the favor, so there ya go." The first man finished his drink and slid his glass forward for a refill.

A burst of shouting pulled everyone's attention towards the back door where five stocky men shoved and jostled each other on their way toward the bar.

The Mafiosi chuckled. "South Chicago," one said to Mona, reading the apprehension on her face. "Listen to their accents. Southside boys are just loud, these guys aren't fighting."

"Give us a couple pitchers," one yelled, slapping a twenty down on the bar.

"Light or regular?" Mona asked.

"Ah, do we look like we're on a diet, lady? Regular."

"You got it." Mona set a pitcher beneath the tapper and handed out the glasses. She made their change and topped off the first pitcher, sliding it across the bar.

"What's this?" one bellowed, pointing at the money she'd left on the bar.

"Your change," Mona told him.

"What the hell, lady? Keep it. Christ, how much is a pitcher here?

179

Four bucks? Listen, toots, every time I order a pitcher, you keep the change—that's so you keep an eye on us all night. Got it?"

"Right. Thank you." Mona topped off the other pitcher and slid it over to the man.

She watched them head to a far table. "What's a pitcher of beer cost in Chicago?" she asked the Mafiosi.

"Depends where you go. Never less than seven dollars, though."

Mona gave a low whistle.

The door flew open ,again—Beau and Jake strode in, their faces red from the wind.

"Mona, Mona, Mona," Beau sang. "Where's Steve tonight?"

"Nice to see you too, Beau. Steve never works Monday nights."

"Huh." Beau turned to the Mafiosi. "Hey, my favorite customers! Catch these two on me," he instructed Mona.

Mona pulled two taps of light and glanced at her reflection in the Blatz mirror hanging behind the spigots. She wished she'd washed her hair instead of pulling it into a ponytail. Images of Jake sitting in some uptown bar with a tall, blonde dressed stylishly in black kept flashing through her mind when she wondered about that night. But he also followed her home the other night. How would she play it with him? Casual, she decided. She'd even ask him about it.

"Here you go." She reached for Beau's pile of bills. "Were you two fishing?"

"Yeah. Everyone's killing them this week," Jake said.

"That's what I hear," Mona replied. "How many did you guys catch?"

"Forty-seven," Beau answered. "But we only got on the river around four."

"Still," Mona said, "that's pretty good." She turned to ring up their drinks.

"How's your leg?" Jake asked.

"Better, thanks." Mona set a dollar down on Beau's pile of money and leaned forward on her elbows. "I worked Sunday without a hitch. Thanks again for the ride and everything. And for checking up on me the other night."

Beau looked at Jake and then at Mona, his mouth opening to release some smart-ass comment. He was interrupted by a crash at the back door and everyone turned to look again. A skinny old man walked through the door, his body covered in metal—pots, pans and utensils dangled from his torso.

"Well, shit!" Scotty crowed from the pool table, raising his cue stick.

"Back at you," the man called back. He crossed the bar, his accessories clanging, and stood next to Scotty and Jake. "Young lady, would you do me the honor of becoming my wife?" he asked Mona while he took off his hat and gave a little bow.

Mona blushed and ducked her head.

"Don't be flattered, he says that to all the girls," Scotty told Mona. "Aren't you already married, Virge?"

The man reached across for Mona's hand and kissed it. "Virgil Simmons here, at your service." He scowled at Scotty before turning soulful eyes back to Mona. "All right, if I wasn't already married I'd ask *you*."

"She's out of your league anyway—Mona's on the town council. She's not just another pretty face." Scotty said and turned around to line up his next shot.

"What can I get you?" Mona asked the man.

"One Jack and Coke," he said, reaching into his pocket and pulling out a harmonica. He attached it to a metal bar strapped around his neck. "What do you want to hear?"

"Excuse me?" Mona asked, bourbon bottle held mid-air.

"Virgil Simmons, one-man band at your service. You name it, I play it. How about *Bicycle Built for Two*?" Virgil banged the cymbals strapped to his knees and pushed buttons on the accordion buckled to his stomach. The bar fell silent while the opening chords floated through the room.

"Mo-na, Mo-na, give me your answer do," he sang in a throaty voice.

The Mafiosi joined in. "We'll go riding on a bicycle built for two."

Mona laughed and clapped her hands when Virgil finished his song and reached for his glass. "Cheers." He drank it in a single swallow and set the empty glass down on the bar. "What do I owe you?"

"Nothing. That was on me," Mona said.

"In that case, let me play you another song, my dear." The accordion's rich tones filled the bar and Mona cocked her head.

"*Paper Moon?*" she asked.

"How does a young thing like you know a song like *Paper Moon*?" Virgil asked, his long fingers moving easily across the keys.

"My grandma," she began, aware of Jake listening to her. "She had lots of old records and I'd listen to them with her when I was growing up."

"Your grandma sounds like a woman after my own heart," Virgil replied, closing his eyes and swaying while he played the rest of the song.

Everyone had a song request for Virgil and the next time Mona looked at the clock it was almost one. It was a fun night with so many different people together at the Pub. Maybe if Bassville grew, it would turn out like this. She checked over the drinks on the bar and seeing they were full, she escaped for the bathroom.

On her return to the bar, she met Jake in the hall.

"You startled me," Mona said, taking a step back and bumping into the wood-paneled wall.

"Sorry." He glanced back over his shoulder at the crowded bar, but didn't move.

"Did you have a good time the other night?" Mona asked, trying to ignore the effect standing near him had on her ability to speak clearly.

"Fine. It was fine. I had a date. Real nice gal. She works in accounts receivable."

"That's nice." Why was he telling her this?

"Yeah." Jake frowned. "Listen, I'd like to ask you out sometime. It's just that I'd already met this other woman. She lives in Northport," he paused. "She's a nice gal, too."

"That's great, Jake." Mona broke in, forcing a wide smile. "Looks like I'm needed back there," she gestured to the bar.

"Right." Jake aside. "I just—"

Mona took a deep breath and turned to look at him, his earnest blue eyes and tanned cheeks. Her cheeks flushed and her heart pounded.

"I just wanted you to know," he finished, staring into her eyes.

"Right."

In the bar Mona started restocking cases of beer into the coolers— so pissed at herself for getting sucked into a stupid fantasy about Jake. Guys like Jake always had a better option than someone like her. Besides, he didn't belong in Bassville if he was dating girls from the city. He was only being nice to her. She was the idiot to read more into anything he said or did. Still, he did say he wanted to ask her out …

"Hey, good-looking," someone said.

She looked up to see one of the South Chicago crew standing in front of her.

"What can I get you?"

"First, smile," he commanded.

Mona forced a smile at him and tried to ignore Jake's return to the bar.

"Second, we need a round of shots—then we're out of here."

"What'll it be?" she asked, lining the squat shot glasses across the mat.

"Let's do five shots of Wild Turkey."

At least it's not tequila. Last thing I want is to deal with is lemon slices and salt shakers right now.

"To Mona!" one shouted, lifting his shot glass in her direction after she finished pouring. "Come on, you bastards!" he hollered to the rest of the bar. "To Mona!"

The bar's patrons raised their bottles and glasses and yelled in chorus. "To Mona!"

She smiled and curtsied, making eye contact with Jake for a split second. "Thank you—and last call everyone!"

TWENTY-ONE

Traffic had slowed to a crawl on Rural Route 20, and the blare of car horns was deafening. Trucks, trailers and cars were parked out to the side of the road and Maw stood behind his cash register, gleefully punching in numbers and stuffing money into the drawer.

Outside at a row of tables his Bikini Fishing Team posed for pictures, flirted and chatted with the customers. Sheila and Jenny wore Maw's signature T-shirts tied at the midriff; the others had cut them off at both neck and tummy to show as much skin as possible. A banner flapped in the spring breeze, advertising the girls, bait, and Dave LaMay's sponsorship. He'd even hired Snuffy to direct traffic, a job Snuffy executed with flair, waving two checkered flags as he routed cars in one end of the parking lot and pointed them out the other. With three times the normal amount of minnows and other supplies on order, Maw had a big weekend planned.

"Are you Maw?" a tall man wearing Ray Bans asked.

"That's me," Maw said. He was making a point of meeting and greeting every customer he could, kissing enough ass to leave his lips raw for a month.

The man stacked his bait containers on top of a case of beer.

Maw stuck out his hand. "First time up to Bassville?"

"No, actually my grandfather brought me up here years ago."

"Where are you staying?"

"At the hotel. We used to rent a cabin down the river, but it's not there anymore."

"Oh yeah," Maw nodded, "Do you like the hotel? Sue and Judi—the gals that run it—they're real nice."

"It's fine."

"How did you hear about my place?" Maw asked eagerly.

"On the radio. They talk about you all the time. You're a celebrity," the man told him.

"No shit? Well if you're a friend of Dave LaMay's, you're a friend of mine. I can give you a discount on your minnows."

"Really?"

"Absolutely," Maw nodded. "And I hope your stay in Bassville is fantastic. Let me know if there's anything I can do for you."

"So far it's been great. I'm even thinking of getting some property up here, it's so nice. You know of anything for sale?"

"Might be soon. There's a farmer up the road fixing to put all his acres up for sale. It's nice land."

"Why's he selling it? Milk prices too low?"

"No, his kid's got cancer and they don't have insurance."

"That's a shame for him, but good for me maybe." The man leaned across the counter. "Say, you're local—got any fishing tips for me?"

Maw scratched his jaw and looked thoughtful. "Well, I shouldn't be telling anyone about this spot ..."

The fisherman glanced over his shoulder at the crowd milling around the bait shop and leaned in closer to Maw. "Look, I won't tell anybody—what's a couple of guys in one boat, right?"

186

"Easy enough to do," Dale told him and started the boat engine. "Come on, Otto. We're gonna pay Maw a visit."

Two pickups skidded into the drive at Maw's Bait and Tackle and three doors slammed in unison. Everyone in the yard looked up.

"There's an open spot back here," Snuffy shouted.

"Hey there, Dob. Dale," Jenny called from behind a table laden with black T-shirts. "You look in a hurry."

"Where's Maw?" Dob bellowed.

"In the shop," Jenny answered. "What's up?"

"Got a bone to pick with that son of a bitch," Dale growled, following Dob and Otto through the crowd that parted for them. Even the greenest-gilled fisherman had sense to step back when two burly Dohill brothers and an ornery-looking Otto Zimm stormed by.

Dob reached the door first and shoved it open with so much force that a display of rods crashed to the floor. The entire store fell silent as the three men searched the shop with stony eyes.

"Gentlemen," Maw greeted them cheerfully from behind a minnow tank in the rear of the store. "Where's the trouble?"

"Trouble's over in Cooper's Bayou," Dale said, his jaw and fists clenched tight.

"What—what do you mean?" Maw's eyes darted from one angry face to the next. He twisted his fingers.

"You know exactly what we mean!" Otto yelled. "You're sending tourists to all the best fishing spots! Bad enough you plug the run on the radio all over Chicago and God knows where else, but now you're sending them straight to where us locals fish." Otto glared at Maw and spat on the floor. "Goddamn sellout is what you are."

Maw held up his hands and shook his head. "You don't honestly believe I'd purposely—"

"Save it, Maw," Dob interrupted. "You don't have any respect for the locals. You'd sell Peg if you could make a profit."

A few customers chuckled, but the mirth died when Dale turned around to glare at the crowd.

"What's he charging you for a dozen minnows?" he asked a man standing by a display of lures.

"Um, I paid a buck for two dozen," the man answered, clearing his throat.

"A buck for two dozen, huh?" Dale jutted his chin at another guy. "How about you?"

"Same," he said.

"That's fifty cents a dozen. We come in your shop all year and buy our bait and our beer and you charge us twice that much—a buck a dozen. These city yahoos who don't know you from their Uncle Harry come in for one weekend out of their lives and get minnows for free. That's bullshit, Maw, and you know it."

"Dale, I'd give you the same discount today—it's a promotional price we're running this weekend." Maw's voice was pleading.

"And you're giving away free fishing tips with the bait?" Otto demanded.

"It was just a couple customers. The one guy used to fish here with his grandfather." Maw stepped toward them. "Honest. I didn't mean to cause trouble. Let me make it up to you." He reached for a rack of T-shirts and began fumbling with the hangers. "What are you, Otto? About a large?"

Otto scowled at Maw.

"I know you two wear a double XL," Maw said, sliding hangers across the metal bar.

"You think a T-shirt will make up for giving away the best spot on the river?" Dob growled, his red-knuckled fists clenching tight at his sides.

"Hey, you know fish—they'll bite in Cooper's one day and further down by the Rat the next. Come on, Dob." Maw forced a smile.

"You know, you're an asshole." Dale started toward Maw. Maw backed up, stumbling over a stack of tackle boxes. He caught his balance by grabbing the side of a minnow tank and turned to face Dale. "Guys!" Maw's voice rose to a shriek and his face paled. "Don't—you don't need to do—"

Dale pulled back one beefy arm and threw his fist square into Maw's face. Maw gripped the edge, but Dale's uppercut toppled him over the edge of the tank, his scuffed sneakers kicking frantically in the air before sinking below the surface. Water sloshed over the sides of the tank and onto the floor; minnows flipped in desperation on the cement.

"You know, I believe I feel better now, Dale." Dob slapped his brother on the back. "How you feeling, Otto?"

"Wish you'd have let me punch him," Otto muttered and followed the Dohills out the door.

Maw sputtered and spat, his beard flattened against his face and a silver-scaled minnow caught in his hair. "A news crew is interviewing me in a half hour, you bastards!"

"Maw?" Jenny entered the shop, stopping short when she caught sight of him standing waist-deep in a minnow tank, blood streaming out of his nostrils and down his chin.

Maw wrung out the bottom of his shirt, exposing the pale bulge of his belly, and wiped his hands over his head. "What, Jenny?"

"Did you fall in?"

Stifled laughter trickled through the bait shop and Maw sighed heavily.

"No, I didn't fall in. What do you need?" He pulled a minnow out of the collar of his shirt and dropped it into the water.

"The guys from Channel 2 are here. Sheila's trying to get the camera guys into T-shirts."

"Shit. Just give me a minute." He looked around the store and hauled one leg up the side of the tank. It took three jumps, but he finally got his body over the edge and slid down to the cement floor with a *Shhhhthunk*. "If everybody will hang on a minute, I'll send a couple of my Bikini Fishing Team in to ring you up and sign autographs. I've got an interview now." Maw unbuttoned his flannel shirt, dropped it on the floor, stripped off his undershirt and walked over to the rack of sweatshirts screen-printed with his new logo. Selecting one, he pulled it over his head. Water spurting from his sneakers with each step, he left the store trailing water.

"Okay, I'm ready!" he hollered to the crowd assembled outside the door.

A petite redhead in a navy blue trench coat pushed through the gathered fishermen and spectators. "Channel 2 here, reporting live from Maw's Bait and Tackle located off of Rural Route 20 in Bassville."

A bright light beamed into Maw's face and he raised his hand and squinted into it.

"We're here with Maw Cooper, the owner of Maw's Bait and Tackle. In a stroke of marketing genius, he has redefined the white bass run in Bassville as we know it. Maw, why don't you tell our viewers about your minnows." The reporter angled her microphone towards Maw's face.

"Well, the minnows here at Maw's Bait and Tackle are special. I've bred them specifically as white bass bait, modifying their genetic structure to increase both their speed and tenacity in the water. That's resulted in three types of minnows: Cantankerous, Passive-Aggressive and Belligerent. Depending on the weather and the day of fishing you're having, you can pick the minnow best suited for your experience."

"I see," the reporter nodded. "And we can see from the crowd in your parking lot how your minnows have dramatically affected the economy here in Bassville."

"That is true." Maw rubbed his hand across his face to check for blood and poked a pinky finger into his ear to clear the water blocking it. "I'd have to say Bassville has always been bolstered by the fishing. Fishing is what keeps this town alive. For decades people have come here and rented rooms and cabins and camped—spent money in our bars and restaurants and bait shops. This town's population quadruples each May with legions of cars, trucks and boats. This year's no different than last—the fishermen always come."

The reporter's smooth forehead crinkled slightly. "Yet this season your bait shop is the centerpiece on radio and television stations all over Chicago."

"Don't forget Los Angeles, New York, Dallas, Tokyo and I-forget-where in Australia." Maw's chest expanded and he reached out to grab the microphone. "When Dave LaMay called me on that dreary March day, I thought to myself, Maw, here's an opportunity. An opportunity of a lifetime. Plenty of locals buy my bait and beer all year long, this store is nothing special. But having my store featured on a big-name radio show like Dave LaMay's—now that's special. How do I make my shop stand out from all the others out there selling the same thing? Simple," Maw paused for effect, staring into the camera. "I market a product never before seen on this river—a product so revolutionary men will take up bass fishing just to say they've tried it. And that, folks, is the story behind Maw's Bait and Tackle."

The reporter reached out for her microphone, but Maw continued.

"Come on down to Maw's Bait and Tackle, folks. We'll treat you right and get you the right minnow for the job. And heck, if you don't fish, you can look like you do with one of my T-shirts." Maw waved over the Bikini Fishing Team, huddled at the edge of the crowd. "My very own Bikini Fishing Team has posed for a calendar on sale here at the store. You can get matchbooks, hats and even can coolers custom-made with the story of Maw's Minnows printed on the side." The girls jostled into position behind Maw, the fishy odor of his clothes and the blood on his hands no deterrent to getting their fifteen seconds of fame on a local news station. The girls elbowed to the front of the group to strike a pose.

"I'm living the American Dream. Right here in Bassville. I've got it all. Beer, babes in bikinis and the best bait money can buy."

The reporter finally wrenched the microphone out of Maw's grasp and smiled into the camera. "And there you have it, Northport. Live from Bassville, this is Channel 2 reporting from Maw's Bait and Tackle—the story of one man and his little dream making it to the big time."

"Aaaand cut," the cameraman announced. The bright light shut off and the crowd burst into applause.

No one mentioned the water that dripped from Maw's pants leg into an ever-widening stream.

TWENTY-TWO

Sunday afternoons had a lazy quality that Saturdays never possessed. The fresh promise of the weekend over, Sundays crept by in a leisurely fashion, dragging its feet before succumbing to Monday morning. People lingered over their Bloody Marys and roasted chicken dinners. Women came into the Pub with their husbands, whole families even came into the bar on Sundays.

Mona was spearing pickles and maraschino cherries on cocktail sticks for several Dohill children who clamored on barstools in front of her. Their parents sat in the dining room, taking turns doling out quarters for the jukebox or the pool table. If she heard *The Lion Sleeps Tonight* one more time today, Mona had plans to shove the jukebox out the door and down the pier, straight into the river.

"Ah-hooo-oooo," the children howled in chorus with the song, "A-we-bum-bum-a-wey."

"Mona, I want two pickles and four cherries. Don't let the cherries touch the pickles, though," a junior Dohill instructed, her round, solemn face peering across the bar.

"Right, no touching," Mona nodded and slid four cherries onto the bright yellow cocktail spear. The door flew open and she looked up to see Jake and Beau walk in and sit at the far end of the bar.

"Thank you, Mona," the children sang to her, sloshing kiddie cocktails across the bar while they slid off their stools.

The herd of children trotted across the floor and around the corner to the dining room. Mona sighed, wiped her sticky fingers on the bar rag and turned to Jake and Beau.

"I'll be right with you guys, I have to mop up that soda before somebody slips in it."

"Take your time," Jake told her and Mona's heart flipped in response to his smile.

Stupid, Mona thought, swiping the mop across the puddle on the floor. *He's got a girlfriend in Northport. Give it up.* Replacing the mop in the kitchen, she steeled her nerves and forced a smile as she walked toward Jake and Beau.

"What can I get you?" she asked.

"A couple of hot blondes," Beau quipped with a wink.

Mona rolled her eyes and looked at Jake. "Does he know any other lines? I've only heard that what—two hundred and eighty times in the last four years."

"I'll have a tap beer. He's an idiot." Jake explained. "I only keep him company because my mom makes me."

"You must really love your mother," Mona told him.

"Get me a Bloody Mary," Beau said.

"What are you two up to?" Mona asked, noticing they weren't dressed for fishing. She held a glass under the spout and pulled the handle. "You want a chaser, Beau?"

"Yeah. We're just hanging around. A couple of single guys with nothing to do."

"Huh." *Single guys.* He said single guys, Mona mused. Beau would know about Jake's girlfriend, she was sure of it.

"You going on a Death March later tonight?" Beau asked.

"Jenny's coming," Mona warned him.

"What do you say, Jake? Want to go on a march?" Beau asked.

Jake shook his head and the falling sensation of her heart reminded Mona how high her hopes had risen. "Some of us working stiffs have places to go in the morning."

"Big day tomorrow?" Mona asked.

"Yeah. We're finishing up at St. Mark's Hospital and then I've got to meet with my boss about a new project."

"Oh yeah?" Mona couldn't fight her interest. "Where's that?"

"Over in Rice Lake."

Mona's heart plummeted further. *It's only a matter of time before he leaves town.* "That's exciting."

Jake shrugged and turned his beer glass in his hands, leaving a wet ring on the bar. "I'm actually holding out for a different job—that foundry addition over in Northport."

"Really?" She excused herself and escaped to the beer cooler where she leaned against a tower of Bud Light cases, the cold cardboard a solid comfort against her back. "Why can't I fall for someone in my league?" she asked herself. Mona banged her head against the wall in the hope of knocking some sense back. Then she braced herself and returned to the bar where a new group of fishermen stood waiting to order.

After checking on every customer, she migrated back to where Jake and Beau sat. Beau finished his drink and stood to leave. "See you later tonight?" he asked Mona.

"Maybe."

She waited for Jake to follow him out the door. Instead he leaned forward and asked, "You really set on going on that Death March?"

Mona shrugged and brushed a strand of hair behind her ear.

"Unless I get a better offer."

"Hm."

Her heart pounded. He seemed … intentional, somehow.

"Thanks." Jake pushed a stack of bills ahead of his glass. Mona waited a beat and then went to wait on the next customer. Jake didn't move.

"So, what are you up to today?" Mona asked him between refills. He wasn't leaving. What if he was waiting for his girlfriend to meet him here? That would be awful. Truly terrible. She took a deep breath.

"Not sure yet. What time do you get done here?"

"Late. I'm on 'til close."

Jake leaned back comfortably and rested his arm across the empty barstool beside him. "You working tomorrow?"

"Noon to eight or so." Mona held her breath until he spoke again.

He stuck his tongue out the slightest bit between his lips and licked them. Then he nodded and asked, "Any chance Steve would let you leave early?"

"Maybe … why?"

"I'd like to take you to dinner if you'd like."

She beamed. "I'll ask Steve."

TWENTY-THREE

Town hall meetings always started at 6:30 in deference to milking and dinner schedules. This left Mona plenty of time to take a shower and wash the thick smell of fried food and cigarette smoke out of her hair after her shift at work. Wrapped in a blue striped towel, she studied the contents of her bedroom closet and realized the universal problem of women: Nothing to Wear. Her prom dress from high school was out of the question and so were the jeans she wore to work. Her one pair of corduroys would have to do, she guessed, pulling them over her hips and buttoning the fly. Discarding a pile of sweaters and T-shirts, she finally opted for a button-down shirt with a collar. *Next trip to town I need to buy an iron*, she thought, shoving the closet door shut with force.

She looked at her reflection in the mirror hanging above her dresser. The ponytail makes me look too young, Mona thought, pulling out the rubber band and tossing it on her dresser. She dragged her fingers through her hair, pulling at the kinks and snarls. Satisfied with her hair, she added lip gloss and mascara—"painting the barn" as Grandma Nancy used to say.

Since she lived only three blocks from the town hall, she decided to walk. The fresh night air and quiet street gave her time to pull her thoughts together. She'd read the meeting order and rules several times and felt prepared to at least sit and listen tonight. It took all her effort to concentrate on the town board and not think about her date last night with Jake. As a compromise, she decided to dedicate one full block of the walk over to remembering how they'd laughed over dinner at a steakhouse in Northport. He'd suggested taking their after-dinner drinks outside to a patio lit up with white Christmas lights and she'd shivered in the crisp night air, despite wearing his camouflage hunting jacket draped over her shoulders. At least he couldn't see how red her cheeks turned under the moonlight when he told her what a nice time he'd had.

She had prayed for a goodnight kiss, but flubbed it royally when she'd tripped on the sidewalk up to her front porch right after he'd brushed his lips against hers. She'd expected him to kiss her on the front porch, not on the street, and he'd caught her by surprise. As he leaned towards her, she stumbled backwards and caught her foot on the edge of the gutter. Feeling the sting of embarrassment and scraped palms from the cement pavers, she'd rushed away calling out, "Thanks, I had a good time." Her face flushed all over again at the memory of the ungraceful ending to their date, but they'd had fun over dinner. She and Jake had discussed Maw, fishing, basketball and what seemed like hundreds of common interests. And he *had* called back to her, "Let's do this again sometime." And he had kissed her. Before Mona finished mentally rehashing their date, she arrived at the town hall.

She saw her dad's red Ford F-10 pickup parked on the side of the road. Mona recognized several other cars and trucks and, taking a deep breath, pushed open the double glass doors. Two long folding tables stretched across the front of the room with seats to accommodate the council members. Twenty metal folding chairs were set up across from the tables in four neat rows. Mona walked over to her dad, who stood talking to Maw and Dale near the front tables. She hadn't seen Maw since the election but he gave her a hearty greeting.

"There's our new councilwoman!" Maw thrust his arm around her shoulders.

"No hard feelings then?" she asked him, returning the half-hug by wrapping an arm around his torso.

"Youth and beauty should always trump age and experience," Maw joked.

"Hey, honey," Loyal said. "Ready for your first meeting?"

She nodded.

"Evening, Mona," Dale said, offering her a handshake, something he'd never done before. "We've got you sitting here on the end. This'll be your seat at every meeting."

"Thanks," she studied the plastic nameplates arranged in alphabetical order, her dad's name next to hers.

"All set?" Loyal asked her again.

"I think so," Mona said, trying to swallow. Her hands trembled and her mouth felt too dry for much talking. She placed her folder square on the table in front of the end chair and sat, looking at the small gathering of people in front of her.

Dale winked at her before sitting next to an older man Mona vaguely recognized.

"The Bassville Town Council will now come to order on this evening of April 16th, 1983," Gene Trayson announced in a loud voice. He led them through the pledge of allegiance, a review of the last meeting's minutes and asked for a motion to suspend Robert's Rules of Order. "First on our agenda is a petition to purchase a culvert, presented by Dale Dohill of 619 Main Street, Bassville."

Mona held her pile of papers, checking off the items on the agenda. Garbage pick-up, weight restrictions on a county road, requests for various permits, a complaint about road maintenance and another about noise from the man renting the apartment above the hardware store next to Grumpy's. Dull as dirt, she thought, no wonder no one attends these meetings. The few times anything interesting comes up probably doesn't outweigh hundreds of boring tax reports and assessments. Still, she did feel very important sitting in front of the small crowd of people in the room and she voiced a clear "Aye," each time a motion was brought to vote.

"Next on the agenda is a request to change the zoning status of the Southeast corner of Trayson Road and Rural Route 20 from agricultural/livestock to commercial and residential. I've filled out a Major Land Division application already. You all should have copies in your files."

Everyone leaned forward and the shift in energy was palpable. Her shoulders tensed and she squeezed her hands together.

Gene paused and spoke again. "As you all know, Angie is sick. In order to pay for the treatments she'll need to fight her leukemia, Dottie and I decided to cash in our biggest asset—our land. We've met with the assessor and by selling our property to a developer we can afford to get Angie the care she needs. I have a plat for you to look over." He stood and passed out sheets of paper. Mona took hers and studied it. The lower right corner boasted the Acre Realty logo in green ink. The plan included six new streets and a pump station. Twelve blocks of identical ranch-style houses with attached garages, she saw. How would people who chose to live in neighborhoods like that get along with Snuffy, a man who slept on the pool table at Grumpy's? Would they insist on paving Main Street and pour asphalt over the ruins of the old button factory to build a new supermarket—putting Bud's out of business? She tried to concentrate on what her father was saying.

"Have you done an environmental impact study for this proposal?" Loyal asked.

"Not yet. There's that little swampy section back by the river road that I've never planted. Someone from the DNR is coming next week to look at it," Gene told him.

"No one's ever switched over land use to this extent before. Is there anything on the books about this?" Otto asked. "I looked, but didn't find anything."

"The county has a fee schedule," Gene answered. "It's on my application form."

Mona thumbed through the papers in her folder until she found it on page three of Gene's application. She raised her eyebrows in surprise. The total price to switch his farm over and sell it for hundreds of thousands of dollars was $875.

Mumbled conversation filled the room and Gene waited for the noise to die down before speaking again. "I know many of you are probably questioning this figure. I know I did when I saw it. What you have to understand is that when these lots are sold and built on, the town will collect ten times that amount annually in property tax. That's only the hard figures. We can't calculate is the other impact— money spent at local businesses, for example."

Movement by the door caught Mona's eye and she watched Jake slip into a seat in the back row. He caught her looking at him and smiled at her.

"While I respect a man's right to do what he wants to do with his private property, I can't support this plan," Loyal said, twisting a pen in his hands. "It sets a potentially bad precedence for future development. What will prevent every other farmer from rezoning? Plus, we can't calculate the hard figures of what this'll *cost* our town. What'll it cost to maintain six new streets? What'll it cost to extend the sewer mains four more miles? What about impact on groundwater?"

Jake raised his hand and Gene called on him to state his name for the record before speaking.

"Jake Paulick." He nodded at everyone in the room and paused for a moment when meeting Mona's stare. "Gene asked me to talk to you about similar projects in other towns like Bassville. Loyal brings up some valid concerns, but from my experience at Beyer's, the good really does outweigh the bad with this plan. Even the most extreme estimates of street and sewer maintenance don't add up to the town losing money on this—at least not over a period of ten years. Realistically, only a tenth of this property will be developed right away, at best twenty percent of the lots will be sold and built up the first year. I realize everyone worries that hundreds of new families are going to move in overnight, but that simply isn't the case."

"Maybe not," Otto interrupted. "But there are other concerns. We've got one deputy for the whole town. What's the safety burden going to look like with a hundred new families moving in? And what about space for these people's kids in our school? Is Bassville prepared to pay for new classrooms and teachers? A town's not only streets and sewer mains."

"You're right, it's not," Jake agreed. He leaned forward, resting his forearms on the back of the chair in front of him. But let me put it to you differently, Bassville's going to change one way or the other. Used to be farming was our economic base—that's not true anymore. Bassville needs to reflect that. You can look down the highway in either direction and see two outcomes: grow or die. Northport grew and people have jobs and opportunities. Zittau has almost disappeared. Their local businesses are down to a gas station and a tavern. Nobody's moving there and most of the buildings and houses are vacant."

"You're presuming that growth is good and no growth is bad," Mona said. She cleared her throat and took a deep breath, conscious of all eyes in the room focusing on her. "As far as I see Bassville isn't stagnant—the hotel's different in the past few years. The Pub added a deck and an outside bar for summer boaters to use. People are having children—Arlyce and Steve have four rugrats running around. Anyway, you can't turn this argument into a question of moral rightness or wrongness."

"No, but if nobody new moves in and the younger generation grows up and moves away because there's nothing for them to do in town, it's a foregone conclusion." Jake shrugged and looked over at Gene.

Taking his cue, Gene added, "I also want to add that it's a question of rights. My family has owned this farm for generations and I figure we've got a right to do what we want with our property. Whether we keep farming it or sell it, it's ours, bought and paid for, so it bothers me to even have to get permission to do something that should be my own business."

"Anyone else have something to say about this right now?" Dale asked.

"This is more than simply an economic issue," Loyal said.

"We're here to make decisions for the good of the whole town, right?" Mona asked. "We can only measure what we know definitively, and that's the cost of development and the cost of services. Obviously this decision doesn't boil down to only economics, but the other reasons will affect everyone differently. Maw will want this to go through, he owns a business and stands to profit. My dad, Loyal, I mean, doesn't want this, he'll get nothing but grief trying to farm around the traffic and complaints. The Dohills will love this, Otto hates it already."

"So, how do we decide, then?" Otto asked.

"Yeah, how *do* we decide?" Maw chimed in.

"I think the whole town should vote," Mona suggested.

Dead silence filled the room.

Loyal cleared his throat after a minute and looked steadily ahead at the small crowd facing the board. "We're elected to handle zoning issues. There's no precedent for a town referendum on a zoning request."

"Ridiculous idea," Otto grumbled.

"We just had an election," Maw added.

Heat flooded Mona's face. *How could I say something so stupid?* She snuck a peek at Jake, who seemed to studiously avoid looking in her direction. "Dumb idea." "What a suggestion." "We're elected to make the hard decisions." The disgusted voices filled her ears and she even heard one woman's voice mutter "Kids these days."

Dale pounded the hammer against the table and yelled for order. After everyone quieted down, he spoke. "Obviously it's a good idea to put the big questions to the town. We aren't even in a position to make a decision on this issue tonight. All Gene's done is file a request. The next step is a public hearing after his request is posted—that'll happen at next month's meeting. We don't even entertain a motion to vote until after the hearing, so unless anyone else has something to say about Gene's request, we're done discussing this item. Are there any questions regarding the Southeast corner of Trayson Road and Rural Route 20?"

"Motion to table Gene's request and table further discussion until the May meeting," Otto said.

"Second," Loyal said.

"All in favor?" Dale asked.

Mona squeaked out her "aye" with everyone else.

Mona's stomach felt sour and the pitying expression on her dad's face made her feel even worse. She was a stupid kid in over her head. After tonight nobody would have any respect for her. Heck, people

206

probably would demand a recall so they could elect Maw. Why couldn't she keep her big mouth shut? Why did she think she had to appease people by making everybody happy? For the rest of the meeting she carefully took notes and kept her head down, avoiding looking anyone in the eye—especially Jake. She couldn't even consider what he thought of her after suggesting such a thing.

An hour later Otto asked for a motion to adjourn.

"I move," Loyal responded.

"Second?" Dale asked, looking around the room.

"I second," Mona piped up, determined to contribute something that wouldn't cause controversy before the meeting ended. She still felt red around her ears from the reaction to her suggestion that the whole town vote. Every person in the room dismissed the idea so quickly that she felt foolish—and having Jake there to watch it all only made her humiliation worse.

"All in favor," Dale said.

"Aye," they chorused in response against the scrape of metal folding chairs, the rustle of papers and jacket zippers. Jake was out the door before Mona got to her feet. She took her time collecting her things, wondering again about Sean's advice. Maybe she didn't belong in Bassville if it was going to change so much. It might be time to think about enrolling in classes somewhere and try a new environment.

"We'll expect you to join our rehash tomorrow morning at the Pub," Gene Trayson told Mona with a smile. "Have a good night."

"You, too," Mona said, pausing to let her father pass.

"I'll give you a ride home," Loyal offered.

They shuffled out of the town hall and into the street, their breath coming in ghostly puffs under the pale light mounted above the front doors. Mona saw Jake standing beside his truck talking to one of the men who'd sat in on the meeting. Their eyes met and he raised his hand to wave at her. She smiled back and continued on with her father.

"I'll call you about that barn roof, Dale," Loyal said, stopping beside his truck.

"Sure thing, Loyal. We'll get her fixed for you. Good night!" Dale patted the truck's hood and walked to his own truck.

"How's it feel to be part of democracy?" Loyal asked after climbing in the cab.

"Important." She repositioned the pile of papers and folders on her knees. "But a little boring sometimes."

Loyal nodded. "For every great debate about raising taxes and assessing property there's about fifty procedural duties that most folk take for granted."

"Like the weight restrictions on the roads," Mona agreed. "I never understood the point of that until tonight. I always knew about them, I saw the signs on the roads, but I never knew why they were there."

"You'll find there's a lot of that. Town and county governments are full of rules."

"How do you keep it all straight?" Mona asked.

"Practice. You hear the same things enough times they start to stick. And if you don't know, there's always some book of codes and whatnot where you can look it up."

"Still, it was kind of fun," Mona confessed.

Loyal pulled in front of her house and looked down at his daughter's face. "Don't know if I mentioned it or not, but I'm proud of you, Mona. Even if you do tend to take the democratic process a little *too* much to heart sometimes."

"Thanks, Dad."

"You can't put every tough decision to a referendum."

"Why not?" she asked, still feeling foolish. "It takes the heat off the board, doesn't it?"

Loyal grunted. "Your sump pump still working okay since I fixed it?"

"Yeah, Dad. Thanks for the ride."

Loyal looked ahead, the lines of his face deepening as he frowned. "I ever tell you about the time I voted against Maw opening up his bait shop?"

"No. When was that?" She couldn't remember Maw not having a bait shop.

"About fifteen years ago. He came to the town requesting an ordinance to rezone—residential to commercial." Loyal's mouth curved into a slight smile. "Everyone voted for him to do it except me."

"Did he know that?"

"Of course. Our votes are open record."

"Was he mad?"

"Sure he was. Didn't talk to me for a month."

"But I don't understand," Mona frowned, "why would you vote against him having his bait shop?"

"I wasn't against him having a bait shop. I was against him having it in his yard."

"But why?"

"When he wanted to open it up, most of the people down the road from him had young children. There were concerns about the noise, traffic, the safety of huge tanks of water so near curious kids … it wasn't as cut and dried as him just wanting to sell some bait."

"And you voted against everybody else."

"I voted what I believed." Loyal put his hand on Mona's shoulder and looked at her. "And it worked out okay. Maw and I are still friends, no kid ever drowned in his minnow tanks and life went on. The point is, don't be afraid to vote what you believe, no matter who's against you. I appreciate you wanting the whole town to have a say in this decision, but that's why we were elected. It's our job. Some of us will be unpopular for a little while depending on the outcome, but that's part of civic duty, Pumpkin."

Mona tossed between the sheets all night, her head full of the meeting, Jake's expression when she spoke up, the explosion of opinion when she suggested the town vote on Gene's petition. Fragments of the meeting kept surfacing in her dreams—images of identical homes lined up for miles, a brand new public library, strip malls full of dry cleaners and hair salons. She'd wake up with her mouth dry and heart racing. I'm going to have a heart attack before my term's up, she thought after waking for the third time on the hour. *Or have a nervous breakdown.*

And to make such an ass of herself right after Jake had kissed her. She groaned and covered her face with her pillow. God, she hoped he'd ask her out again.

At five she finally rolled out of bed and grabbed a notebook and pen from a kitchen drawer. While she wrote, the trailing vines of Mister Stripy tomato plants on her kitchen table brushed her hands. She wrote down every single reason she could imagine for and against Gene's request. By seven she had writer's cramp and felt tired enough to go back to sleep. Didn't that figure, and now it was time to get ready for work she realized. In four weeks the board would meet again to continue their debate and possibly vote. With Gene abstaining, there was a good chance of a tie. Mona knew she'd get an earful of everyone's opinion until that night—and she'd get a fresh onslaught after she voted—one way or the other.

TWENTY-FOUR

"Judi, can you take it?" Sue yelled across the lobby where she balanced on a ladder hanging a new Old Style sign from the beer distributor.

Judi set the stack of towels down on the edge of the desk and grabbed the phone.

"Bassville Hotel," she said, instinctively pulling the reservation book in front of her.

Frowning, she paged ahead in the binder and ran her finger down the page. "Sorry, sir, but we're booked solid that weekend." From opening day of fishing season through June, no one in a fifty-mile radius had a room to let.

She flipped the pages ahead to July's dates and nodded. "I have a room that'll sleep six."

Finishing the reservation, Judi hung up the phone and grabbed the stack of towels again.

"Any chance you can finish the liquor order? I have to change a light bulb up in five." Sue reached for the towels in her daughter's arms.

Judi sighed and trudged towards the bar. Her mind felt numb and her body ached from the constant rush of the season.

She stood in the bar taking inventory, making out the order for next week when they'd be in full swing. Sixty-eight degrees and sunny with a mellow breeze, it felt like summer. From the report at the bait shops, the fish thought it felt like summer too, they weren't biting at all. The lobby was quiet all day—their guests were all out on the river today—so it surprised her to hear someone walk through their front door.

Judi recognized Mona Butterfield from the few times she'd been in the Bassville Pub.

"We're out of rail rum and Steve sent me to ask if you have any bottles to spare." Mona's cheeks were tinted by the sunshine and Judi wondered how she got any color—Mona must work just as many hours as she did. Judi heard from The Pole that their cook quit after coming down with the chicken pox. During her sick leave, she decided that she'd rather work at a day care with children than flip burgers and prep chicken. Everyone was pulling double shifts at the Pub.

"I'll go look."

"Thanks," Mona nodded. She looked around the lobby, seeing it for the first time in broad daylight through completely sober eyes. "It's pretty in here." She walked to the framed photos arranged on the wall and reached up to touch one. "That's taken from the pier right outside the pub. I'd know that angle anywhere." Her finger traced the curve of the river, a glossy grey blur beneath smudged glass.

"I found those during the renovation."

"Nice." Mona peered at the next one.

Judi regarded Mona's faded blue jeans, scuffed sneakers and red polo shirt. She seemed older than Judi had always thought. "How are you making out this season?"

"Pretty well." Mona turned her attention from the photographs on the wall and back to Judi. "Got my eye on a new mountain bike—I always splurge on one big thing at the end of the season. Makes the hard work feel more significant if I do that."

"A mountain bike," Judi repeated.

"Yeah." Mona walked to the desk and leaned on her forearms. "Last year I bought a new TV and a kitchen table. Year before I got my bedroom furniture."

"You live in that brown house just off of Elm Street, right?"

"Yep. You must not get much privacy living here," Mona observed.

"I do, sort of." Judi chewed at a hangnail. "Not really. It would be nice to live someplace else. Where do you go biking?"

"Lots of places. A few state parks nearby have good trails."

"I used to bike—years ago."

"When you lived—?" Mona deliberately left the question open. No one in Bassville really knew where the Sue and Judi were from, a mystery of the same proportions as the pyramids or Stonehenge.

The door blew open again and three men bustled inside, their faces red from the sun and wind. "Hey, Mona," one of them called. The other two waved at her.

"You guys aren't done for the day are you?" Mona asked.

"No, just taking a break for lunch. We'll see you later tonight."

"I'll have a pitcher waiting on the bar," Mona promised.

"That's our girl," another called back over his shoulder and their footsteps echoed down the hall.

"How's it going with the town council?" Judi asked.

"It's going," Mona shrugged. "It'll be crazy in a couple weeks when we vote on what do to with the Trayson place."

"I can imagine. From the little I've overheard, people seem pretty divided on it."

"They are, and both sides make a good case."

"Do they?" Judi slid the reservation binder aside and leaned towards Mona companionably.

She really seemed interested, Mona thought. Jenny hadn't asked about any of it—the only mention she gave was complaining about a broken nail when she'd gone to vote. Everyone at the bar only wanted to convince her to take their side on the matter. Judi was the first person who wanted to talk to her and it felt good. "Yeah, they actually do. I agree that a person should have the right to sell their own property. That's nobody else's business. And I've known the Traysons my whole life; I watched Angie grow up, so I want them to get the money they need to help her get better."

"So, you're for it," Judi smiled.

"I don't know. The impact of all that change scares me—what kind of people will move here? Will Bassville become a sanitized version of a town and look like every other city in America? What about the farming and the wide open spaces that make this a great place to live?"

"Sounds like there's a solid practical argument for it and a philosophical argument against it."

"Well, when you say it like that it does sound that way."

"I give you credit," Judi said, looking Mona in the eye. "At least you're involved and being thoughtful about the decision."

"Thanks," Mona rubbed her sneaker toe against the side of the hotel's front desk. "I'm trying my best anyhow."

"I'll go get that rum for you. Will three bottles be good?" Judi asked.

"Perfect."

Mona occupied herself again studying the photos on the wall until Judi returned with a paper grocery sack.

"Thirty bucks sound fair?"

"Shit," Judi laughed. "It's Heaven Hill brand, not top shelf. Give me twenty."

Mona handed Judi two tens. "Thanks a lot."

"No problem."

Mona was halfway out the door when she paused. She'd noticed the slight flicker of what? loneliness? sadness? that crossed Judi's face. With her hip bracing the door open, Mona called out to her. "Sunday night I'm going on a Death March with a bunch of people. If you want to join us, we're leaving from the Pub at eight."

Judi beamed, surprised and pleased. "Thanks. Maybe I'll see you."

"I hope you do. Later then," Mona said and headed down the street.

Judi stood contemplating this invitation until her mother interrupted her. "Honey, can you sweep off the deck now?"

Sunday nights were a race to see who could close first—the last place open had to play host to the crowd of bartenders, waitresses and cooks whose weekend now started with money and stress to burn. Mona hustled Jenny and Sheila out the door and turned to give Spade a pleading look. "Please," she begged.

"Well, since you said please," he grumbled, scooping up his change and jamming it into his front pocket.

"Meet us down the street! Scotty'll be there. And maybe Beau ..." Mona tried to make the offer sound enticing. She loved Spade, she really did, but she didn't want to host the party at the Pub. She wanted to be partying down the street and if she didn't lock the doors fast, they'd all end up on the other side of *her* bar.

"I know when I'm not wanted. You'd think a regular like me would be welcome here with all the money I spend," Spade said.

"Thank you, Spade." Mona shut the door behind him and turned the key in the lock. Unplug the dart machines, lock the kitchen door—she'd done everything else earlier while Jenny and Sheila nursed tap beers and waited for the rest of the customers to clear out. She slung her purse over her shoulder and jogged around the side of the building to see a tall figure standing in front of the Pub entrance.

"Mona?"

It took her a moment to recognize the voice in the dark street. "Judi?"

"Are you headed home for the night?"

"We're just getting started," Mona assured her, remembering her invitation. "Come on—they're waiting for us at Riverside."

Judi fell in step alongside Mona. "I'm glad you decided to join us," Mona told her. "You'll like Sheila. Jenny's a real pain in the ass, but she's fun to go out with."

Cheeks red from the cold wind, Mona and Judi stepped into the Riverside and simultaneously rubbed their hands to erase the chill.

"It sure cools down at night," Judi said, shuddering at the sudden warmth in the bar.

"Yeah, it does. Hey!" Mona called across the bar to where Jenny and Sheila waited for her. Scotty had already racked the balls on the pool table and Spade stood with his cue stick ready.

"Hey yourself," Jenny replied. "I got you a beer already." She slid a fifty-cent tapper over to Mona and raised her eyebrows in reference to Judi.

"You guys know Judi, right?"

Jenny nodded and Sheila leaned over and offered a greeting.

"We know Judi. Good to see you out," Scotty said, cheerfully raising his beer at her.

"How's your sister doing, Scotty?" Judi asked.

"Shitty," he told her. "But my bone marrow's a good match."

"Oh my God! That's great news!" Mona wrapped her arms around his neck. "Why didn't I hear this sooner?"

"We just heard from the hospital Friday. They have to run a few more tests to confirm, but if all goes well, they can do the procedure in a couple weeks—right at the end of Angie's chemo treatment."

"Let me know if there's anything you need. I mean it," Mona told him, cupping his cheeks with her hands before sliding onto a stool next to the pool table. Any movement on your farm?"

"None until the zoning gets approved. Right now dad's done all he can. Sure seems like the money's there for the taking, though. You should talk to your dad about it sometime. Lot more money in selling land than there is in milking cows. But I bet Sean already told him that." Scotty chalked his cue stick.

"You know it." Mona nodded.

"You shoot pool?" Spade asked Judi and motioned at the table.

"No, not really." Judi sat on a barstool beside Mona and smiled tentatively at him.

"Let me get you a drink," Mona offered, reaching into her purse. "What'll you have?"

"Beer's good," Judi answered. She looked around the tiny bar, marveling at the old-fashioned bar lights and checkerboard linoleum. "I've never been in here before. This is like a step back in time," she said to Mona.

"It is—Rosie, can you bring us a pitcher?" Mona turned back to Judi. "Rosie's owned this place forever and she keeps it real clean. Mostly the old-timers come in here. They close early and keep it basic, it's a good spot to start a Death March."

"You said Jake was coming," Jenny interrupted. "Where is he?"

"Hell if I know," Mona shrugged. "I'm not his mother." She wished she knew his plans, but he'd been out of town for work. Each time she passed his house she looked for lights or his truck, but no dice. At least, she reasoned, his being out of town explained why he wasn't calling her.

"Well, no shit," Jenny snapped, tapping her long nails on the bar.

"Judi, have you ever talked to Maw about being on his bikini fishing team?" Sheila asked. "He's always asking us girls if we know anybody else willing and able."

"Judi's not the bikini team type," Mona said. "Are you?" She turned to Judi.

Judi laughed and shook her head. "Not really. I don't even own a swimsuit. Anyway, weekends are busy for me. Only time it gets slow at the hotel is Sunday after everybody checks out. By Tuesday we're filling up again. Especially in spring."

"That's how it is. I love fishermen," Jenny agreed and blew a kiss at a cluster of fishermen sitting across the bar from them. "You guys are the best!" she told them.

Scotty bent forward and lined up his shot. "Nine ball, corner pocket." The cue ball hit the nine ball with a clear, quick snap and sent it rolling directly to the pocket.

"Nice shot," Judi told him.

"Thanks. Seven," Scotty nodded at the table and looked up at Spade. "Taking candy from a baby."

"Quit yapping and take your shot already," Spade said and circled the table while considering his next move.

Scotty drew the cue back and pushed it forward. The seven ball missed the pocket by a half inch and spun back towards him. "Shit."

"Don't tell me you're choking under pressure already," Spade sneered.

"I don't know why we bring them along," Jenny complained. "All they want to do is gamble."

"They probably don't know why they bring us along," Mona answered. "All we want to do is drink."

A sly look crossed Sheila's face. "Except for Jenny. All she wants is *that*."

218

Mona and Judi followed her gaze across the bar to where Beau stood by the door. Alone, Mona observed. Jake was probably home and sound asleep by now.

"Ladies," Beau greeted them, "and gentlemen," he nodded at Spade and Scotty.

"Hey, Beau," Mona answered. Judi and Sheila smiled while Jenny turned up her nose and looked away.

"Jenny, Jenny, why the cold shoulder?" he asked, pulling up a barstool between her and Judi and straddling it in a cloud of Drakkar Noir.

"Rosie, get him a glass, please," Mona said. "Beau, you know Judi from the hotel, right?"

"The pleasure's all mine," Beau told Judi, who gave him a look that could cool molten lava.

"Nice to meet you," she returned before shifting in her seat to face Mona.

Beau turned his attention to the pool game and set two quarters on the edge of the table.

"Looking for some easy money?" Spade asked.

"Only question is whose money is easier to get," Beau said.

"Hope your pockets are full, Beau." Scotty eyed him before turning to the girls. "Any of you want to play?"

"Nope, you boys go on ahead," Sheila told them. "We're here to drink."

"I say we head over to the hotel next," Jenny suggested.

"Aw, Jenny, Judi's probably had enough of the hotel by tonight. Let's skip it and head to the Log Cabin."

"That's all right, Mona," Judi said. "I don't want to mess with tradition."

"It's up to you," Mona said. "I know how glad I am to sit in someone else's bar—I almost never hang around the Pub when my shift's done."

Three hours later they ended their march at Grumpy's. Jenny had warmed up to Judi after watching her rebuff Beau at every opportunity, and she leaned drunkenly against Beau's side. The rest of them played Ship-Captain-Crew, Snuffy even joining in the dice game.

"Boxcars!" Judi cried jubilantly. "Come on, baby needs a new coat," she sang and shook the dice cup twice before slamming it down on the bar.

"Aw shit," Scotty moaned and stood. "I'm out." He walked over to the jukebox and Judi passed the cup to Mona.

"Beginner's luck?" Mona asked Judi.

"No—I'm always lucky at dice." Judi grinned.

Mona seized the moment. "Where did you live before you moved here?" she asked.

A guarded expression crossed Judi's face while Sheila and Spade looked up expectantly.

"We've moved around a lot. Last place we lived was Toledo. We playing dice or what?"

"We're playing dice," Spade said and took the cup from her.

"Toledo, Ohio?" Mona asked.

"Yeah," Judi frowned.

"What did you do there?"

"What do you mean?"

"Like were you a student or what?" Mona pressed.

Judi tapped her beer bottle on the bar. "I was an undergrad at the university," she said. "I studied French."

"Really? Then why did you come *here*?" Sheila asked.

"Aces!" Spade cheered and passed the dice cup to Sheila.

"My mom wanted to try something different." Judi paused and watched Sheila shake the dice, farm out a two and shake

220

again.

"Nothing," Sheila muttered. "You win again," she said to Judi.

"Snuffy, catch them a shot on me," Judi said. "All of us. You, too."

Everyone shifted their attention to the prospect of another drink, except Mona who puzzled over Judi's evasiveness.

"So, Beau," Mona began, emboldened by alcohol, "how come Jake isn't out with us tonight?" She tried to make her tone sound casual, like she asked about Jake all the time.

"Jake?" Beau narrowed his eyes. " "He's working up in Rice Lake, I think."

"No reason, I just wondered."

"Uh-huh." Beau shrugged. "Hard to have fun with that workaholic."

"Drink up!" Sheila urged, elbowing Mona in the side. Mona contemplated the shot glass Snuffy set in front of her. The sharp sting of tequila hit her nostrils and she closed her eyes. Picking up the glass, she tossed it back and grimaced when the drink burned the back of her throat.

"You swished it!" Beau yelled, gulping his shot in a quick swallow. Jenny drank hers and slid the glass back toward Snuffy before standing up and grabbing Beau's arm.

"Let's go," she whined to Beau. They staggered out the door, Beau's hand buried in Jenny's back jeans pocket.

"I should get going, too," Judi said and grabbed her purse off the bar. "Thanks, guys."

Mona followed Judi and Sheila out the door after leaving Snuffy a ten-dollar tip. He'd drink it away, but maybe he'd use it for a couple meals. The girls walked down the street together and breathed in the fresh air.

"Thanks for inviting me tonight," Judi said, stumbling over the curb and reaching out for Mona's arm to get her balance.

"I'm glad you came. It's always the same people—nice to mix it up a little."

"Especially with *nice* people," Sheila added. "I've known Jenny my whole life, but she can be a bitch. You're a good addition to our crowd of townies, Judi."

They parted ways at the hotel and Mona jogged the remaining five blocks to her house, hugging her arms tight around herself to block out the cold breeze.

Later, Mona took two Tylenol and sank into bed. It was good that Judi had come out with them. Her head throbbed and she closed her eyes. Jake hadn't said anything about her to Beau. Was that good or bad?

Judi awoke and headed straight for the sink. Her mouth felt chalky, her head felt cloudy and her body ached. *This* was why she was better off staying home, she thought, brushing her teeth and spitting.

"What time did you get in last night?" Sue asked her daughter when she walked into the lobby at ten o'clock.

"Two-thirty," Judi told her. "It was fun, actually. Nice group of people."

"What did you do?" Sue prodded.

"Went to every bar in town for a drink, shot pool and played dice."

"Bassville is a bastion of high culture," Sue said dryly.

"It was a good time," Judi said, feeling defensive. "You can't expect me just to work all the time and not make any friends or go out or anything."

"I didn't say that," Sue said, setting a cup of coffee in front of her daughter. "I'm glad you had a good time." She left the lobby and Judi sat down at the desk, resting her head against the cool varnished wood.

TWENTY-FIVE

B<small>Y THE END OF</small> the week everybody in Bassville had heard about the town board's upcoming meeting and Maw's latest marketing ploy: a bikini fishing guide service. A steady stream of fishermen flowed through town and a giant *For Sale* sign was posted on the edge of Gene Trayson's hundred-acre field on the west side of town. The Traysons had decided to sell the farm regardless of the board's final vote. Scotty started taking vitamins to stay healthy while Angie lay propped up on paper-thin pillows on her hospital bed in Milwaukee, finishing her chemotherapy.

"Did you hear how much he's charging?" Dill Dohill asked.

"Who? Gene or Maw?" Spade returned.

"Either—for God's sake, the whole town's suddenly up for sale." Dill pulled off his cap and rumpled his hair.

"You want to buy a bar, cheap?" Steve asked them. "Might as well get on this boat before she leaves shore."

"You'd never sell this place," Spade told Steve. "You couldn't handle the working world."

"Funny," Steve shot back, "coming from a guy who still lives with his mother." He turned his back on the locals crowded at one corner of the Pub to wait on the customers walking through the door.

"I think I need a fishing guide," Beau mused, staring at the poster Maw hung on the wall earlier that afternoon. It advertised "Your own personal bikini fishing team guide on the Wissipaw River—Available at Maw's Bait and Tackle."

"Anyone take him up on it yet?" Dob asked.

"Not that I've heard," Steve said. "But I guarantee if I did, Arlyce would nail my nuts to the floor."

"You're not the only one," Dale agreed.

"It's a damn good idea though," Dob said.

"Yeah, until every decent fishing spot on the river's been found out," Otto grumbled. "And then everything will get fished out and what will be left?"

The men nodded, sobered by the potential impact of Maw's scheme. Nobody enjoyed predicting the river becoming *that* commercial.

"Sure would've liked to seen Peg when she found out," Steve remarked, eliciting a new ripple of chuckling.

"Yeah, how's that go again? 'Hell hath no fury like a woman scorned?'" Dob asked.

"Nice," Dale said, elbowing his brother in the ribs. "Miss Schmidt taught you real good."

"Well," Dob retorted. "She taught me well."

"LET ME OUT!" Maw's voice was raw from yelling and his hands were sore from pounding on the door. He stopped his tantrum for a moment to listen—silence. He pressed his ear to the door and heard nothing but the hum of the refrigerator.

"Goddamn it!" he cursed and kicked the door with the heel of his foot before sitting down to stew and rest on the floor.

News of the bikini fishing team guide service had hit Peg in the worst imaginable way. She'd picked up the kids from school and stopped by Bud's for a gallon of milk when she saw the new poster. A color photograph of Jenny and Sheila standing in a boat, holding up silver-speckled white bass, toothy smiles and curvy flesh stunned her into silence while the cashier repeated the total to her at the register.

"That'll be $4.57." The cashier followed Peg's gaze to the wall. "Oh."

Shaking, Peg looked back at the cashier, her expression livid. "When?"

"He hung that up this afternoon—about two," she'd answered, keeping her eyes lowered.

Peg pulled out a five-dollar bill and laid it on the counter. "Keep the change," she called, grabbing the milk and running out the door.

Frank and Nancy jumped at the squeal of her tires pealing out of the parking lot. Peg held a hand up to them as she passed and growled to her children, "Sit back, we're going home."

Somehow she'd kept her cool while she reminded Maw he had bills and paperwork to take care of, so why not get it done tonight before it got busy tomorrow. After turning the key in the lock, Peg screamed, "Bikini fishing guides my ass! You can go to hell!"

Then she grabbed her purse, locked the front door behind her, and drove the children to her parents' house. By five o' clock eighteen cars had pulled into the parking lot at Maw's. The bait shop was dark and the door was locked. A hand printed sign on the door read: Closed For Repairs.

"I just heard Maw's is closed tonight," Steve said, returning to the local end of the bar.

"No way," Dob said. "Who told you that?"

"Bunch of guys just came in asking about it." Steve nodded at the men sitting at the corner table.

"Maybe he's got something really big planned for tomorrow," Dob suggested.

"Maybe he's out showing all the good fishing spots," Otto said.

"I like to believe the best about people," Steve grinned. "He's probably enjoying a nice quiet night out with the wife before all hell breaks loose tomorrow."

"How come you aren't doing that with Arlyce?" Ben asked Steve.

"Good point," Steve laughed.

Saturday morning, Dave LaMay returned to town for the inaugural bikini fishing team's guided tour of the river. Maw had invited him, as his guest.

"Promise him girls in bikinis and he's in the car with more enthusiasm than a frat boy chugging on a beer bong," William muttered under his breath, checking his watch for the tenth time while they banged on bait shop door.

"Where the fuck is he?" Dave asked while giving the wooden door a frustrated kick with the toe of his Air Jordan.

"Can I help you gentlemen?" The sound of a woman's voice made them jump and spin around. Dave's face fell as he looked Peg up and down, taking in her blue jeans, battered sneakers and baggy sweatshirt.

"Where's Maw?" Dave barked.

"He'll be out in a few moments. I'm Peg," she held out her hand to Dave and returned the appraising glance. "While we're waiting, I'll brief you on events here since you last spoke to him," she continued smoothly. "There was a ... er ... *misunderstanding* on the phone about the fishing guides. Today the girls will take you out on the river. This is a one-time deal, special, just for you for featuring Maw's shop on your show. As far as any further guided fishing expeditions on the river, you get those from Maw. Are we clear?" Peg narrowed her gray eyes at Dave.

"Will Maw come, too?" William asked

"Maw has to run the shop today," Peg told him. "But I'm sure he'll be glad to take you out another time."

"Why the change in promotion?" Dave asked.

"Let's just say some doors were hard to unlock." Peg's lips tightened into a thin line. "Follow me and we'll get your bait."

The two men followed Peg into the shop and waited while she turned on the lights and started the cash register. Grabbing a bucket, she leaned over one of the tanks and began dipping minnows into a small Igloo cooler. "The boat's all ready for you—you'll meet it off the public pier over by the Pub."

"What time?" William asked her.

"In about a half hour. You've got the girls until mid-afternoon and then they'll drop you back at the Pub."

"Sounds great," Dave told her. "We can get a twelve-pack while we're over there," he muttered to William.

Peg handed William the cooler and shoved a Styrofoam cup of grubs into Dave's hands. "There ya go. Have fun!" She hustled them out the door, flipping the sign on the door to read "Open."

"I'll be right back!" she shouted to the trucks idling in the parking lot and raced into the house. Unlocking the closet door, she glared at her husband's whiskered face, his reddened eyes and rumpled clothes.

"Peg—" Maw began hoarsely, his anger rising.

"You've got twenty minutes to shower and get your ass in that shop. I sent your DJ out fishing with the girls for today and that's the end of it. Say another word—I mean it, Maw," Peg held up a finger in warning, "and that's it. Don't push me another inch." She turned on her heel and strode back down the stairs to the bait shop.

"Woman, you have no business messing with my business," he argued.

"Twenty minutes!" Peg yelled before slamming the door shut.

Maw scrambled to his feet and ran down the hallway to the bathroom.

"For the love of God," Mona said in disgust, watching the scene outside the Pub. A pontoon was parked at the public pier where the bikini fishing team had drawn a large crowd. Two news trucks and several cameramen lined the pier. They parted suddenly to make way for two men—the DJ from Chicago and his manager.

The customers in the Pub breathed heavily against the windows, panting over the exposed flesh, their hot breakfasts forgotten in the excitement.

"Now that's what I'm talking about," one man in a flannel shirt said. "Beer, bikinis and fishing. Maw knows where it's at."

Traffic on the river had stopped, every face turned toward the pier. Jenny waved at the boats and turned up the radio. Dave LaMay began gyrating to the music and danced up to Jenny, who snaked her arms around his waist and ground her hips against his. Mona rolled her eyes but kept watching the pier.

"Why aren't you out there?" Scotty Trayson asked her. "Don't tell me Maw didn't ask you."

"He did. I won't compromise my dignity just so he can peddle a few minnows. Besides, didn't you know Steve keeps me prisoner in here until Memorial Day?"

"Uh-huh." Scotty stuffed the last of his toast into his mouth and chewed, his attention fixed on the drama unfolding outside. "By the way, that was real nice of your mom to come over and spring clean for my folks this week."

"It's the least she can do. Your mom and mine are like sisters. I know she wishes she could do more to help out."

"The cleaning was huge. I think all the time Mom spends sitting with Angie while she's getting chemo just gives her more time to worry. She's sort of stuck there with nothing to do except make lists of things."

Mona reached across the bar and laid her hand on Scotty's forearm. He shook his head and exhaled a long sigh. Scotty was a good egg, his whole family was good people, they didn't deserve this. Maybe the silver lining would be them selling the farm and walking away rich, Angie cured, Gene and Dottie free to relax some.

"It's like a bad movie," Mona said. "Could it get any worse?"

In answer to her question, Beau appeared on the pier and joined the party on the boat.

"Oh geez," Mona muttered and jutted her chin at the scene outside. "It got worse."

The pontoon began to glide towards the center of the river and make its way beneath the bridge. A cameraman and a reporter Mona recognized from Channel 2 ran up to a couple of fishermen in a boat nearest the shore. To her amazement, the boat pulled up to the pier, collected the two men, and followed the pontoon's course south.

"Wouldn't you like to fish like *that*?" one man remarked in awe.

"Wonder what they'll catch," Mona said and smirked. "Probably a cold dressed like that today."

"Did you see that one chick wearing a *thong*!" another man said.

Scotty and Mona exchanged a look of mock horror. "Jenny!"

Scotty chuckled. "What time they coming back?"

"Do me a favor, Scotty," Mona told him.

"What's that?"

"Drool outside. I've got enough to clean up without having to wipe your mouth."

The door slammed open again and Mona grabbed menus and

followed the new customers to the only open table. Her movements had become automatic, her mind disengaged. Until the season ended, there'd be no breaks for the working people.

The register drawer jammed twice and Maw sent Peg to the garage for his carpenter's apron. Filling the pockets with change, he tied it around his waist and took care of business by milling around the store. Peg was stationed in the back, pouring minnows into bait buckets and advising which type of fishing jigs and crankbaits to use. His daughter sat at the front counter helping people fill out fishing licenses. The bustle of the store cheered him like it did every year— the entire fishing season held all the promise of Christmas morning.

"Sunny day like today, I'd go with Passive-Aggressive," Peg explained to the line of customers waiting with their bait buckets and coolers in hand. "It's your best bet, unless you want to catch them hand over fist, in which case I recommend Belligerent."

Maw gave his wife a fond smile. Sure she ruined a brilliant promotional idea, but he'd forgotten how comfortable it was to work side by side with Peg. Unlike the bikini team, she didn't require coddling or special favors. She knuckled down and did what was needed without bitching about a chipped manicure or being too cold, too hot or too tired.

Today he'd sell out of almost everything. In fact, he kind of wished they would so he could turn the sign back over to "Closed" and take Peg out for a nice steak dinner over at the Pine Tree Supper Club. What the hell, maybe he'd just do it anyway—after a call to his breeder when the traffic slowed down.

At twelve-thirty the fishing party returned to the Pub and Mona discovered the girls had acquired glowing suntans instead of frostbite. She scowled at the pasty white of her own arms while dumping a bucket of ice into the bin. The unexpected turn of weather brought a range of customers through the Pub—bikers, country drivers, fishermen and families.

"You think we should let her sit on a barstool like that?" Steve asked Mona while he filled a pitcher of beer from the tap. "It might be against some health code or something." He gestured toward Jenny's rear end, perched on a stool by the window.

"It's appalling," Mona said, wrinkling her nose. "Should I bring them menus or do you want to?"

"I've got them," Steve told her, topping off the head on the pitcher. "Your favorite customer just walked in." He nodded toward the door.

"Grandma and Grandpa?" Mona asked, turning around to look. Her face flushed when she recognized Jake's profile towering over the rest of the crowded bar.

"Go get him, kiddo." Steve winked. He grabbed a fistful of menus and hurried across the bar before Mona could protest.

She waited for Jake to finish greeting people and sit down before approaching him. "How's it going?" They hadn't really talked since their one date, but they'd both been busy. That's what she kept telling herself each passing day.

"Good. Real good. That job up in Rice Lake kept me busy." He looked at her so intently that Mona wondered if she had food in her teeth or a pimple blooming on her forehead.

"What can I get you?"

"I'll have a tap beer please, and catch those guys over there," Jake gestured to the assembled locals at the corner by the door.

When she returned with his beer, Jake's attention had turned to the fishing party. Jenny waved him over and Beau shouted at him over the din of the jukebox.

"Here you go," Mona said, willing him to stay put.

"Look, I have to get going in a minute. I really stopped in to see if

231

you wanted to have dinner tomorrow night when you're done with work."

Mona felt her smile nearly split her face in half. "Absolutely. I can be done here by six."

"Perfect. I'll come by and pick you up." He finished his beer and waved before walking out.

A block down the river the hotel bar was quiet. William stood in the doorway debating where to begin looking for Judi. Before he'd reached any conclusion, she called a greeting to him from the lobby behind him.

"All done fishing?" Judi asked.

"I am." The dopey grin stuck despite his efforts to look casual.

"Now what?" Judi flopped a stack of white towels onto a chair and the clean smell of bleach drifted up. She bent over to tidy the brochures for boat rentals on a nearby table. William's presence today unnerved her. A tingle of expectation electrified the air around him.

"Now it's time to see if you care to join me for dinner later."

More pleased than surprised, she answered, "Let me check with my mom."

"Funny, I haven't heard that line from a woman in years."

"Because you haven't asked a woman out in fifteen years?"

"Sure."

"I'll be right back." Judi walked back to the kitchen and after closing the door behind her, jumped up and down. "Mom?"

"Yes?" Sue bumped her way out of the walk in cooler and dropped two bags of bread dough onto the stainless steel countertop.

"You're working in the bar tonight, right?"

"Yes." Sue looked up sharply at her daughter.

"Can I get tonight off, then?"

"Does this have anything to do with that Dave LaMay?"

232

Judi's eyes widened. "What? Oh God, no. No, Mom. *William* asked me out to dinner."

Sue exhaled a sigh of relief. "Good heavens, now that's another story entirely."

Judi giggled. "You didn't really think—"

"I don't know what I was thinking." Sue laughed. "Have fun. Yes. Go."

William had no compunction about leaving Dave on his own at the Bassville Pub. Maw or one of the girls would steer him somewhere safe when the bars closed. He grabbed the keys to Dave's Ferrari and checked his reflection in the flaking mirror above the dresser in their room—Judi's room, actually. He'd fought temptation to rifle through her belongings and instead studied each item in the room, trying to fathom her history. The stack of art books, a collection of incense burners and a pile of sweaters and shirts on the dresser gave him little to work with—but it was a start.

Smoothing his hair, he stood straight and headed down the hall for the hotel bar. Herb Townsend raised his eyebrows when William ordered a seltzer and lime, but William didn't want alcohol to mellow his senses; he wanted to stay sharp for Judi. The women he met in Chicago were all the same—plastic-looking carbon copies of one another and being in their company required some form of anesthesia. Granted, this probably was due to the social scene Dave enjoyed. William knew he should try to cultivate an interest beyond the nightclubs on the Loop, but there never seemed to be time.

Who would've guessed that in a town exploding with men—hell, there were probably twenty men for every eligible woman in Bassville tonight—he'd get a date with someone beautiful and intriguing. Yet here he sat, tapping his fingers nervously on the bar and drinking seltzer water, waiting for Judi.

"I'm ready."

William started, knocking over his drink. Judi wore an orange blouse that clung to curves he'd suspected she had and make up that shimmered lightly, catching the flecks of gold in her brown eyes. She'd left her hair down, and it bounced in loose curls around her shoulders. She looked amazing and he froze when he saw her.

"Sorry," Judi smiled and the color rose in her cheeks. "Didn't mean to startle you."

"I didn't hear you come in." William reached for a stack of cocktail napkins and began sopping up the mess. "I like your hair like that."

"Thanks." She reached up and brushed it behind her shoulders.

"Sorry about the mess," he told Herb, who'd come to his rescue, stoically removing the glass and lime slice from the bar.

"It's only water," Herb said, whisking the remains away with a rag. "You kids have fun tonight."

"Thanks, Herb," Judi said and took the arm William offered her.

He would never forget how she smelled, like oranges and vanilla. Like spring sunshine.

TWENTY-SIX

Sunday afternoon, mona waited for the first lull in the steady traffic of customers and raced for the bathroom. Makeup bag in hand, she freshened up face and hair and sprayed herself liberally with Jontue to mask the smell of deep-fried food and cigarettes. She'd change her clothes at the last minute, just in case she spilled something. Back behind the bar, she straightened the chips display repeatedly until Spade yelled at her.

"Stop it, woman! You're making me nervous! A guy comes in to relax and you're fussing around like my mother. Sit down!"

Mona looked at him, hunched over his soda, his faded green T-shirt fraying above his pale, skinny arms. Spade met her stare. "What's going on with you today?"

"Nothing." Mona glanced around the bar and satisfied that no one was in earshot, told him in a low voice, "I'm going out to dinner later."

Spade raised his eyebrows over the rims of his glasses. "A date? Who's the poor bastard?"

Mona scowled and reminded herself that Spade was not known

for his tact and good manners. "Jake."

"Really? Well, I'll be … how do you like that?" Spade mused over this bit of news and Mona felt oddly relieved. It struck her how it *did* matter to her that certain people approved.

Mona pushed open a cooler door to begin straightening the stacks of soda cans when Arlyce's three sons came running through the front door tallest to smallest.

"Where's the fire?" she called after them.

"Hi, Mona!" they chorused over their jostling for the kitchen. "Dad's gonna be on TV!" the oldest yelped before colliding with his mother.

"What's that?" Arlyce asked, scooping him into a hug and ruffling his feathery brown hair.

"Dad. He's gonna be on TV. For catching fish," he panted to Arlyce, grabbing his stomach and bending over.

"How do you know?" Arlyce knelt to tie the youngest son's shoelace. The she licked her thumb and used it to wipe a smear of dirt off the his cheek.

"'Cuz some lady came and talked to him while he was out in Helmut's Bayou. Guy with a camera filmed us and everything!" Her son danced from foot to foot, his brown eyes shining with pride.

"Where's your baby sister?" she asked.

"In the boat with Dad," the middle son told her.

"Maw was there, too," the youngest added from where he clung to Arlyce's leg.

"Your father was with Maw?" Arlyce asked sharply.

"No," the oldest said, tugging at her apron with impatience, "Maw was with the TV lady."

Arlyce looked over at Mona and Spade. They shrugged in return.

"Last I heard Peg had him under house arrest," Mona said. "Steve better get back in time for his shift."

236

"Maybe she let him out to do interviews," Spade suggested to Arlyce.

Arlyce bent down and ruffled her youngest boy's wiry hair. "That's great, guys. I'm glad you came to tell me." She kissed the top of each son's head and herded them toward the door. When it slammed behind them, she shook her head. "First Maw's famous and now Steve. What's the world coming to?"

"I'm telling you, Bassville's the center of the known universe lately," Spade said.

"Seems like anything's possible anymore, doesn't it?"

When Steve strolled in thirteen minutes late for his shift, Mona dashed to grab the clean clothes she'd hung in the storage shed behind the Pub. The center of *her* known universe was picking her up any minute. She slid out of her jeans and polo shirt emblazoned with the Pub's logo and stuffed them in a shopping bag. Hurrying because someone might barge in on her at any moment, she yanked on fresh jeans and buttoned up her shirt, knocking over a box of plastic cups in her haste. Struggling to slide them back into the box—the slippery plastic sleeves collapsing in her hands, she cursed under her breath. Her plan was to wait casually for Jake in the bar, but by the time she finished picking up the shed, she stepped outside and saw his boat leaving his house.

Walking to the docks lining the riverbank in front of the Pub, Mona watched Jake glide across the river toward her. He pulled up along the only empty dock and squinted at her, the sun directly in his eyes. "You ready?"

"Ready for what?" Did he mean to take her fishing for dinner?

"Dinner," he said, reaching out to grab the edge of the dock. "Climb in."

Hesitating only a second, Mona joined him in the boat. "Where are we going?"

"Pine Tree," he said. "Northport's too far a drive this late at night and I thought you'd like to eat without Beau leering at us from the bar, so the Luau Club's out. And you probably get sick of eating at the Pub, right?"

"The Pine Tree sounds nice." Mona leaned back in the seat of the boat and watched the cottages and trees pass by as they headed up river.

"The river's pretty this time of year. I thought you might like to take a boat ride," Jake continued.

Mona looked over at him and smiled, pleased at his perception. "This is great. I don't get to be out here much in May."

After Jake docked the boat and gallantly offered Mona his hand, they headed into the Pine Tree, a spot known for its potent cocktails and huge steaks. They sat next to each other at the quiet bar and Mona ordered a beer. It was hard to get too gassed on beer and she was determined not to stumble over a curb or otherwise make an ass of herself. The place was almost empty, just a few tables talking low over their drinks. The hostess and the bartender, both former classmates of theirs, looked bored and two waitresses rolled silverware into napkins at a nearby table. They waved to Mona and the bartender lingered to talk about football with Jake.

"I bet you don't want to order fish," Jake said after the bartender served up their drinks and menus and went to fill one of the waitress's drink orders.

"That's right," Mona answered while reading down the menu. "The tenderloin sounds good, but I never get to eat stuffed pork chops."

"You can't lose with a steak out here," Jake advised. "Have you decided how you're going to vote on the Trayson deal?"

Mona closed her menu and set it down on the bar. "Yes, I have. Did you ask me to dinner to lobby me? If that's the case, I have to turn in the receipts to the Ethics Committee."

Jake laughed. "I'm not trying to lobby you. I just think it's amazing you're involved like this."

"Maybe it's in my blood. You know, Dad and all."

"Could be. You had my vote."

"Thank you. I've got absolutely no experience and a lot to learn."

"You're smart." Jake shrugged. "You'll figure it out."

"I didn't go to college like you did," Mona said, wiping her finger across the condensation on the side of her beer bottle. "I'd be embarrassed to tell you the grades I got in high school."

"What do you mean? I always thought you were one of the brainy girls."

"Whatever gave you that impression?"

"Always quiet—I remember you dodging around the football team to get in and out of your locker quickly and I assumed you were in a hurry to get to class. And didn't your brother rake in all kinds of scholarships?"

"What do you mean by that? Quiet girls are smart girls?" She couldn't believe he remembered her having a locker near his.

"No—well, yeah, I guess so. All the mouthy girls I knew were dumb as bricks. Take Jenny for example."

Grinning, Mona nodded. "I can see why you'd think that, but no, just because I was quiet didn't mean I was smart."

"At the construction company I work with all of kinds of people," Jake took a drink of his beer. "Some of them have college degrees, some of them are high school drop outs. What makes them smart or stupid has nothing to do with their diploma. It's how they treat people and how they solve the problems put before them."

Mona considered his remark before asking, "Did you get the foundry job?"

Jake shook his head and her heart fell. Beyer's would send him away.

"I don't know yet. That won't be decided for a couple weeks. Meantime they just stuck me on a job they're trying to wrap up—I'm over at that new high school they're building in Clearwater."

"What do you do besides work at Beyers?" Mona asked. "I know you fish and hunt, but what else?"

He grinned. "You're more interested in other people than talking about yourself."

Mona blushed and looked down at her hands. "It's habit. I collect information about people—like a game. I ask people what they do and then I save the interesting bits." She looked up and encouraged by his smile went on. "I once met a guy who repaired dry cleaning equipment for a living. I mean, everyone knows about dry cleaning, but who'd think about repairing dry cleaning machinery? I've met a world champion wrestler whose stage name was 'The Undertaker.' One day, a traveling blues musician came into the bar and I got to help him write a song. I guess you could say I collect people's occupations the way some folks collect spoons or license plates."

"And you remember them all," Jake said, admiration in his voice.

"It's a gift."

In the candlelit dining room, Mona felt certain everyone in the room noticed them. She tried to not stare at Judi and Will, the DJ's manager, sitting together at a corner table. Their heads were close together, they were so absorbed in each other, they never looked up. Mona grinned at the thought of Judi finding true love. He seemed like a nice guy

"Can I bring you anything else tonight?" the waitress asked, clearing away their plates. "Need a doggie bag for the rest of this steak?"

Jake raised his eyebrows at Mona and she shook her head. "I'm stuffed. Everything was delicious."

"We'll have an after dinner drink at the bar," Jake told the waitress while he pulled out his wallet and placed a credit card in her hand.

"What would you like?" Jake asked Mona as he led them back into the bar.

"I don't know," she said. "I don't usually do after dinner drinks at home. They always seemed too fancy next to my TV dinners."

Jake smiled. "Bailey's on the rocks," he told the bartender. He turned again to Mona. "I had a good time tonight."

Heat crept up Mona's cheeks while she nodded her agreement. A couple Mona recognized walked past and waved at her, the woman looking at Mona inquisitively. *Yes! We're together!* Mona wanted to shout. Instead she smiled and agreed with Jake.

When they left Pine Tree, Jake again held the door for Mona. The river shone silvery under the starlight and the air blew cold. "Here," Jake tossed Mona a wool blanket from beneath a seat cushion. "I figured you didn't dress for a night out on the water."

Mona tilted her head back and for the first time all month saw the stars overhead. Everything seemed clear the moment she moved her gaze upward. She'd been so busy thinking about the Pub and the farm and now town politics, she'd forgotten to look up and wonder. Stars made you do that, she thought. Probably why God placed them above us. We wouldn't look at them in the same way if they were below us. The wind rushed across her cheeks, refreshing like a cool shower.

The lights from shoreline cottages and the red glow of boat lights marked their journey back down the river and twice Mona saw a fish break the water's surface to jump out of its world into hers. When they reached the landing she noticed the parking lot was still full and wondered how many of those people were in the Pub. She pushed aside the urge to go in and help. Steve was the better bartender; he could handle any crowd.

Jake turned toward his house and cut the motor. They drifted through the hum of insects and slopping of the waves against the pilings. "I'll drive you home," Jake told her, reaching out to grab hold of the dock.

"That's okay, I can walk from here." Mona felt foolish the minute she said it.

"You're not walking home, I planned to drive you," Jake said.

"Thanks."

Mona studied the inside of the boathouse, the first part of his house revealed to her. The walls were bare, the high water mark staining them a muddy brown. A bare ceiling bulb illuminated the space and reflected off the water.

"What do you do when the river floods?" she asked.

"Good question. I tie my boat off on the deck and pray the water doesn't get as high as the floor boards."

"Has it ever?"

"Not yet. But you can see it's gotten pretty close."

She followed him to the steps up the side of the house and across the deck.

"I'd invite you in, but I've got to work at six tomorrow morning," he said.

Mona didn't know what to say, so she just nodded. Was he insinuating he wanted to ask her to stay? Or did he mean he wanted to drop her off and get the night over as soon as possible? He opened the passenger side door of his truck and waited for her to climb in.

"I appreciate that you're not bleeding all over my floor mats this time," he said while backing out of his driveway.

"Happy to oblige." Mona laughed.

"How's your leg anyway?" Jake asked.

242

"Fine, like it never happened."

"Good."

They fell into silence for the rest of the drive, listening to the wail of a country singer's heartbreak. When he pulled up in front of her house, she turned to look at him. "Thank you, Mona. I had a great time." The truck cab seemed impossibly wide and there was no way he'd reach across to kiss her goodnight.

"I'll walk you to your door."

She nodded, loving the way he made her name sound special, saying it with equal emphasis on each syllable. She reached for the handle and let herself out of the truck. The street felt cold and solid beneath the soles of her sneakers and she paused a moment to find her equilibrium before walking up the sidewalk to her house.

He stood at the edge of her porch while she turned around, determined not to flub it this time. This is it, the end of my second date with Jake. She took a deep breath and looked up at him, a tiny bubble of joy growing bigger in her chest when he stepped closer.

"Let's do this again." His breath felt warm on her face.

"I'd like that a lot."

Then he leaned forward, and placing his hands on her shoulders, he kissed her softly on the lips. She closed her eyes, let her feet, knees, legs melt away, and returned his kiss with the longing of four years and more restraint than she thought possible. When he pulled away it took her a moment to speak.

"Thanks again," she said hoarsely before heading into her house. This might be what a heart attack feels like, she thought as she watched him walk down the sidewalk to his truck.

TWENTY-SEVEN

CARS AND TRUCKS AND trailers followed one another up the single-lane highway. The breaks in traffic were almost imperceptible, and June Butterfield timed how long it took her to cross the intersection on her dashboard clock each time she headed in to town. Her record was seven minutes of steady traffic—all headed in the same direction: to the water.

Last week the *County Post* published the headline, "Rare Karner Blue Butterfly Found on Trayson Property." The article had gone on to discuss the sudden discovery of a nearly extinct and federally protected species of insect on the edge of the Trayson property—a wet and swampy section just before the county road ran parallel to the river. Dottie had called that afternoon, her voice choked with fury.

"Goddamn butterfly wasn't bothering anyone when the county put in that road ten years ago. Now when it's our turn, suddenly it's 'Oh no! What about the environment! You should protect that!' Hypocritcal bastards!"

"How did they find it?" June asked, fearful of the answer.

"Otto. He kept pushing for an environmental impact study. The DNR sent some college kid doing an internship out to survey the property. You only got to hear about the freaking butterfly. The *Post* didn't run the rest of it—fertilizer runoff, manure treatment, silage storage. They can build a new high school over in Northport next to the old landfill, but now the state's raising questions about whether we should build houses over an old cornfield."

"I'm so sorry, Dottie." June wished they were talking in person; she'd pull her friend into a hug and try to absorb some of her grief.

"You want to see contamination, look at what goes through those storm sewers in town—I've seen the nasty foam on the river when it rains hard. And here's the kicker: that butterfly isn't even supposed to be this far south. I told the kid, 'Move it to some north woods and let it live in peace there,' but noooo, some damn insect gets lost and we can't move it. That would be *cruel*, he said." The bitterness and pain in Dottie's voice was so palpable that June's ear burned next to the phone receiver.

"Is there anything you can do?" June asked, feeling somehow responsible. "I wish Loyal had voted yes right away. I wish Mona wasn't on the board to have any say in this business. Oh, Dottie, I wish they'd have approved the zoning two months ago when they approved so many other requests. Tell me," June pressed, "what can I do?"

"Nothing we can do but wait and see. *Worst* case, they say we'll have to set aside twenty acres for protection—can't farm it, can't build on it. Meanwhile I guess we just push ahead with our plans until someone says otherwise. I don't know anymore," she wailed.

"Well, then go ahead with your plans," June declared. "If the zoning passes, who's to stop you from building? Maybe you'll get it pushed through before they finish the impact study. These things can take years, it's all red tape and paperwork. You'll be able to sell your farm. It will work out."

"Ah, June." Dottie gave a gasp of a sigh over the phone. "She just gets weaker and weaker—she's always got headaches now and the light hurts her eyes. I'm so worried something else is going to happen and she'll get worse. I just wish I could fold her up inside of me and absorb the cancer for her."

June couldn't think of what to say to her friend; her mumbled sympathy felt inadequate.

"Remember when she started kindergarten and her favorite color was pink? She always wore that pink sweatshirt and pink corduroy skirt. She'd pull it out of the laundry room—I could hardly get it washed in between wearings. And that charm bracelet Gene's mother bought her when they went to Tennessee. It had all those horses dangling from it and the bracelet was cheap so the horses fell off. I spent so much time finding them and repairing that damn bracelet." Dottie laughed through her tears.

"I do," June sighed. "I remember everything."

Later, June drove past the Trayson's farm on the way to town and looked hard at the small cluster of trees next to the county highway, hoping, she realized, for a glimpse of the tiny blue-winged creature causing the wheels of progress—or whatever this was—to stall again. At least for now nothing could change—including Angie's chances for recovery.

She pulled up to the intersection across from Maw's and watched the traffic moving in and out of his yard. Peg was out behind the shop tending to one of the tanks. Even with all the excitement of fishing season, it could be a boring month if you didn't fish and didn't have to take care of those who did, she thought.

Otto whistled two sharp, high notes which brought Rex trotting to his side, panting and eager for their next adventure. His boat launched, cooler and bait bucket stocked, lunch packed and he was ready for the day ahead. Knowing traffic on the lake and river would be heavy, Otto planned to head past the Rock River today, taking his chances on the Little Eddy. Ordinarily this section of the river was impassible by boat but the flooding earlier in the spring had cleared out huge sections of wetlands—pulled whole islands of earth and grass and trees miles down the Wissipaw and deposited them along the eastern shore of Long Lake.

Last week Otto watched one of these miniature islands slowly drift past. A squirrel ran up and down the length of a Swamp Oak's trunk, excited or terrified by the experience of floating away. A mallard flapped her wings, guarding her nest supported by the reeds and grasses, dirt and roots entangled beneath her. Her panic was a strange contrast against the clear blue sky and the river's calm surface.

In 1937 a Conservation Corps had dug a series of canals down by the swampy edge of the Wissipaw and Rock Rivers in hopes of creating passage for duck hunters and alleviating some of the flooding on the farm fields. Now they were saying those canals had allowed floodwaters to peel away layers of swamp and protective cover, stripping the riverbanks bare. But Otto recognized a fresh fishing spot opened up in the nick of time. Next year he'd head north to fish, he promised himself while scratching Rex behind the ears. He'd get the hell away from all the craziness of Bassville. Maybe he'd even settle up there after retirement.

He drove past another cluster of boats, ignoring the polite waves of their passengers.

Ordinarily Mona didn't like the two o'clock lull between lunch and happy hour interrupted by stray customers, but she'd been chomping at the bit to dish about her date with Jake and seeing Judi walk through the door was a welcome surprise.

"Let me guess, you're out of rail rum," Mona grinned, wiping her hands off on a towel.

"Nope, I'm in the mood for one of your burgers. Works, please."

"You got it. Want something to drink?"

"Iced tea." Judi sat down.

"I saw you had a hot date the other night," Mona said, after calling back the order. "That Will's a cutie."

Judi flushed and nodded. "It's true."

"And?" Mona probed.

"We had a really nice time. William's lovely."

"Lovely. Not sure I've ever heard anyone describe a guy like that before."

"You've never heard anyone describe William."

"So?"

"So what?" Judi stacked two packets of sugar on top of each other and opened them both with a single rip.

"You going out with him again?"

"He'll be back in June when things slow down. It's safe to say our interests are mutual."

"Cool. I saw you two, you know, Sunday night while I was at dinner with Jake—"

"Jake Paulick? The hunk that came into the bar with a huge walleye last month? How did this happen?"

It was such a relief of internal pressure to tell Judi about her date— better than telling Jenny. Judi asked all the right questions and didn't give any advice.

"Are you going out with him again?" Judi asked when Mona finished her story.

"Yes. Definitely. I think your burger's ready, I'll be right back."

She returned with the burger and fries nestled on wax paper in a plastic basket. Sliding it in front of Judi, she reached into a cooler for ketchup and mustard. "You want any Tiger Sauce?"

"What's that?"

"Horseradish and mayo—it's good with your fries."

"I'll try it."

While Judi dug into her food, Mona boosted herself onto the cooler across from her. "I heard another rumor about you. Did you really pay The Pole and Scotty with hunting packages to Canada for building your deck?"

"How many people in this town actually get paid through a payroll?"

Mona considered this. Most of Bassville bartered or paid cash. Some took folks fishing for cash and sold fish to restaurants down the river for cash. The Dohills often traded labor for boats and snowmobiles. Dottie Trayson had knit dozens of thick wool hunting sweaters in exchange for various odd jobs around their farm. "How did you get them a trip to Canada?"

Judi wiped her mouth on a napkin. "My uncle owns a charter flight business and drops guys off in the woods for those hunting trips—you know, for bear, elk, moose."

"Up in Canada?"

"Yeah. He's always offering Mom and me vacations. But getting dropped in the middle of the forest with nothing but your packs and a tent isn't our idea of a great vacation. People have died on those trips."

"Is your whole family from Canada?"

Judi nodded and took another bite of her burger.

"But I thought you said you were from Toledo."

"When my dad died he left no good memories and a mountain of debt." Judi smoothed her napkin across the bar and traced a pattern

250

on it with her fingertip. "After the life insurance check came, Mom cashed it and we hit the road. Mom had a cousin who talked about Bassville and fishing. It sounded like a good place to start over."

"That must have been hard." Mona tried to imagine leaving Bassville without saying goodbye to anyone.

"Not if you knew Ludlow. It's a pit." Judi rested her chin on her palm. "The toughest thing, really, was learning how to say 'out' without the accent."

"If you had any idea the stories people floated about where you're from and what you're up to." Mona slid up onto a cooler and reached for her water glass.

"Like what?" Judi's eyes sparkled with amusement.

"My personal favorite is that you and your mom are in the witness protection program."

"That's a good one!" Judi considered it for a moment. "Any chance we can make people believe that's true?"

"Sure. It's easy. All I have to do is mention it to a couple people and it's God's truth." Mona leaned forward on her elbows. "In fact, I'll start tonight."

"Brilliant." Judi reached in her pocket and dropped a ten-dollar bill on the bar. "Keep the change. Back to the grind now."

For the rest of her shift Mona devised how to resurrect the rumor about Judi's past with witness protection—when she wasn't dissecting every moment of her dinner date with Jake.

TWENTY-EIGHT

A FTER THREE DAYS OF thunderstorms, the sun broke through and the lilac trees exploded overnight, bright sprays of purple and white fanned out from the windbreak behind the Bassville Town Hall— nature's signal that the white bass run had reached its peak. Their heavy perfume carried down the street, and every now and then a person would stop in the course of their day and inhale the scent of sweet spring. Scotty Trayson cut a branch of them off the bush outside the Bassville Hotel and brought it inside to Sue and Judi.

"For your front desk," he told them. "I thought they'd look nice."

"Thanks, Scotty," Judi said, sticking her nose into the tiny flowers and tight, dark buds. "They smell beautiful."

"Better put them in some water," he warned her before heading out the door to the deck where he and The Pole were putting the final touches on the railing.

"That was sweet." Sue took the lilacs from Judi and inhaled deeply. "There's good people here."

Judi gave her mother a long look. "There's good people all over, Mom."

"Happy Mother's Day," Mona told June, placing cocktail napkins on the bar in front of her parents. "Sorry—again." Every year Mother's Day fell on a Sunday during fishing season and Mona always spent the day behind the bar. Every year she felt indescribably guilty.

"Thank you, dear," June said and centered her napkin in front of her place. "I'll have a vodka tonic. With a lime."

"Dad?"

"Whisky Old Fashioned. Sour." Loyal pushed a twenty-dollar bill toward Mona. "Keeping up with this okay?" He gestured to the crowded bar.

"It's not too bad today. " Mona grinned. "It's better with locals to keep me company."

"I'm sure. Have your tips been good this season?" June asked.

"Still on my way to my first million," Mona said. "It's been steady. No big fights since those bozos trashed Steve's lumber pile. If anything, all the new business from Maw has made it busier but less crazy. Maybe we're just too busy and too crowded for any trouble."

"Let's hope so," Loyal said. "I know Steve looks out for you, but I still worry about you working at night surrounded by a bar full of drunks."

Mona sliced a lime and squeezed a piece before dropping it into her mother's drink with a flourish. "As long as Steve's around, you don't need to worry, Dad. A bar fight is the least of my worries compared to the council meeting this week."

"Were you here when they brought in that fifty-pound catfish?" June asked, changing the subject.

"Disgusting. The Pole just laid it out right here on the bar—its barbells were thicker than my fingers." Mona shook her head. "Not as bad as a sturgeon. But I wish they'd keep fish outside instead of bringing them in here to show off."

"Maw tells me they're entering that one in the records book," Loyal said.

"That so? It was a huge fish." Mona lifted the bar mat up with her fingertips and drained it into the sink—it had been a busy morning for the Bloody Mary crowd. She'd drained the mat three times already that day.

"You're still coming for dinner, right?" June asked.

"Wild catfish couldn't keep me away. Can I bring anything?" Mona asked. "Arlyce might have an extra pie or something back there."

"Just bring yourself. I've got ham, cheesy potatoes and rhubarb pie for dessert."

"My favorites. Be there by five." Mona nudged the bar mat back into place. "Is Sean coming?" She had talked to him earlier in the week, begging him to join them for Mother's Day in hopes that the occasion would get him and their father talking again.

"As of this morning he was."

"Good." They just need to sit down and talk things out, Mona thought, picturing Sean and Loyal reaching a peaceable agreement. She tried to read her father's expression.

"See you at five," Loyal said as he and June moved aside to let a new customer place his order.

"How's my favorite bartender?" the man asked.

"Just great. And how's my favorite fisherman?" Mona returned. Her way of making each customer feel special had resulted in a small pile of gifts in the back cooler.

"Brought this especially for you. Italian sausage from my brother's shop." The man handed her a package wrapped in brown paper.

"Wow. Thanks a lot! Is it spicy?" Mona asked.

"A little. He uses garlic and peppers from our mama's garden."

"Wonderful. I can't wait to eat it. I'll save it for a special occasion!"

After settling the man in with his whiskey and water, Mona carried the sausage back to the cooler and laid it on top of two pheasants in a plastic bag, a box of Frango chocolates and a T-shirt from a bar on Beacon Street in Chicago; the day's haul. Fishing season was second only to Christmas for the presents she received. She patted the sausage that she would keep, along with the chocolates and the shirt. She'd pawn the pheasants off on her mom. Men were kind of like pets sometimes, bringing her dead animals to show their regard.

Stopping home for a quick shower and change of clothes, Mona paused by her kitchen sink. According to everything she'd heard and read she could safely move her plants outside after today. She filled a glass with water and drizzled it onto the squash plants. Her dad had a tiller she could borrow to work up the ground in the back yard. She'd ask him about using it tonight.

In her enthusiasm for getting the seeds started, Mona now realized she'd probably have to till up the entire yard. "Oh well, you don't have to mow a garden. You just have to weed it." She shrugged and grabbed the box of Frango chocolates on her way out the door.

"I'm so glad you came," Mona murmured to Sean while wrapping her arms around him.

"Town councilwoman. I'm proud of you—you'll stay and make something good of this town. I can picture it." Sean returned her hug and then pushed her back at arm's length to study her face. "Taking after the old man, right?"

"Could be something like that."

"Any new news about Angie?" Sean asked.

"She's living at the hospital now and they're waiting until she's done with chemo. But the good news is that Scotty's a match."

"That's great!" Sean looked at the box of chocolates in Mona's hand. "For me?"

"For Mom," Mona told him, slapping his hand away. "Have you

and Dad talked?"

"Sure. We've covered how school's going, have I had any car trouble this spring, and my general health and well-being."

"Uh-huh." Mona narrowed her eyes at him.

Sean frowned. "Look, what's done is done. He's not going to disown me just because I don't want to be a farmer. And I'm not changing my mind. We can fight about it every time we see each other or ignore it. I prefer ignoring it."

"That's healthy. No closure—just ignore the problem altogether."

"Yup. Works for me."

Sighing in irritation at both of them, Mona brushed past her brother and into the dining room where June was setting the table.

"Mom, I should be doing that. It's Mother's Day." Mona grabbed the forks from June's hands and handed her mother the chocolates.

"How nice! Thank you, Mona."

Sean sat at the table and helped himself to a dinner roll. "How's town council work treating you?"

"I don't know. It's different."

"Mona's doing a great job." Loyal stood in the doorway, his tall frame looming authoritatively over Mona and Sean. "It makes a man proud to see his child follow in his footsteps."

"Loyal," June warned in a low voice.

"Well, it does," Loyal said, sitting down to join them.

"I think it's great you're getting involved in town politics," Sean added. "They need some fresh blood to help bring Bassville into the next century."

Mona pulled at a hangnail. "I don't know if I want anything to change," she said. "We'll see. There's a lot to be considered before making any big decisions these days."

"So I hear. But I don't totally understand it. Who cares if the Traysons want to sell their property? It's theirs. What gives anyone else the right to judge that?" Sean said.

"Because their decision affects their neighbors—and last I heard, your freedoms end where the freedoms of others begin." Loyal clenched his jaw to suppress his annoyance.

"But what's the point of owning property if you don't have the freedom to control what you do with it?" Sean asked.

"Can we *please* discuss something else?" Mona interrupted.

"Sure." Sean shrugged. "What would you like to talk about?"

"The weather, religion, I don't care." Mona stirred the potatoes on her plate, her appetite fading as her apprehension grew.

"The weather then. It's been a great spring—excellent for fishing. Fishing's good for Bassville." Sean couldn't help goading her further.

"So's farming," Loyal added.

"Who's ready for dessert?" June asked, standing and pushing back her chair. "You know what *I* think is good for Bassville?" She answered her own question. "Families that get along with each other."

Mona glared at her brother and her father while they exchanged sheepish smiles. At least ganging up on me gives them common ground, she thought.

TWENTY-NINE

Maw loved his new celebrity status. Just yesterday at the gas station, five people asked him about being on TV and meeting Sergeant Slaughter, the WWF hero. One night he took Peg out for dinner at Red Lobster over in Northport and spent the whole time shaking hands and answering questions about minnows, being on TV and fishing.

"Maw! I saw you on TV the other night. Sounds like the bait business is treating you well."

Maw stood and extended his hand to the man standing by their table while Peg rolled her eyes. "The bait business is going great. Have a seat."

The man pulled an empty chair over to Peg and Maw's table.

"What channel did you see me on?" Maw asked.

"Channel five."

Maw nodded. "That was a good interview. Not as good as the one I gave to the *Tribune* while in Chicago, but still it was all right for a local news show."

Peg ripped a garlic-cheese biscuit in two and crammed one half in her mouth. The man shrugged off his coat and draped it over the back of his chair.

"I'm going to be on TV in Australia next week," Maw said. "Imagine that. My little bait shop going worldwide."

"Wow! That's incredible. Did you go to Australia?" he asked.

Peg ground her teeth, willing the man to appreciate the fact that he'd just interrupted their first night out without kids in two months.

"How is everything?" their waitress asked.

"Terrific," Maw enthused. "Can you get my friend here a drink? What'll you have?"

"A whiskey and coke," the man told the waitress. "Thanks, Maw."

"Just put it on my tab," Maw instructed her. "Catch my friends over at table ten, too, while you're at it."

Peg swallowed and stood.

"Going to the bathroom?" Maw asked.

"Going to get my coat. Get the check. I'll meet you at the car."

"But—I" Maw half stood and reached over to her.

"It's date night, and I didn't plan on spending it with every freeloader who recognizes you from the TV or newspaper." Peg strode towards the coat room and Maw hurried behind her.

"Peg, you're being rude."

She whirled around and jabbed her finger into his chest. "You're the one being rude." She looked over his shoulder and caught their waitress's eye. "Check, please."

When she saw the total a growl escaped her lips and she thrust the bill at Maw's face. "Seventy-three dollars?" she shrieked.

"Peg," Maw began, reaching for the bill.

She elbowed him away and pulled out her wallet, and slapped money onto the hostess stand. "Keep the change," she said to the waitress who stood by, uncomfortably shifting her weight from foot

260

to foot.

On the car ride home, Peg unloaded two months' of grievances. "Seventy-three dollars on drinks for total strangers. What are you thinking? You're a sucker, Maw. A sucker for anyone who'll pay you a second of attention."

When they pulled in the driveway, she got out of the car and slammed the door shut behind her. Maw threw the car in reverse and drove to the Pub where he bought a round for every person sitting at the bar and everyone in the dining room too, for good measure.

Maw adored being famous. He wore a Bikini Fishing Team T-shirt every day so people would be sure to recognize him. And on the outside chance that anyone didn't, like the night he'd ended up at the Beach Club dancing with his bikini team and their assorted groupies, he made sure they did. One college kid with wavy blonde hair and an entourage of women wore a Maw's Minnow's T-shirt and Maw headed straight for him after finishing the Electric Slide with the Bikini Team.

"Nice shirt, buddy," he said, pointing at his own.

"What? Oh, thanks, man." The kid nodded briefly before turning back to his group.

"Where'd you get it?" Maw persisted.

"My uncle got it for me," was the reply casually tossed over a shoulder.

"No kidding? Who's your uncle?" These kids would never believe their luck when they learned they were talking to the man himself, Maw thought.

The kid turned around, resigned to talking to a sweaty, middle-aged stranger. "Stan Engel."

Maw shook his head. "Don't know him. But then a lot of folk come through my store lately buying T-shirts." He noticed the glimmer of recognition on a few of the faces surrounding him. "Ever since Dave

LaMay from Chicago put me on his show… " he trailed off and sat down at an empty table.

"*You're* Maw from Maw's Bait and Tackle?" one asked him.

"The one and only." Maw modestly raised his bottle of beer.

"Well, no shit," said the kid with the minnow T-shirt. "How about that?"

"Weren't you just on TV the other night?" asked a woman with curly red hair pinned back in a banana clip.

"Probably," Maw nodded. "Every day lately I have another interview or celebrity appearance."

"I went white bass fishing one spring," said another young man. "With my grandpa on Long Lake."

"Sure, sure, that's good fishing," Maw told him. "Hell, it used to be solid boats up and down the river years ago. It's still pretty nuts, though."

"Maw!" Jenny Bender screamed for him to join them again on the dance floor.

"Guess I better go join the girls." He winked. "They're on a mission tonight." Maw grinned at the redhead. "Care to join me?"

By the end of the night Maw was surrounded by the crowd drawn to him by the lure of free drinks and his modest fame. Maw Cooper was the most popular guy in the club that night despite being the least likely to get laid.

Dry weather from a low pressure system meant washing windows and Mona was hard at it. Using a razor to scrape away dried bugs, she eyed the top edge of the sill with caution. The barn spiders that nested in the siding of the Pub grew as big as two inches across—and then there were those legs. Mona didn't notice Maw until he was standing right behind her.

"Hey," she said, looking at his red eyes and rumpled T-shirt.

"What's up?"

"I need coffee," he rasped.

"Looks like you could use more than coffee. What've you been up to?"

Maw sat down at the nearest picnic table and shook his head.

After returning with his coffee, Mona finished polishing one window and then hopped off the ladder to move her supplies to the next. If she focused on the robins singing, it took her mind off the webs covering the eaves above her head and the possibility of a huge brown spider dropping onto her hair.

"I think Peg might kill me," Maw told her.

"Why's that?"

"I told her I'd be home early and I wasn't."

Mona knew when a customer needed an attentive ear, so she dropped the dirty rag back into the bucket and gave Maw her full attention.

He studied the dregs of his coffee cup. "That was on Friday."

"Today's Monday," Mona pointed out.

"I know. That's why she's gonna kill me."

"What happened?" Mona tended to reserve judgment until she'd heard the whole story, but experience had taught her that men behaved like children, leaving their wives no choice but to mother them—and the wife that became a mother was in danger of losing her husband because men don't want to be mothered. She'd seen it with Chad Longwell—he'd be in the bar every night of the week and his wife would call the bar to nag him to come home. "Chad, it's Helen," Mona'd tell him, holding the phone out towards him.

He'd wave her away, "Tell her I'll be home when I get there." Helen labored to pull him in line, berating him, screaming threats, her anxiety rising with his insistence to join every fishing trip, hunting trip or snowmobiling trip. Then at a bachelor party two years ago he met a stripper who admired his boyish charm and fun-loving ways. Chad came back to Bassville to pack his things, telling Helen that he'd fallen in love with someone else—someone who better understood him and loved him for who he was.

Last Mona heard, Chad was still in Eagle River, treating his new girlfriend the same way he'd treated Helen. Dob reported a snowmobile trip last winter he'd run into Chad at a bar and the phone rang, it was the girlfriend telling the bartender to send Chad's sorry ass home already. Mona hated how women acted so desperate, but men provoked them. When angry women called the Pub during her shift, she always silently handed the phone over to the man in question. No way would she put herself smack in the center of anybody's marriage problems.

After rumpling his hair and combing his beard with his fingers, Maw continued his story.

"We were on the river Friday afternoon to do a photo shoot for *Fin and Feather*. The girls wanted to stop for a quick bite before heading back, and the place was packed. By the time we finally got a table it was past seven. Then we ran into some people Jenny knows from Clearwater and they invited us to a party.

"I was too drunk to drive safe, so I stayed over at this guy's house and I swear, I wanted to come home."

"But—" Mona let the question hang in the air.

"I had to get back to my boat."

"It didn't occur to you to call Peg?"

"Didn't want to bother her. She was busy with the kids and I had Snuffy lined up to work the shop for me anyway."

"Uh-huh." Mona's lip curled with disgust.

"Then the motor wouldn't start so I figured I'd just hitch a ride back to town."

"Right. Good idea." Mona glanced at the docks where a boat was

264

pulling up. Maw had about four minutes to finish his story.

"Beau showed up and said he'd take me, but he was on his way to the Beach Club in Clearwater. I rode along with him and he stayed there until bar time and then headed to an after bar party. When we got back to his place, he insisted I get some sleep there before heading back home."

"And you still didn't bother to call Peg," Mona guessed.

Maw sighed. "I couldn't just leave my boat behind. So I finally got a hold of Dob and he took me out to Long Lake to get it."

"And then you went home," Mona said hopefully.

"By the time I got my boat, I had to catch him a drink for giving me a ride and then a bunch of guys I'd hooked up with a fishing package came into the bar and bought me a drink ..." Maw hung his head.

"Count yourself lucky if she hasn't changed the locks, Maw."

"I know, I know. This whole spring everything has gotten completely out of control."

"You need to fix it, Maw." Mona tried to sound encouraging. "If you grovel enough, Peg *might* forgive you someday. She's a stand-up gal. You need to go home."

Memorial Day weekend was traditionally the last hurrah in Bassville before folks settled into the steady summer season. Fishermen collided with pleasure boaters, vying for every bed and barstool. The week before D-Day, as the locals called the weekend looming ahead, everyone bustled about the business of taking care of the last of the serious fishermen in town. With less than two weeks to keep the pace, Maw walked over the bridge and had climbed the steps to the front of his bait shop when he realized the sign read "Closed" and the parking lot was empty.

He tried the door. The deadbolt was locked.

He climbed the steps to the house. Locked out there too.

Ringing the doorbell, he pressed his face against the window to look inside. No one came. He tried the back door with no success.

Resigned to waiting until Peg returned, Maw plopped down on the stoop in front of his shop and watched the traffic pass. The field across the highway was on everybody's minds these days when they weren't thinking about fishing. If they approved rezoning it to commercial property, Gene stood to make two million dollars when the ink dried. A number of developers had presented their drawings and plans, everything from a subdivision of houses to strip malls and mini marts. Maw still could not comprehend how this could hurt Bassville. It was just a farm field that Gene wanted to sell to help his daughter beat cancer. Who could argue against that?

Loyal had tried to explain to Maw the strain on the roads and tax dollars required for infrastructure like storm sewers and garbage collection. He brushed Loyal's arguments aside, quipping, "You gotta spend money to make money." Otto kept complaining that their peace and quiet would be disrupted with such aggressive growth.

Maw spat on the gravel walk and listened. It was plenty quiet, what harm could some extra traffic cause? It was *too* quiet, he thought after another moment. He stood, the realization chilling the blood in his veins, forcing his headache to the back of his mind while he walked around to the back of his shop where the minnow tanks usually swirled and bubbled—the water circulation was as critical to the life of a golden shiner as to any other fish breathing under the water's surface.

A stillness met his ears and eyes and he stared with disbelief that boiled into rage.

The tanks were unplugged and the corpses of thousands of minnows bobbed gently on the water's surface in all three tanks. The stock for the weekend ahead worthless and starting to rot under the hot sun.

As if in answer to the questions spinning in his brain, a seagull with mottled grey feathers glided in and perched on the edge of the farthest tank. It reached its beak into the water and started to eat.

THIRTY

THE WHITE BASS SWARMED beneath the Wissipaw's surface in excited masses, dodging and darting around each other, turning sharply to swallow a falling insect or nip at a passing clump of algae. The residents of Bassville anxiously rushed around each other on both sides of the Wissipaw as the town board meeting approached. They paused to dissect every theory and bit of gossip on the street, in the canned goods aisle at Bud's Supermarket, and at the gas station while filling up their cars.

Between obsessively analyzing her fledgling relationship with Jake and the vote looming Monday night, Mona was distracted. She poured drinks wrong and screwed up one order so badly that the customer stiffed her on the tip, something that never happened during a white bass run. Like an automaton she cleared glasses and wiped tables clean with her bar rag, her attention focused across the river.

She and Jake had gone out two more times—they'd gone to the new James Bond movie playing in Northport, and they'd spent another evening walking around the quiet evening streets of Bassville as they talked about ... well, thinking about it now, they hadn't really discussed much of anything, but the conversation about nothing sure came easily for them. Both nights had ended with some pretty good kissing on her front porch. He'd called her two other nights, late, too late for him to meet her out and yet early by her bartending schedule. The fact was clear despite her fleeting moments of insecurity: she and Jake were becoming a couple.

Around Mona, the speculation continued.

"People hate change. It'll be a no vote for sure," Otto Zimm insisted. He'd been one of the first to hammer a "No Grow!" sign in his front yard. He glared at the Dohills.

"I agree. Best thing for this town is what Maw's done with the fishing. If more people did what he did, we'd be just fine and everyone'd leave us alone the rest of the year," Snuffy added.

A few stools down, Dob and Dale forecasted future construction jobs resulting from the new zoning.

"We could see as many as two hundred new houses go up in next three years," Dale said, scratching his head with a pencil.

Dob chuckled. "Next thing you know, we'll be the next Clearwater. We'll be ordering traffic lights by the dozen."

"Sounds good to me." Beau grinned. "Liven this place up a little."

It was better to obsess about Jake, Mona thought. The uncertainty of Bassville's future made her stomach cramp and her head ache.

"How's Angie?" Arlyce asked Dottie when she sat down to the Stitch and Bitch table.

"She's ready for the transplant. One treatment to go, but she is *ready*. You probably heard that a few of the girls in her class—and a couple of the boys, too—shaved their heads in solidarity. When I brought her the photo of her entire class, most of them bald, holding up a sign reading 'Get well soon Angie!' she had the biggest smile on her face." Dottie dabbed at the edges of her eyes with a tissue. "It still makes me cry to think of those kids doing that for her."

"Well, it wasn't *that* much of a hardship for them to shave their heads. Mine couldn't wait to grab a razor when he came home from school last week."

Dottie chuckled. "My girl's a trendsetter, then." She looked gratefully at the two friends who were making this struggle easier. It wasn't just the casseroles they brought over, it was the constant encouragement they doled out to her throughout each week, phone calls and little visits that kept her spirits from crashing.

"And did you hear about Peg?" June asked, her fingers pulling the yarn over and around her knitting needles faster and faster.

"The girls at the Hair House say it'll cost Maw five grand to replace his stock," Dottie said, pausing to take a drink of her iced tea. "That's two month's profit."

June slid her chair over to get rid of the sun's glare in her eyes. With the balmy weather, they held their weekly Stitch 'n Bitch on the deck outside. June pushed aside the sweater pattern she'd been studying and picked up her needles again. "Don't you think it was a little rash?"

"How do you figure?" Dottie demanded. "He disappeared for a whole weekend with a boat full of girls wearing bikinis. I'd say he's lucky that's *all* she did."

"I'm not saying she shouldn't be mad," June hastened to explain, "but Maw's loss is hers as well. She cut off her nose to spite her face, you might say."

"I think putting Maw out of commission is exactly what she should have done. Steve said he might not even get a new supply by this weekend."

"Will they close the store?" June asked.

"Someone needs to pull him back in line. I love Maw as much as the next person, but he's been out of control all spring. It's one thing to try to make a little extra money, but TV crews? Bikini fishing teams?" Arlyce pursed her lips in disapproval.

"Peg says he's spent whatever he's made chumming it up with anyone who mentions that DJ's show," Dottie added.

"Mona said he spent three hundred dollars buying that DJ and his manager drinks and dinner the other weekend," June said.

"That's nothing," Arlyce told her, "what do you suppose he spent going to Chicago that weekend?"

"I don't think some people will ever forgive him for giving up some parts of the river." June squinted her eyes and looked towards the Wissipaw, blinding at this time of day when it reflected the midday sun.

"You mean Otto?" Arlyce asked. "There's more than one local who'll never spend a dime in his store again." She'd never alienate a local customer that way. Maw was too short-sighted in her view.

"If the board passes that zoning ordinance, Maw can sell the whole bit off and start fresh, right?" June suggested with a shrug.

"How do you think the vote will go?" Dottie asked. "I'm pretty sure Otto's a no, and we all know how Loyal will vote."

"I don't know," June mused. "People are so divided and it'll probably come down to Mona's vote in the end. And I have no idea how she's leaning."

"If it were up to Jake Paulick she'd vote yes," Arlyce said.

"It's not up to Jake Paulick," June snapped. "It's up to Mona, and she'll decide whatever's best. She'll choose based on more than what one man has to say.

"Your girl's got a good head on her shoulders and she'll vote her conscience, we can all agree on that," Dottie said, reaching across to rest her hand on June's knee. And her conscience, Dottie thought,

272

would be affected by Angie's desperate situation. How could Mona possibly look at the picture of her daughter every day and not feel torn up?

"It's going to work out," June said, dropping her needles and placing her hand on Dottie's. "One way or another, it'll work out for the best."

Later that afternoon June Butterfield put a vase of lilacs in every room of her house, careful to check each cutting for ants. The fresh smell invigorated her as she set about the last of her spring cleaning. Mona was coming over to help her get the garden planted. Standing on the bed to reach the last ceiling fan, June gave it a good swipe with the dust cloth and heard her daughter's voice calling from the yard.

Skipping down the steps, June grabbed her gardening gloves and beat-up straw hat from the kitchen counter on her way out the back door.

She stopped mid-stride when she saw Mona—or rather Mona's legs supporting what she presumed to be Mona's body, holding a cardboard flat overflowing with foliage.

"Don't plant until after Mother's Day, that's what they always say." Mona set the flat down on the porch and called back over her shoulder, "I'll be right back. I've got two more boxes in the car."

"What on earth, Mona?" June asked, inspecting the plants on her porch. She lifted a tomato plant, already ten inches tall and bushy with leaves. "This is from your kitchen? I thought you were planting this in your own yard."

Mona nodded. She slid another box next to the first, its bottom scraping against the grit on the porch. "It's only half of what I started. I'm saving the rest for my own garden." Her smile was proud.

"These are beautiful." June watched Mona pull a third flat of plants from her car.

"Mr. Stripey," June read off a popsicle stick in one container. "Is this a tomato?"

"Yes. They're heirloom plants. They're supposed to taste better and grow better than the hybrid seeds they sell at the store."

"How did you learn so much about these?" June turned the tomato plant over in her hands and examined its leaves.

Mona shrugged. "Found a couple books at the library and studied up."

"I must say, you have a green thumb, sweetie. These look incredible."

"They do, don't they?"

June studied her daughter's pleased expression. "Farming's in your blood. You know, your father always wanted to be a crop farmer but he stayed with dairy farming because that's what his father did."

Mona nodded. She'd always been June's girl, Sean was Loyal's boy. But she *was* Loyal's girl, too, wasn't she? "Who'd have guessed?" She grinned and gestured to the boxes overflowing with leafy seedlings. "I'm a farmer, too."

"Something to think about," June said, handing her daughter a trowel.

The shadows lengthened across the yard by the time June and Mona reached the edge of the garden. Empty plastic containers littered the rows between the plants that now looked much smaller once tucked into the earth outside.

"Anything to report about Angie?" Mona asked, crawling across a row of squash plants to dig up the ground for peppers. She pulled two dandelions, their long roots pale in the sunshine.

"Sounds like a week from now they'll be ready to do the transplant. They have to coordinate with the end of Angie's chemotherapy treatments. It's marvelous that Scotty was a match."

"And by then they'll know soon about their land," Mona said, pushing dirt in a mound over pea seeds.

"How do you think it'll go?" June asked, trying to sound nonchalant.

"Don't know. After the last two months I believe anything could happen. Anything at all."

June didn't press her daughter any further on the subject. Mona would do the right thing, just like she had faith Angie would get a transplant and it would take and everything would work out just fine.

THIRTY-ONE

THE NEXT MORNING JAKE invited Mona to go fishing on her day off. "I'll never get to see you if I don't take a vacation day—your hours at the Pub aren't exactly compatible with my construction schedule."

Flattered that he'd use a vacation day, Mona agreed, even though fishing wasn't her first choice for fun. But what else was there to do in Bassville at nine in the morning? She met him at his house, determined that the pleasure of his company and the beauty of the river would offset her distaste for sitting still, waiting for some fish to bite on her hook.

"How are things at work?" she asked, leaning back against her seat.

"Crazy. I'm waiting to hear about a couple different projects."

"Where are they?"

"One is the new high school in Northport. The other is a paper mill in Oklahoma."

Mona's chest tightened and she sat up. "Oklahoma?"

"Nothing's decided yet," Jake said, trying to reassure her by leaning forward and putting his hand on her knee. "Really, I'd much rather stay in Northport."

She swallowed and nodded, afraid to speak. There it was. He wasn't going to stick around Bassville. Jake was just like T.C.

"Big night tonight," he said to her, reeling in his line and casting it out again in a graceful throw.

"Yeah." Mona appreciated his changing the subject. Maybe he really didn't want to leave. She sat back again. A mosquito hovered near her right arm and she caught it in her hand, smearing it into grey powder.

"You'll support the future of Bassville, right?" Jake asked.

"What do you mean?"

"The vote for Gene to sell his farm for his daughter. It's the best way to start improving things around here."

Mona turned to look at him, her fishing pole forgotten and half submerged in the water. "And if I vote against the zoning I *don't* support Bassville?"

Jake smiled, unaware of his offense. "Isn't that what a 'no' vote would mean? I've explained this to you already. There is no tax base in agriculture. Residential and commercial land use is how Bassville grows."

She cocked her head and studied his expression. Birds chirped in the trees overhead, their cheerful singing continuing without regard to the two people below. "So I *don't* support the town if I vote *against* the zoning request." She didn't want to misunderstand him.

"Is there any other way to look at this?" Voting against the rezoning meant keeping things the same, no progress, no growth, eventual death for any small town. And few reasons for change were more compelling, Jake thought, than giving a family a chance to save their daughter's life.

"How can you say that? If I didn't love my town, why would I run for town board? Why is it bad if things stay the same? Maybe by voting against this I *am* supporting Bassville—saying I like it just the way it is and I don't need anything to change."

The silence that followed her speech felt horribly long until Jake spoke again in a steady voice. "You'd honestly vote against Gene and Dottie getting the money to treat their daughter?" He knew it was an emotionally manipulative thing to say, but really didn't the vote boil down to the Traysons' rights?

Mona's eyes burned with tears and she looked away. A swell of nausea rose in her stomach and she wished she were anywhere but stuck on this boat in Cooper's Bayou. Anywhere but trapped so close to Jake. "That's not how it is," she said.

"I don't know how you can see it any other way. It's so simple, really. You can't *not* support the Traysons' right to sell their farm to save their daughter's life. No reasonable person could vote against Bassville having the chance to be prosperous and grow."

Another long silence covered the boat and Mona reeled in her line and set the pole on the bottom of the boat. "Please take me back to shore."

They didn't speak until he pulled up next to the dock by his house. Mona climbed out, feeling exposed and awkward as she scraped her right shin along the jagged edge of a wooden plank. She turned and looked down at him. "I don't know why you think this is an easy decision. You're bullheaded. You're looking at this from a construction standpoint—just another job for you. That doesn't make it all right for you to judge *me* for thinking differently. Or my father. It doesn't bring in as much tax money, but that doesn't make farms useless. They feed people, which is pretty important if you ask me. I don't agree that voting 'no' is a death sentence for Angie either, there are grants, we could raise money with a fundraising event, appeal to a foundation that helps kids with cancer. And another thing." She took a sharp breath before continuing. "You don't get to have an opinion

on this town's future if you're not sticking around to see it through."
She strode across his lawn and got on her bike, wishing she had
driven because then she might have spun her tires in the gravel drive
for effect. Her silent departure on a bicycle felt impotent.

THIRTY-TWO

THERE WAS STANDING ROOM only by the time Loyal called the meeting to order. A hush rippled across the crowd. Dottie Trayson clutched her purse with both hands to hide how they trembled. She tried to arrive early to get a seat but got there too late. She stood in the back of the hall wedged against a table loaded with tax forms and informational brochures about how to recycle and where to license your boats and ATVs.

Mona fought down the urge to run out the door and head for home. Her armpits felt cold with sweat and her shoulders were tense. The only comfort she found in the room was Grandma Nancy's beaming face; Grandpa had parked her close to the front and she twinkled up at Mona. Solemnly, Mona ticked off the first item with her pencil and voiced approval of the minutes from the last meeting before looking over at her father. His expressive jaw was clenched, she could see the muscles bulging beneath the skin of his cheek.

"Next is the contract for ditch cutting. Ben Barlow has put in a bid for $500 a month—he gave the only bid." Loyal's voice sounded quiet in the crowded room.

"I move we grant Ben the contract," Otto said.

"Second," Mona said.

"All in favor?" Loyal asked.

"Aye."

The meeting moved swiftly from approving variances, hearing committee reports, and granting a temporary liquor license to the VFW for their annual chicken barbeque. People leaned forward with each passing item and by the time they reached the rezoning request their faces seemed too close, Mona thought. The lone fly buzzing over the heads of the town council flew in slow circles—struggling to move its wings in the thick atmosphere.

"The session is now open for discussion before the vote on Gene Trayson's request to rezone his property from agricultural and livestock to residential and commercial." Loyal cleared his throat and looked ahead at the crowd. "Maps of the proposed development have been posted by the doors."

The board waited, pens and fingers tapped the tables.

Otto was recognized to speak first. "As anyone knows from driving by my front yard this past month, I'm against this." Muffled chuckles filled the room and the mood shifted like Teutonic plates sliding miles beneath the earth's surface. "While I agree a man's got a right to sell or trade what's his, I think he's got to sell it as is. A farm's a farm and I think Gene ought to keep it as such. That said, I also think we've got a responsibility to keep things from getting out of hand. People have safety concerns, traffic concerns. I've talked to at least twenty people who're dead against this."

The board members nodded; Loyal wrote something on a legal pad.

"Bassville's good right now, and I don't see how having a hundred or so strangers move to town is going to make it better." Otto nodded to acknowledge the scattered applause around him.

And so it went for and hour and sixteen minutes, citizens of Bassville saying their piece one by one. Dob presented a chart describing the economic growth of the town with the new development, claiming a 27% increase in tax revenue. Pat Bender argued that the cost of new roads, new classrooms, increased police force and streetlights would destroy Bassville's financial integrity. Even Grandpa chipped in his two cents about paving Main Street, "to make it accessible for all kinds of traffic," he said while gesturing at Nancy's wheelchair. Mona kept track of the comments in the margin of the agenda, hash marks on the left to count those for, hash marks on the right to count those against. She hoped one column would show a clear lead, divining for her the sway of her vote. The opinions supporting Gene's request had a clear lead by the time Dottie Trayson took her turn to speak.

"While on the surface this is about money, it's also about two other things. Personal freedom and my daughter's life. Gene and his family have farmed that land for over eighty years. If anyone here thinks turning all that hard work over to a couple of strip malls and fifty ranch-style homes is an easy choice, well, they're wrong. Deciding to sell our farm is the toughest decision we've ever had to face." Dottie's voice cracked and she pressed a tissue against the corners of her eyes before continuing. "We've worked hard to keep this farm running. It's ours. It's ours to do with what we want. If we want to sell it, that's our choice and I don't think anybody else should have the right to tell us we can't." Dottie's nose shone bright red. Loyal looked down at his calloused hands and Otto shifted in his seat, his boots scraping the floor.

"This issue is about our personal freedom in this country to sell our property *if we want to*. And to tell you the truth, we don't want to. God," Dottie shook her head and grimaced through her tears, "I'd love for Angie to be well. I don't want her to be sick, maybe die. I'd love for this nightmare to end so I could wake up and ask Gene what they're paying per gallon of milk instead of wondering if our baby's going to get better. I hate selling our farm to pay doctor's bills. But goddamn it, we have to. And because we *have* to, you *have* to let us." She sat down amid the silence around her.

Loyal cleared his throat again, his cough invading the room like a shout. "Are there any other comments from the floor?"

Everyone looked around, but no one raised a hand.

"Do I have a motion to vote?"

"I move we vote on Gene Trayson's zoning request." Mona said, her voice sounding harsh to her ears after not speaking for almost two hours.

"I second," Otto said, looking at each board member in turn.

"All in favor?" Loyal asked.

"Aye," Gene, Dill, Mona and Loyal said, their voices tired, their faces drawn.

"Opposed?"

Otto's voice rang out in solo protest. "Nay."

The room vibrated with the hum of conversation. People began standing and moving around the room before Loyal could call for a motion to adjourn. The board members shouted over the noise in the room, reading each other's expressions as a cue to stand.

Otto walked across to Gene and offered his hand. "I hope there's no hard feelings, Gene."

Gene took his hand without a word.

They stood across from each other for another moment before Dottie interrupted them, pulling her husband into a bear hug, tears streaming down her cheeks in rivulets of black mascara. Gene held her close, his flannel shirt absorbing her tears. His shoulders shook as he shut his eyes against the room.

Maw edged through the room to where they stood. "Good of you to come around tonight," he said to Loyal. His smile looked too bright and false under the blue glaze of the fluorescent lights. Loyal passed him and silently stalked outside.

"What? What did I say?" Maw asked, turning to Mona, his hands outstretched.

"Sometimes," Mona said quietly, "you need to learn when to quit."

THIRTY-THREE

Peg and maw had driven separate cars to the town meeting. They'd slept in separate places all week, he on the couch beneath a ratty afghan, she in their bed using all the pillows to prop her head. He pulled in the driveway behind her and they got out of their cars at the same time.

Maw watched his wife slam the door and turn back to look at him. Acting quickly, hoping she felt some goodwill toward him after the meeting, he called out to her, "Good news, isn't it?"

She hesitated and he jogged a few paces and stopped in front of her. He looked at his wife. She hadn't spoken to him in a week. Instead, her directives had come via their children. "Tell your father dinner's ready." "Tell your father his mail is on the hall table." Shut out of her world through her silence and avoidance, he realized he had become afraid. Not lonely, not angry, but scared. All his failures, risks, flaws and fears kept him awake at night and pricked at his thoughts during the day. Peg, he learned, was the dam that kept these things at bay. Her constant confidence in him kept him afloat, her haranguing kept him steady.

"Peg." He studied her face, the familiar lines and creases in her skin and the lipstick bleeding past her lips; he missed her snappish wit and her laughter. "I am sorry. I was wrong. I was acting like an adolescent ass."

She stood still. Not what he wanted, but it was better than her turning away and walking up the steps into the house.

"Can you help me make this right with you again? You know I love you. Whatever it takes. I'll do it."

"Whatever it takes?" Peg asked.

"You name it. It's done." Maw crossed his fingers behind his back for a second before uncrossing them and amending his promise. "Almost anything."

"Almost anything," Peg repeated.

"Tell me what you want me to do."

She considered him for a moment and then head up the stairs to the house. "Start by cleaning up the yard. You want to stay in business, you have to keep things looking nice around here." She paused on the top step. "And when you're done with the yard, and that includes weed-whacking and taking out that overgrown honeysuckle bush in back, then you've got over a month's worth of bookkeeping to do. I'll probably have to lock you in that closet for a week for you to get it all done."

"I love you," Maw shouted as she shut the door to the house. He turned to survey the yard and picked up a skateboard.

THIRTY-FOUR

TUESDAY MORNING MONA GRABBED her helmet and hopped on her bike. She'd look down at Bassville from Bunker Hill and sort the thoughts clamoring in her head. The peace and quiet of the hillside would put her mind at ease as much as the workout.

Breathing heavily, she stood on the pedals and pushed herself to the highest spot. From there she could see the entire landscape. Her dad's farm was quiet and she could watch a tractor moving along Trayson's field. Traffic came steadily over the hill and passed down the highway, the faint hum reaching her ears from two miles away. Traffic across the bridge was sparse, but boat traffic on the river was heavy today.

Mona squinted her eyes, trying to see the Trayson farm more clearly. It looked as still as her dad's place except for the tractor. She realized she'd half-expected to find bulldozers leveling the barns, clearing the land for the surveyor's to set up their flags and signs. But it was only one farm going under and the process would take time. Who knew how long it took to transition from cornfields to neighborhoods. Tonight she was going to meet her parents for dinner to discuss the future of their farm and her plans for it. The Butterfields would continue the tradition of farming; she and her mom would convince Dad of that.

Reaching for her water bottle, she leaned her bike against a tree and sat down on a rock. After today, maybe next year or maybe even this summer, the new houses would be built. Families from the city would move in and join the Dohills and the Traysons and the Barlows and everyone else on a Friday night eating and drinking at the Pub. There'd be a new convenience store for fishermen to stop at next spring—maybe they'd even sell bait. The library might get more money and Main Street would finally get paved, but would the new people wave to her grandparents when they passed by?

Judi and Sue always did, she reasoned. And they were new to town. Plus she'd heard that Sue gave Snuffy free breakfast leftovers and let him use the hotel's shower once a week. Perhaps a town could change people as much as people could change a town.

Jake's big chance could come true now. The way was clear for him to build and build and build with no end in sight. Mona wondered if she could ever look at him the same way once it started.

The noon whistle whined in the distance, a faint echo through the treetops and up to where Mona sat. She stood, feeling the coldness of the rock seep into her spine after sitting for so long. Straddling her bike, she started back down the hillside, remembering the last time she came this way she got fourteen stitches and dinner with Jake Paulick. Riding home, she felt increasingly disappointed when she didn't see his truck on the road. By the time she reached her house, disappointment evolved to anger. Fuck him. Stupid, dumb, idiot male. Town's full of men right now, plenty of fish to catch in Bassville.

Maw gnawed on a pen cap, the steady pressure of the plastic between his molars both painful and satisfying while he looked across the road. He'd been up all night making amends and now faced a day of taking care of a stream of fishermen. The ones that came through early in the day were all business, just hand over the bait and we'll be on our way, thank you very much. That was fine by Maw; he was too distracted for small talk.

The Trayson place was quiet. Maw wondered if they'd gone to the hospital for the day. A lone pickup truck had pulled out of the drive at seven and Maw assumed it was the hired help finished with the morning milking. The raw earth was dark with rain, straight furrows plowed across as far as he could see. He tried to imagine it looking any different; a strip mall, a subdivision, rectangular blocks cut through by streets denoted by narrow white signposts reading Pheasant Run, Briarcliff Drive, Oakdale Court. As much as he hated to admit it, Loyal was probably right. People who lived in places like that didn't fish and if they did, they weren't coming to his place for gear. They'd buy stuff at the big sporting goods store at the mall in Northport. They'd only stop in his store for the occasional bucket of minnows or dozen crawlers. He sighed and replaced the pen cap, reaching for his coffee mug when the door swung open.

"Morning, Maw."

"What's the word out there, Dob?"

"It's a good day for fishing." Dob dropped his Igloo cooler on the counter and headed for the back coolers. "What're they biting on?"

"Hell, they'll bite on your finger for another week. Heard Steve ran out of bait the other day and started using venison sausage he'd packed for his lunch. Said those fish hit on that about as well as anything else he'd ever tried."

"Is that a fact." Dob pulled a six-pack out of the cooler and tucked it under his beefy arm. "Get me three dozen shiners."

"You got it." Maw took the cooler back to the minnow tank and started dipping. "Going out alone?"

"Dill's meeting me later. He got called to a job this morning." Dob set a bag of chips and three strips of beef jerky on top of the six-pack.

"Anything else?"

"Nope, breakfast of champions," Dob quipped, biting into the jerky.

Maw grimaced even though he'd had a bag of Cheetos and a can of Mountain Dew at five-thirty. He handed Dob his change. "I didn't charge you for the shiners."

"Why the hell not?"

Maw shrugged. "You're local."

"Thanks. We'll catch you later." Dob shoved the door open with his shoulder and Maw heard him greet someone in the parking lot. The door swung open again, this time a man ducked in, his two sons in tow.

"Four dozen shiners and the kid here needs a new rod," the man said, ruffling his youngest boy's hair. "He busted it last week pulling in a catfish."

"You keep the fish?" Maw asked him.

"Hell yeah, she weighed twenty-eight pounds." He laughed. "Probably should talk to somebody about mounting it."

"You should," Maw agreed, dipping the minnows into the man's bait cooler. "A catch like that's something to be remembered."

THIRTY-FIVE

Mona parked her bike by the barn and walked through the open door into the darkness. Her eyes adjusted and she inhaled the sweet smell of hay and manure before sneezing once.

"Bless you," Loyal said, his voice from the third stall to her right.

She picked up a shovel and began clearing out the stall next to his. "Thank you."

"This is a surprise," Loyal said, glancing up at her.

"I need to talk to you about something." A nervous tremor jangled in her arms and hands.

"What's that?"

"Dad, I want to take over the farm." She spoke quickly to prevent his interruption. "I can grow things, and I've done the research. The guy at the extension gave me information about all kinds of stuff—soil testing, pest control and even some government funding I can apply for since I'm a woman. There's a market for produce around here—good produce, like organic tomatoes and beans and squash—

and nobody else is tapping into it. I want you to let me have five acres to plant on for one season. If I can break even the first year, we'll add a little more and over time convert the whole farm out of dairy and into vegetables. We'll go slow so I can prove myself to you and if it doesn't pan out, then it won't hurt you too badly." She drew in a breath. "What do you think?"

Loyal scraped his shovel along the concrete floor of the stall and propped the shovel against the wall. He wiped his face with his shirt sleeve and adjusted the brim of his cap. "This is a pretty big thing to do," he said.

"I know." Mona swallowed. Please say yes. Please consider this. Please don't say no.

Loyal shrugged. "Draw up a plan, and we'll look it over after I get the corn planted."

Mona jumped up and wrapped her arms tight around her father's neck. "Thank you! I can't wait to show you what I've been working on! We can even do worm composting and maybe build some hoop houses …"

"We can still keep the tractors, right?" Loyal asked.

"I don't plan to plant five acres of vegetables by hand," Mona said, laughing with happiness.

The Pub's dining room was empty and Mona scrubbed the corner window, erasing the streaks in a final swipe. She looked across the river at the blue cottage and wished she could erase her longing and the sick taste of desperation as easily as she could clean fly spots and fingerprints. The door slammed in the bar and she wadded up the paper towel in her fist.

She was just past the dart machines when she saw him standing alone at the bar, his jeans and boots dusty from work. Jake leaned forward to look into the kitchen and jerked back when he saw her round the corner and stop short.

"Hi." Mona walked to the edge of the bar, five stools down from where he stood.

"Hi." Jake's greeting hung in the air, thick as wool.

"You need something?" she asked.

"I didn't think I'd catch you alone in here. I'm glad." He took a deep breath. "What I said to you was uncalled for. Unforgivable. I can't even offer you an explanation for why I said it. It was stupid of me."

Mona nodded, any response lodged in the plaster that had become her tongue.

"I know you're thinking I'm only here because of how last night's vote went, but I'm not. I'd be here anyway. I hope you can believe that."

"I think I can."

Jake took a step toward her, his sun-bronzed hand grabbing the back of the barstool next to her.

"Do you forgive me for being an asshole?"

"Isn't that a pre-existing condition when you're male?" she asked.

"I'm serious."

"So am I." She paused before heading behind the bar. Jake didn't move.

"I don't deserve it, but can we try this again?"

The sour ache of desperation, hours of longing and watching, shattered, replaced by the floating, light-headed realization that Jake Paulick could fall in love with her, a farmer's daughter who tended bar and was about to launch her own career as a vegetable grower.

While she smiled and told him yes, and tomorrow after six would be lovely, she thought maybe he already had.

Acknowledgements

This book has been almost twenty years in the making—I started collecting stories at a bartending job that got me through college and introduced me to my husband (see what I did there, Doug? I put you first!). Years later, I wrote horrible early drafts that didn't make any sense. In 2007 I optimistically saved and printed sixty-three pages and brought them to a Screw Iowa Writers Workshop where Marni Graff, Mariana Damon, Lauren Small and Nina Romano agreed with how terrible they were. Their skillful editing, patience and encouragement were vital in shaping this novel from a blob of crap into this final version.

I also need to give a shout-out (and probably send drinks down the bar) to: Gordon Pagel, the editor of *Wolf River Country,* discovered my work while researching the original Maw Cooper and validated my efforts. Troy Vosters and Bob Tellock answered my questions about dairy farming. Per Henningsgaard and his editing students gave me marvelous feedback. Dr. Donald Small generously advised me on the medical history of leukemia treatment. Becky Brown dragged me to the Erma Bombeck Writers Workshop and convinced me to keep writing. Mitch Miskoviak designed the amazing cover and Beth Cole at Bridle Path Press handled the book design and other details. Finally, I am grateful to a legion of friends, my loving family, book club, supportive readers and even my high school students (you get soda, not beer) who asked me questions about this project over the years, which prodded me through the grueling final revisions because once you say "I'm writing a book about a fishing town," people expect you to actually finish it and get it in print.

I continue the strange, but (mostly) true tales of Bassville with the next installment of this trilogy: *Down the River.*

About the Author

Melissa Westemeier's also the author of *Whipped, Not Beaten* and *Kicks Like a Girl*. She lives with her husband and three sons in northeastern Wisconsin where she teaches high school English, reads and messes around in the garden.

The author, age 6, serving up drinks with a smile behind her grandparents' basement bar.

www.ingramcontent.com/pod-product-compliance
Lightning Source LLC
Chambersburg PA
CBHW022138170626
46807CB00005B/1990